The Seduction
of the Glen

~~ The Glen Highland Romance ~~
Book 5

Michelle Deerwester-Dalrymple

Table of Contents

Chapter One: The King's Decree

Auchinleck Castle, East Ayrshire, 1307

Another victory over the English meant even more drinking and celebrating. From his vantage on the second story of the Dumfries keep, recently freed from English dominion under the Earl of Pembroke Aymer de Valence, he watched his men, the faithful clans of Scotland in their bright and earthy plaids sing and cheer, and oh, how the whiskey and ale did flow.

Only King Robert the Bruce didn't celebrate with them. He sat alone in the second-floor study, a low fire casting fearsome shadows on the coarse stone wall. He hated what he had to do next, but there was no choice. 'Twas nay the same as MacCollough's sister, he tried to justify to himself. That Scottish lass had been a loyal woman, sister to a loyal Laird, one of the King's closest advisers. And if MacCollough's sister managed to outsmart the Bruce and wed a clansman she cared for, well, he could nay fault her for those actions. Said man was a loyal Scot as well.

But this? With the de Valence sisters? 'Twas different. This time 'twas not a loyal woman. 'Twas not the sister of a clansman and close adviser and friend. Aislynn de Valence was the niece of the now defeated Aymer de Valence. She and her sister, Agnes, must be sent north, whether as captives or for future bargaining, the Bruce didn't yet know. All he did know was he wasn't about to let these assets go.

He flicked his eyes to the sturdy door, waiting for the knock. Asper Sinclair would be none too happy at this assignment, yet 'twas necessary. Someone needed to take the lasses far into Scotland, hide them from the English, keep their location secret. A brave, honorable man who could keep the lasses safe. And so, what if the Bruce was selecting men sworn to bachelorhood as their escorts? If any of the Sinclair men found their way into the hearts of the lasses, matrimony would only solidify the Bruce's position as king. And, perchance, form an alliance with the English instead of fostering an enemy.

The sharp rapping at the door finally arrived, and the King bade the man to enter. Asper Sinclair strode in, his head of thick red hair peering around the door before his battle-hardened body followed.

"My King. To what do I owe this honor?" His deep voice rumbled across the shadows of the study as he gave a curt bow. The King kept his eyes on the celebratory men below.

"Dinna call it an honor, yet, Sinclair."

***

Aislynn's slender arms clutched at her sister's muscular shoulders, trying to shake some sense into the young woman. Though Aislynn was but a year older, and the women resembled each other well, sharing the same light-brown hair and peridot and hazel eyes, sometimes she felt more like a mother than a barely older sister.

And now she pleaded with Agnes, begging her to reconsider as she looked on her sister's costume with horror. Agnes, dressed in a man's dusky tunic and baggy brown braies that gathered at her calf and tucked into loose-fitting leather boots, neatly passed as a fresh lad.

With her hair hacked off by a dull knife and tucked under a dirty bonnet, Agnes felt secure in her appearance. No man would think her a lass or try to assail her. She could move freely across the lowlands before the pretend king decided her fate, which is exactly what she wanted. Aislynn tried to convince her otherwise.

"Please, Agnes, you will not make it dressed as a lad! You were raised as a lady! Please don't try something so dangerous!"

"Dangerous?" Agnes screeched, her high pitch causing Aislynn's panicking eyes to flit to the door, convinced someone had heard. "'Tis much more dangerous to remain here and have the Bruce imprison us, or worse! The man is a villain, bent on the destruction of all things English, including us!" Agnes breathed in and tempered her anger, her face softening as she lovingly begged her sister. "Aislynn, I would feel safer if you came with us. We can make it to England, to our uncle, King Edward, and find sanctuary with his court."

Aislynn looked over her shoulder – was someone at the door? Her sister's bold gesture was playing tricks on her nerves. "Nay, please, I've heard the Bruce is considerate, that he —"

"After Uncle Aymer kept that bastard's wife and daughter captive for so long? Do you think he will have mercy for any de Valence?" She shook her head and yanked her arms away. "No, sister, there's nothing for us here. Look." Agnes jerked her head to the window. "The men are below. We can ride for England. But we must leave now."

Agnes was always the impulsive, impetuous one, the tiny sister who got into trouble then looked to Aislynn to help her get out of it. While this time was no different, Aislynn was terrified she wouldn't be able to do that. Here, under the command of the Scottish King, Aislynn knew there was little she could do to help either of them.

Then Aislynn did hear something on the other side of the door – the sound of heavy footfall on stone. Scotsmen were coming down the hall. Aislynn turned back to her sister, her eyes wide with fright and confusion. Indecision rooted her to her spot.

"Then you remain here," Agnes told her. "You've made your choice, such as it is. Let them do with you what they will. I will return with King Edward's army and find you." Agnes lunged toward Aislynn in a quick move, kissing her cheek. "I love you, sister. Look for me to return for you."

Then Agnes was gone, slipping over the windowsill, down a rope made from ripped sheeting the women had torn from the bed. Aislynn leaned out the window, eyes wide with terror as her sister worked her way down and leapt onto the waiting horses below. Two English soldiers, men loyal to Commander Aymer de Valence and the English cause, followed her, riding off into the slippery night. Aislynn sighed and unwrapped the cloth from the bedpost, letting the fabric drop to the dirt of the bailey. The door flung open with a crash, and Aislynn spun around.

"Ye must come with us," the monstrous men in strange, skirted clothing commanded, stepping into her chamber. "The Bruce will see ye now."

One man grabbed her arm and hauled her toward the door. The second man peered around the room, on the far side of the sturdy, four-poster bed.

"Where is the other one?" his guttural voice boomed.

Aislynn feigned ignorance, shrugged, and kept her mouth shut. While she may not agree with her sister's actions, she wasn't a traitor. They would have to beat the information out of her.

And as the Scotsmen dragged her toward the study at the far end of the castle, Aislynn paled, praying it wouldn't come to that.

***

The bare-legged giants all but threw her into the study, where she landed unceremoniously in a hunter-green *tiretain* pile at the foot of the infamous Robert the Bruce. Aislynn rose with as much grace as she could muster and brushed at her lush gown. Her eyes remained downcast, but she did catch the Bruce giving a dirty look to the men at the door. He waved them off, and they slammed the door, leaving her alone with the false king.

Or, at least she thought she was alone. Keeping her eyes away from the Bruce – just as she would never look at the Devil, she couldn't bring herself to look this vile man in the eye – Aislynn let her gaze drift around the rest of the study. Her mind churned in a heated rush, trying to figure out her fate at the Bruce's hands, when her eyes caught the leather-wrapped feet of a man standing in the shadowy corner. Aislynn started. So, she wasn't alone with the Bruce.

The man was a Scot, 'twas no doubt as to that. His plaid draped around his shoulders and hips haphazardly, as if he dressed quickly and in the dark. *How is it these Scots run around in little more than a blanket? The indecency of their bare legs and chests? Why didn't they dress like real men?* Aislynn judged the man before her eyes even moved past his chest.

Which wasn't bare, much to her surprise. He wore a rough-hewn, woolen tunic under the plaid, with wide sleeves that didn't hide the largest of his muscled arms or chest. Fear forced bile into her throat. *Would this savage man be the one to punish or kill her?*

Her dreadful thoughts didn't stop her from taking in the rest of him, especially the shock of deep red on his face and hair. And was his hair shaved on the sides? *Oh, it was.* Just when she believed her position couldn't get worse – the man in the room was an uncivilized heathen, what she'd heard the Lowland Scots call Highlanders, and Aislynn knew this man was not present to aid her in any way.

She was shaking in her thin slippers by the time she finally turned her head to the pretend king. Compared to the barbarous man in the corner, the Bruce appeared normal, almost plain. The King's brown hair was brushed back in smooth waves, and he wore civilized trews like a man should. The only garment that made him stand out as nobility or royalty was the heavy black cape edged in black fur and secured at his neck by a detailed brooch. When he gazed at her, his own brown eyes were soft, not harsh, and Aislynn had an inkling that the King might be more forgiving than the uncivilized brute in the shadows.

Robert remained silent, evaluating her as though she were a piece of meat served up on a platter. Unsure of what else she should do – *how did one engage with a false, heathen king?* – she curtsied low.

"Rise, my lady," the King's rich voice commanded kindly.

Aislynn obeyed, keeping her head bent, watching the Bruce from under hooded eyes. The King shifted his attention to the door, as if waiting for something. After a moment, his deep brown eyes flashed at Aislynn.

"Where is your sister? Didn't she accompany ye here?"

Aislynn shook her head. The King didn't even have to move, as the other Scotsman jumped at the door, yelling for the two Highland guards in the hall to search for the other English lass. The men, both Asper and the King knew, would send soldiers out in search of the errant lass without delay.

"Where is she?" His voice sounded less kind. Aislynn's knees knocked together under her gown.

"I don't know," she answered honestly, her voice a light whisper. "She slipped out the window with some soldiers, riding for safety."

The king's groan of displeasure was unmistakable, but he gathered himself and returned the inquisition back to Aislynn as the large, austere, red Scot resumed his position in the corner of the room, crossing his trunk-like arms over his chest. The men shared a knowing look before the King continued.

"Your uncle, he has retreated north, supposedly to Bothwell Castle, and barricaded himself inside. I am no' surprised, but I am mildly interested as to why he left ye and your sister behind. 'Tis less than considerate to leave women exposed to the bloodthirsty conduct of men. Did he nay fear for your safety or your virtue?"

Aislynn had no voice. In truth, 'twasn't possible for her to defend her uncle. He *had* left her and her sister behind, the remnants of his beleaguered army riding for Bothwell without them. Her dismay regarding her uncle marked her milky face. Aislynn was never one to mask her emotions, nor did she want to. She grimaced at the thought of him and despised her uncle for this predicament in which he placed her.

Her only hope was that the time she spent in the presence of this northern king was enough for Agnes to escape. This king may seem sensible, but who knew what he may do when crossed. Men's behaviors were fickle when it came to power, Aislynn understood well enough.

"'Tis especially troublesome," the King continued, "as your uncle has my wife and daughter imprisoned with Longshanks. If I were your uncle, I would worry that the King of Scotland might want to extract a measure of revenge on his own kin."

There it was, the threat Aislynn had been waiting for. A white flash of fear burst through her whole body, every inch of her shaking. *Was this the end for her? Would the King strike her down here and now? Or worse, imprison her in a cage? Toss her to his army?*

"'Tis fortunate for ye, lassie," the King resumed, "that we Scots are nay the brutal manner of men your English brethren have shown themselves to be. Rest assured, neither your sweet life, nor your virtue, will end this day."

Aislynn exhaled the painful breath she had been holding as she awaited the King's decision. At least 'twasn't death. But what retribution would come? Imprisonment in some dank, Scottish dungeon? Held for ransom? Bartered as an indentured servant? Perchance there were other punishments worse than death or dishonor. Aislynn kept her head bowed, trying to hide the panic and tears that threatened to spring forth.

The king exhaled his own breath, coming to terms with his decision. Laird Sinclair wouldn't care for it, undoubtedly. But he would do what Robert asked because he was a fierce supporter of the Bruce. The King was fortunate in men like Sinclair and his kin.

"I canna return ye to your family, that ye well ken. And until my wife and daughter are returned to me unscathed, ye shall remain under my protection, in the far northern Highlands with my man, Laird Sinclair, and his family." The King gestured to the Scot in the corner.

"What?" The ruddy Scot bellowed, what skin that could be seen above his beard flaming more red than his hair.

"What?" Aislynn echoed.

The Highlands? The far north Highlands? Aislynn's head swam in a faint, and her fingers reached for the desk to brace herself. Her whole life had been spent in the borderlands, the Lowlands of Scotland, where people at least spoke a passable English. The Highlands were home to barbarians, large monstrous people who spoke a strange, guttural language. And she must make the journey with the prodigious red Scot in the corner? The room swam before her eyes at that prospect.

"His kin shall watch o'er ye," the King spoke as though he heard nothing, "protect ye, and aye, ye will have to work – we all work hard in Scotland. No spoiled nobility here."

Aislynn scoffed under her breath at his assessment of English ladies.

"But ye will be treated with respect due any other clansman or woman. Ye shall have no contact with your family. Once my wife and daughter are returned, we shall escort ye back to your uncle's home, wherever and whenever that may be."

King Robert waved his hand toward the glowering Scotsman in the corner. The man moved to the door again, recalling the Highland soldiers.

"My men will take ye back to your chambers, where we shall ensure your windows are tightly barred." He sent a wry look to the Sinclair, who only shrugged at the king's implication. "When we find your sister, she shall be sent to another clan in the north. Dinna fret for her safety."

The King jerked his head, and the two Highlanders returned to Aislynn's side, forcibly accompanying her back to her chambers where they fitted the window slit with wooden planks to prevent her from following her sister. Their grip on her arms was almost welcome, for surely, she would have swooned to the floor without them. They slammed the door on their way out, and she heard a clunking sound – they were barring the door from the other side. She was locked in.

Her sister was wrong. Aislynn hadn't made any decision. Once again, for a number of times so high she couldn't count, the course of her life had been decided for her.

Abandoned by her uncle, despondent that her sister had escaped, and scared of what her future held, Aislynn threw herself on her lush brocade bedding and cried herself to sleep.

***

Once Asper Sinclair closed the study door behind the departing English lass, he shifted to look his king in the eye.

"Please tell me ye are joking," he begged Robert. "Ye canna mean for me to leave ye now, at the height of your war, to escort a lass up north? A lowly merchant could provide ye such a service!"

"Aye, indeed, he could," the King agreed. "But this is de Valence's niece. She is of royal blood, if remotely, and the King of England will nay take her capture well. I need her protected, to be accepted into your clan without acrimony. 'Tis more than an inconsequential errand, Asper."

The red giant pursed his lips. Robert watched the mechanics of his warrior's mind working quickly. Asper rubbed at his thick russet beard, selecting his words carefully.

"What if some of my men transport her instead?" Asper offered a new strategy. "She will still be well protected, spoken for by the Sinclair clan, and my men will be just as strong warriors as I."

"What's wrong with ye, Asper?" Mirth danced across the King's face, and Asper didn't like what he saw. "She's a comely lass. Surely, she was enough to encourage ye?"

"What?" Asper's eyes bulged from his face, and the King burst out in a peal of laughter at his kinsman's unease. "To take advantage of an English lassie? One of noble birth? What do ye make of me, Robert?"

The King calmed his breath and slapped his man on the shoulder. "Nay, nothing of the sort. As I told the lassie, we Scots are of a much nobler temperament than those English rutting dogs. But if we are to house the lass for a spell, what better way to help set ourselves up and force

England's hand than some well-matched marriages? Kingdoms have shifted and been conquered by a solid wedding 'afore."

Asper shook his head. The King had a twisted way of playing matchmaker, and many a Scotsman had become intimately familiar with this trait.

"I am no' in the place to take a wife, milord," Asper said flatly.

Understanding dawned across the King's features. "Aye, 'tis true. I had forgotten your recent handfast 'afore ye came south. And she is keeping an eye on the clan for ye."

The King's mild dejection at failing to make a solid match encouraged Asper's mind to work again.

"I have a suggestion," he intoned, a hint of a smile pulling at his heavy beard.

"Oh," the king responded with interest. "What would that be?"

Asper drew himself up to his full height, his wide shoulders and barrel chest crowding the narrow confines of the study.

"I think ye need me here, your Grace," Asper began. The King raised one bushy eyebrow.

"Ooch, do ye now?" he joked. Asper narrowed his dark green eyes.

"*Aye*, ye do. But ye are correct, someone responsible needs to escort the lass north, keep her from the English, and protect her honor along the way. Even perchance wed the young woman. Ye need a strong Sinclair man to do this task."

Robert the Bruce remained quiet, waiting to see where Asper was going with this lecture.

"Or perchance, two. My brothers, John and Marcus, they are a strong pair. With a few other Sinclair men, they could see the lass north safely."

Asper Sinclair paused, and the Bruce's eyebrow rose impossibly higher on his forehead, waiting. "And?"

Asper's furry lips twitched in anticipation of his next words.

"And neither brother is spoken for. Both Marcus and John are fair enough on the eyes, or so I've been told, and John's light-hearted character is well known amongst the clans. Marcus is considered a charmer. If ye want a young lass perchance to find a mate with a Highland clan and solidify your position, I ken of no one better suited to woo a lassie than my younger brothers."

The Bruce bit at the inside of his lip, considering Asper's proposal. 'Twas sound, to be sure. Asper was a chieftain, a close adviser, and betrothed, so his ability to make the lass swoon was limited. The red-headed warrior spoke true – his younger brothers would be much more engaging to a lass who lost her family, her home, and was being secreted north. While the odds of the lass falling for any Highland man was nothing more than a wishful chimera, the odds indubitably improved if the men involved were the Sinclair brothers.

Their ability to woo, to make lasses giddy, to bring smiles and blushes to the most staunch young women, was renowned in the Highlands. Coupled with their immense sizes and ability to fight (even fight dirty if the cause arose), the brothers made perfect candidates for this endeavor. The Bruce nodded slowly as he wrapped his mind around the idea. And the longer he considered it, the more appealing the idea became.

"Asper, I do think ye have found a sound solution. While John may complain about leaving our battle front, having strong escorts and loyal swords to rout any rogue English in the north may be ideal." Robert clasped Asper's forearm in a strong grip. "Gather yon brothers and let them know the good news of their royal task."

Flicking his gaze past the King to the rousing hubbub coming in from the window slit, Asper shrugged.

"Perchance 'twill hold till morning. I dinna think my brothers will be in any shape to accept royal decrees this night."

Chapter Two: The Wager

The slit of the tent was wide enough to allow a piercing ray of sunlight through and radiate on John Sinclair's eye. Blinking at the offending light, he snapped his eyes shut to stop the dull throb that started behind his eyes and encompassed his whole skull. The rays of early morning sunrise only made the throbbing worse.

Fecking drink, he chided himself.

John shifted to his side, hoping to fall back asleep once out of the sun's dreadful gleam, but his aching head wouldn't give any relief. Nor did his aching bladder. Hungover and tasting the sour remains of whiskey in his mouth, he barely made it past the tent flap before dinner from the night before found its way up and out. Whiskey had flowed far too freely yestereve, and his gullet was going to punish him for his excessive libations.

Rising slowly, he shifted his swollen, aching eyes around the bailey, praying no one watched him lose his stomach like a sloshed lad. To his good fortune, the rest of the men, his layabout brother included, still snored the morning away. Stepping past the make-shift tents, he made his way to the horse trough, and taking a deep breath, he dunked his head into the icy water.

Shockingly cold, but effective. 'Twas nothing like ice-cold water to chase away a night of drinking. The shock forced his aching head to calm and helped him fully open his eyes. And his now empty stomach was much relieved to boot. As much as he would have liked to have slept longer, the sun was up, and so was he. Time to take on the day.

After emptying his throbbing bladder and ducking back into the tent, John toed at Marcus, his snoring brother, to wake him. Always a heavy sleeper, the man was oft impossible to wake. John kicked him again, harder this time, the tip of his leather boot finding Marcus's rib cage.

"Wha—? What?" Marcus mumbled, rolling to his side. A pain-fill grimace crossed his face.

"Get up, ye lugabout," John scolded. "Come dip your head. We have a busy day ahead."

"What day? Why are ye up with the chickens?" Marcus rubbed his hand across his dark amber hair that matched his brother's and readily marked him as a Sinclair. "Ye are the only one up at this time, to be sure."

"Nay, ye are just lazy. We may have won the battle yesterday, but there's much to do today. The King will have assignments for us," John spoke as though he hadn't recently remedied his own drunken morning ills.

Marcus threw off his covers, reminding John of a trampled urchin. His stained tunic rucked above his well-muscled belly, and John had the sense that if he stepped closer to his younger brother, the man's stench would make his eyes water.

John grabbed Marcus's tunic by the shoulder and dragged him toward the water trough.

By late morning, Dumfries Castle bustled with energy, spirits still high after the astounding defeat of the Earl of Pembroke's much larger army at Loudoun Hill. The Bruce's funneling tactics worked once again, and the English battalion in Galloway fell in a single line under the Scots' onslaught. The funnel of death created an ample killing field, and the Scots reveled that their recent military tactics worked as well as they had.

After ten years of clawing at an uphill battle for liberty, this series of victories under Robert the Bruce inspired the men in a way not seen in over a decade, since the great Wallace had led the first Scots uprisings.

The Seduction of the Glen

John and Marcus spent most of their morning running banal errands for surgeons and tending to animals — refilling the horse trough in particular. Their older brother, Laird Asper Sinclair, remained locked away in the study of the stronghold with several other chieftains, planning their next strategies. The men working in the bailey were placing their wagers on whether that meant moving north and east to rout the English presently on Scots soil, or if they were to march south to meet the King of England and his factions head on.

Covered in horse muck and peat from cleaning out the barn, John and Marcus didn't hear their brother's footsteps until the red giant was right behind them. He coughed discreetly. His brothers jammed their pitchforks into a mass of caked, brown grass and each turned in a lazy half-circle to face him.

"Brothers," he spoke, nodding slightly. "Get yourselves into some clean clothes. The King demands your appearance in the hall."

Asper's enigmatic words left a poor impression on his brothers. Neither one moved toward the tents.

"What kettle of fish have ye gotten us into this time, Asp?" John asked.

Marcus's cheek flexed, knowing that every time Asper gave them a command, 'twas not the best news. Since they were children, John and Marcus had been pulled into all sorts of misadventures due to Asper's actions. They weren't ready to jump at his request now.

Asper ran his fingers through his wild thatch of hair. Though he may have brushed it down earlier in the day, every hair stood on end, a red mane around his head. John and Marcus gave less thought to their similarly colored hair – John kept the sides of his locks clipped, similar to Asper, to tame the deep vermilion waves, while Marcus cut all his hair shorter so it hardly skimmed his neck.

"Can ye just make yourselves presentable? 'Tis the King who wants to see ye!"

Asper stormed off with aggravated stomping. John and Marcus faced each other; mirrored smirks plastered on their lips at getting their brother's goat again.

"Ye look like shite," Marcus observed.

"No less than ye," John retorted. He glanced down at his manure stained tunic. "I guess we should go change. No use meeting the King in shit-stained plaid."

John threw his pitchfork into the corner of the barn and headed to the horse trough for the second time that day.

***

King Robert was finishing a midday meal with his closest advisers in the main hall when John and Marcus arrived. The scent of bread, honey, and cheese lingered in the air, and John's stomach growled in response. He hadn't eaten yet and didn't think to snack as he scrubbed his skin before his conference with the King. He hoped someone offered him food.

Asper, Laird of the Sinclairs of Reay, met them as they approached the tables, leading them to the King. At least both brothers had the good sense to wash their faces and change into fresh tunics, Asper noted. All three of the Sinclairs marched in long strides to the King's table, grasping the hilts of their swords when they bent low in deference. Robert tapped on the table, waving at them to rise.

"Please, do not. We have an important matter to discuss. Have ye eaten yet?"

Thank the Good Lord. John, mouth watering, flicked his eyes heavenward before shaking his head nay.

"Here," King Robert waved his arm again, this time over the trencher before him. "Load up a platter, then join me."

In a swift move and with a swirl of his black-furred cape, the King stood and departed for the hallway. John and Marcus scrambled to throw vittles onto a plate and chase after Robert and Asper.

They followed their brother into the study off the main hall where a massive, ornately carved desk held court in the center of the room. Light from the window slit was interrupted only by the shadow of Robert, who gazed out into the bailey where his kinsmen and army were making themselves at home.

"Gentlemen," the King began in a tone that caused John to take the grouse leg from his watering mouth and drop it onto his plate. This meeting with the King, 'twas more than just a conference regarding military movements. John flicked his intense verdant eyes to his brother, who stared straight ahead at Robert, hard and unflappable.

John's lips pressed into a thin line. His older brother and chieftain knew why they were having an audience with the King and, John had no doubt, this would not be a welcome assignment. Further, this unwanted assignment was Asper's doing. *Feckin' Asper and his machinations*, John grumbled to himself. He dropped his platter onto the fine desk and crossed his arms, letting his body display the ire that his mouth daren't speak in the presence of the King of Scotland.

"We have an important task for ye both. Your brother and I believe ye are the best men to complete this assignment with success. Ye'll also need to select two other men to accompany ye."

John and Marcus shared a deliberate look. One of John's dense russet eyebrows rose high on his forehead as he spoke.

"Accompany us where?"

"Back to Reay keep," Asper answered for the King.

"What?" Marcus wasn't able to keep his shock hidden. His whole body stiffened.

John rested his hand atop Marcus's arm, trying to subdue him, even though he wanted to respond the same way.

Leave the King's army in the midst of this glorious war of independence? John was incredulous. *Just as they accomplished their first significant victory?*

"We have an asset," King Robert answered simply. "We need you to bring this asset north, hide it well. And if we manage to retain this asset," Robert shrugged casually, "the more the better. 'Twould be all the better for us if we keep this asset for as long as we can, so I dinna ken when ye will return."

"Asset? What kind of asset?"

John's eyes rifled back and forth between Asper and Robert as a creeping sensation snaked up his spine. Something significant was amiss. Otherwise, why all the mystery?

"So, will ye do it?" Asper asked, keeping his face to the King. He daren't look his own brothers in the eye. *Just how bad was this assignment?*

"Do I get to ken what the task is 'afore I accept?" John ventured.

"Nay," the King responded.

"I told him ye would do it, already," Asper admitted.

Both John and Marcus turned their gape-mouthed faces to Asper. What, exactly, did he volunteer them for?

"We would do what?" Marcus tried to get an answer.

"Will ye accept this task?" the King asked again.

The silence in the room was thick, and breathing was like trying to catch one's breath after being submerged in a loch for too long – painful and wavering. John and Marcus caught each other's gaze once more. How did one say *no* to the King? Especially when their brother already confirmed their participation in this scheme?

"Aye," John broke the silence. What other option did he have? "Aye, I'll do it." He tipped his head toward Marcus. "We will do it. And I ken who we may bring to help us in this endeavor. So, what is it? The asset?"

John thought he saw the King's lips twitch under his light beard – *was he trying not to smile?* Tales of the King's strange sense of humor ran rampant among the clans.

"I'll have the asset brought here. Asper?"

The Sinclair Laird nodded and stepped from the study, speaking to the Highland warriors standing guard in the hall. After several minutes, they returned, a third person held firmly between them.

John's eyes widened in shock.

A woman. A nervous, beautiful young woman with earthy hair and dressed in forest green, resembling a fairy plucked from the trees.

What manner of prisoner was this? Did she have the asset?

***

Aislynn's arms were secured behind her back, but that didn't stop the lassie from holding her head high, so high that she seemed to be looking down her tiny, straight nose at them. Her pale hazel-green eyes were hard, an expression unfamiliar in women, at least to John. A golden net snood gathered most of her fair brown hair at the base of her neck, but several loose tendrils framed her milky face. Her gown, a shiny green cloth embroidered in a silver thread, bespoke her status. This wasn't just any woman. She was noble, perhaps, dare he guess, *regal?* And definitely not Scots. Who was this woman?

John's breath stuck in his chest. *Christ's blood, was she the asset?*

Robert answered his silent question. "Allow me to introduce Lady Aislynn de Valence, niece to the Earl of Pembroke and to King Edward Longshanks himself." Robert all but spat out the names as he spoke them.

John snapped his mouth shut. After Aymer de Valence absconded, leaving Dumfries to be overtaken by the Scots with their success at

Loudoun Hill, John assumed the Earl took the entirety of his household with him, including his surprisingly attractive if pretentious niece. Who left a defenseless young lassie behind?

Marcus and John shared the same curious glance before returning their attentions to the King and the woman by his side. She ignored them all, as though she wouldn't be treated like Highland cattle for barter.

"The King has requested ye bring the lassie deep into the Highlands. Undoubtedly, 'tis no place deeper than the Sinclair lands of Caithness." Asper's bright head nodded as though he agreed with his own statement.

So like Asper – John also kept that thought to himself.

"What would ye have us do?" Marcus's perplexed voice resounded. "Kidnap the lass? Take her home?" A look of insult shadowed his face. "Are ye sending us home, brother? Do ye no' need us here?"

John barked out a laugh at his brother's indignation. He sounded truly wounded. But John too wondered at the reasoning behind asking the Sinclairs to take the lass. Surely other clans would have been just as able to handle this task and keep the Sinclair warriors close to the battle for Scotland?

"I need as many here as I can get," King Robert agreed in a flat tone. He flicked his soft brown eyes to the lass next to him. If John didn't know any better, he would have thought the King was uncomfortable with this endeavor. "But I need men I can trust, men who will assure her safety, and –"

Shifting his head to the King at the abrupt pause, John squinted his eyes. "And what?"

A sharp elbow forcibly struck him between the ribs. John's angry gaze turned on his older brother.

"I will tell ye all ye must ken for this task," Robert finished. "For now, ye are here to meet the lass and prepare yourselves."

John looked between Asper, the King, and the proud, petrified lass standing by the desk. Shrugging one shoulder in acceptance, he moved closer to the pasty Englishwoman and bowed before her.

"Milady," he said in a low voice as he bowed, "My name is John MacInnes Sinclair. I am at your service."

When she didn't respond to his introduction, he stepped back and let his younger brother step forward.

"And I am Marcus MacInnes Sinclair. Also, at your service," he told her as he gave an abrupt bow.

"These men," the King gestured to John and Marcus, "shall be your escorts north."

***

Aislynn tried to keep her wits about her as she watched the engagement between the men. The three on the opposite side of the desks were brothers, 'twas as obvious as the sun on a summer day. Similar in height and build – dreadfully tall, with thick chests and powerful legs, they shared several other respects: dull green and blue plaid wraps that hung from their bodies as though they considered dressing for royalty a bother, and shades of dark burgundy-brown hair, a color of which Aislynn had never before encountered on a person's head.

The older of the three men, the one with the fullest head of hair that boasted shaved temples and small braids near his face that matched the lighter red of his beard, was the same immense warrior present the first time she was dragged to the King's study. *My uncle's study,* she thought indignantly.

The other two men were perchance half a score younger. The one with an easy smile but fearsome green eyes who introduced himself as John, kept his locks full across the crown and back but short on the sides, almost as though 'twas shaved, too. While not quite as tall as his older brother, the strangely shaved-yet-full hair gave him a more frightening appearance.

The other man, Marcus, didn't smile as readily, but his green eyes seemed softer. Aislynn could easily mistake that as kindness – most likely it meant he was just a youth and less jaded regarding the harsh realities of the world. *Poor young man,* Aislynn thought. *He will learn the evils of the world soon enough.* Unlike the wild hair of his brother, Marcus kept his hair clipped short, which only made him look even younger. *How is a lad so young part of the army?* Pity for the young man washed over her, and she shook it off, refocusing her attention to the man introduced as John.

She probably should have acknowledged his introduction, shown that she was still noble despite her present captive circumstances, but the thought of touching one of the wild Highlanders made her stomach churn. She'd heard stories of how they lived in squalor and wore little more than those colored, plaid wraps (and Agnes even joked once that she'd heard the men wear naught beneath when the plaid is wrapped around their hips! Aislynn's sister was nothing if not shameless).

Thoughts of her sister pulled achingly at her heart, and her proud gaze dropped to the floor. She blinked back her tears, determined not to show any measure of weakness to these villainous men.

***

"Lassie?" One of the men asked her in his guttural Scots affectation. Blinking quickly several times, she peered at him from under hooded eyes. "Are ye well? Ye suddenly dinna look hale."

'Twas the Highlander named John who spoke. His voice had a kindness to it, but she wasn't tricked by any niceties on the part of these men. They were infamously vile, uncivilized, and any polite manners were undoubtedly only a ruse to gain her trust and use it against her uncles. She shook her head in response.

"We shall get ye back to your chambers," the King commanded in a soft tone, one she had heard from him before but didn't trust.

At every moment she waited to hear her final punishment. Though, she must admit, being held captive deep in the Highland wilds seemed as horrible a punishment as she could imagine. Strange people, odd customs, and their general hatred for all things English. Death would be more welcome. In the obscurity of Northern Scotland, who could come to her aid? The possibility of her sister finding her was unlikely. She would be at the mercy of men ready to snatch her innocence from her. She'd end up a tainted, abused woman, trapped in an uncivilized land for the rest of her days. Her bleak future. Yes, death surely would have been better.

The King had moved to the door to recall the Highland guards when the savagely shaved John moved forward and gently clasped her elbow in his large paw of a hand. She wanted to shake him off, hide from this dire fate, but the weight of his warm hand on her was comforting. He didn't hold her like a guard, rather more of an escort.

"I can take the lassie back to her chambers. If we are to travel north with her, she should ken who she is traveling with."

'Twas the most sane statement Aislynn had heard since this warring turmoil in her life began months ago. Her uncle had preached the great hope of English rule in Scotland, only to be run off his claimed land once Robert the Bruce returned, leaving her and her sister abandoned. Then to be captured and at the mercy of the Scots, 'twas any wonder her mind still functioned with any rational thought!

Yet here, after all this, one of these uncivilized monsters had a care about her. Aislynn swallowed her shock and waited for the King's answer.

"Aye," he nodded, his lips thin with consideration. "Please escort Lady Aislynn to her chambers."

Perchance Asper Sinclair had the right of it, the King reflected. While John and his brothers were oft seen as crazed and carefree, John's behavior changed once the woman entered the study. If the King needed someone to get close to the lassie, make an *alliance,* John Sinclair may well be the man Robert needed. King Robert flicked his eyes to Asper, who didn't try to hide the wry grin that parted his wine-colored beard. *Ooch, the Sinclair bastard knew what he was doing the whole time.*

***

Aislynn thought it wise to keep silent as they walked the shadowy halls toward her chamber-prison. Surrounded by luxuries, true, the lock on the door and guards right outside bespoke the truth. She was no guest, merely a prisoner. And the last thing she wanted to do was strike up a conversation with one of her guards.

John, conversely, had no such compunctions regarding his ward. His courteous words about Auchinleck Castle bordered on jocularity. When he did ask a question that she refrained from answering, he skipped over it with no comment, providing his own response. Only when he began to ask about her family did she respond.

"Have ye any family here in Scotland? Other than your uncle, I mean?"

"No!" she bit out, rather too quickly in John's estimation. Probably hiding the truth, and he couldn't blame her. 'Twas difficult to be fully honest in a precarious situation like hers.

"Ooch, weel, I did no' mean offense. I'm just curious, ye ken?" His pace slowed as he chatted, and he raised a bushy eyebrow at her. "Ye have family in England then, I must presume."

"For a man of your stature, you do have an impeccable vocabulary," she told him in a flat, condescending tone.

He didn't let the insult halt his movements, but her statement gave him pause. What manner of men did these English think they were?

"Of my stature, lass?" He wanted to know exactly what she thought of him.

"I mean no offense," she repeated his words, dryly. "But all the tales I've heard of Highlanders, and most Scots in general, truth be told, say that ye are nothing more than an uncivilized bunch of clans with no reason or education."

"Mmmm." John had heard the same tales among English and Scots in the Lowlands. If she meant to shock him, she wasn't successful. He'd heard worse from his own kin.

"Yes, my family is in England," she continued. "My mother died when I was a child, and my father is close to the King, and has no need for daughters, other than to make a marriage match. Until that inevitability, my father, the Baron of Winchcombe, found it more expedient to send us away until such a time as he found us useful. Scotland seemed as good a place as any, I suppose."

"Us?" John probed. He'd heard another de Valence niece had escaped. Perchance this was the same lass?

Aislynn stiffened, realizing the mistake of her words. She tried to cover herself with a moue of untruth.

"Yes, a younger sister who departed earlier this year."

There, not an honest statement by any means, but it paralleled the truth. Agnes did leave a few days ago, so it was earlier in the year. *God save me from such lies,* she prayed and hoped the wild-haired man moved on in his questions.

"Do ye miss her, your sister?" he asked, a question which took her by surprise. She'd expected probing to find the missing sister, not an inquiry into her emotions. Aislynn shrugged offhandedly.

"Yes, of course. Hopefully I will see her again soon."

Yes, John thought, *hopefully.*

He pressed a large hand against her upper arm, halting her before the formidable door of her chambers.

"Here ye are, lass. I ken ye are cloistered here, but once we leave for the Highlands, and ye can breathe fresh air and see the expanse of Scottish soil, I hope ye feel less of a prisoner and more of a guest. Though your movements may be guarded, the King is a good man and desires ye to be treated with respect. Of that I am certain and can promise that fealty to ye."

Aislynn's light hazel green eyes squinted at his kind words. She continued to stare at him while he held open her door as though he were an escort, not a jailer. John waited patiently until she nodded her fair head, silently bidding him good day, and stepped into her room.

Just as John moved to close the door, she shifted slightly, turning her profile to catch his gaze over her shoulder. Time spun out for a brief, heated moment, holding each other's eyes, then John nodded in return and closed the door, securing it behind him.

***

John returned to the King's study to find his brothers' heads bowed over the desk with the King, their words low.

"So, what is truly going on with the lass?" John asked, his booming voice disrupting their hushed conversation.

The King's eyes flicked from Asper to John to Marcus, and he pinched his nose. When he didn't answer, Asper straightened his deep green plaid and began to speak.

"The lass is a prisoner, aye," Asper confirmed what they already knew. "But her positioning close to the Earl of Pembroke and the King himself is a strong one. If we were to wed her to a man of high status here in Scotland, 'twould solidify our positioning, and perchance the English would nay be so ardent in their aggressions on our soil. If one of their own were a Scot, that is."

Asper let the implication hang, hoping he wouldn't have to explain this opportunity in full detail. His brothers were not stupid, just guileless. The light of understanding dawned on John well before it did on Marcus.

"Wait, brother. Ye, and the Bruce here, ye want one o'us to wed the lass?"

Marcus was silent but looked as though his brother hit him across the face with a plank.

The King and Asper Sinclair nodded together.

"As the brothers of Laird Sinclair of Reay, ye hold positions of power. 'Tis a sound match," King Robert intoned. He moved around the desk to place a hand on each of their shoulders. "And ye would be wed to royalty. A niece twice removed from the great King Longshanks of England? Your bairns would have royal blood."

"Why would I want English blood in my bairns' veins?" Marcus seemed horrified at the prospect, but John, having just spent a few close moments with the lass, was intrigued.

"She is bonnie, to be sure," John countered. "Haughty as one would expect from the highborn English, but nay cruel. There are worse wives to be had."

Marcus's eyes brightened with a green light at John's defense of the English lass.

"Do ye want her, then? Do ye think ye can claim her?" Marcus asked. A sardonic grin tugged at his scruffy, bearded cheeks.

"Why, do ye want to claim her? Ye have no' even talked to her."

"Want to wager on it, Johnnie lad?" Marcus asked.

"Who are ye callin' a lad, laddie? And 'twould nay be a fair wager. What manner of woman wants a weak lad such as yourself? Any lass would prefer a strong man like me," John teased his brother, puffing up his chest, and Marcus's face set hard.

"A wager, then. A silver to the man who wins her hand."

"Wait," the King interjected. "Ye shall be her guards, aye. In truth, she is a prisoner. 'Twill take much for her to want to wed either of ye, Scots blood notwithstanding."

"Nay a'tall, once she gets to know me," John announced.

"Once she gets to know me, ye brash *scunner*," Marcus taunted back.

"Ooch, weel then." Asper knew that one Sinclair brother would undoubtedly win the lass – these two were naught if not staunch competitors. Mayhap not romantics, but what they lacked in wooing skills, they made up for in ardor. They could make her forget her imprisoned state. The lass would have to fight the brothers' attentions off with a stick, Asper knew without question. He grinned at King Robert, who gave his final instructions.

"But she is also a guest of the crown, a respected noble lady. Ye are to protect her from those who may want to cause her harm, and ye'd do well to remember that. Perchance then ye will have a chance with the lass. May the best man win her hand," the King said, and waved them off with a flick of his hand. "Ye leave on the morrow."

Chapter Three: A Long Voyage North

The horses huffed with anticipation of the journey ahead, their breaths small puffs around their muzzles. They were packed with every manner of foodstuffs and many of Lady Aislynn's belongings. Marcus took the initiative to escort the prisoner to the inner bailey where John waited with the horses. Two other Sinclair men waited with him – the graying Oggie Sinclair and the pink-eared youth, Etan. The four men made up the party escorting the lady to her new home with the Sinclairs.

As Marcus walked with Aislynn, he explained that the Sinclair lands lay in the far north of Scotland proper, beyond the Great Glen, buttressed by Pentland Firth and the mighty North Sea itself. With luck, they could make the journey in a fortnight or so.

When they stepped towards the yard, John looked up and several flashes of conflicting emotions thrummed through him. The first was a twinge of awe. The Lady Aislynn was stunningly attired in an earth-toned chestnut riding gown and a rich hunter-green cape that flattered her coloring. Her hair had been elegantly coiffed in a deep brown caul that held her shining locks off the delicate bones of her face.

Truly, he had nary seen such an image of pristine womanhood in his life, and his manhood flexed beneath his tunic and tartan. Throwing his plaid casually across his chest and over his shoulder, he marched toward the Lady and his brother.

For that was the second emotion that overwhelmed him – jealousy. Unlike the stiff and rather abrupt conversation he'd held with the lassie, she seemed at ease with his brother, her hand placed lightly on Marcus's arm as they walked. That same sense of ease danced over her fair face, and John envied their relaxed interaction. His insides roiled watching them, and he had a worrying sense that 'twas more than just the wager with his brother that caused him such internal distress. His reaction to Aislynn was visceral, animal, and for the first time since they were young lads, John wanted to rip out Marcus's throat.

John couldn't stop himself; he rushed the couple exiting the main hall and clasped his hand around Aislynn's arm. She raised her soft brown eyes to him in surprise.

"Here, milady. Allow me to help ye onto your horse."

"I can help the Lady just fine, brother," Marcus retorted with a touch of ire.

"Aye, ye can, but your horse still needs ye to load your pack, so I will help the Lady."

Marcus cut John a hard expression, then gave a courtly bow to Aislynn before ambling off toward his ride, yelling at Etan for not finishing his chore of loading the horses.

Aislynn continued to stare at the brazen Highlander from beneath hooded eyes. Surely, a lowly prisoner was not worth the effort to quarrel over who would assist her onto her horse. The strange behavior of her sentinels caused her to fret more than she already was.

And she was fretful. She'd nary traveled farther than Dumfries, having resided much of her life on the civilized estates of England with the royal family. Now she was to be forcefully removed to the far north at the edge of the world, where only uncivilized barbarians were reputed to live. Her insides shook and quivered like a Christmas pudding. The odd behavior of her captors only worsened that quivering.

"Come milady, permit me to assist ye," John spoke with an air of formality. "Your gown and the lass who wears it are both too fine to risk a fall in the dirt."

At first, she thought him mocking, his intense green eyes watching her every move. The look of him, however, appeared earnest, and his hard body was poised to lift her into the saddle. Sweet words may pour honey into her ears, but she was not of a mind to fall for it. Why should he treat a prisoner of war with such geniality?

The warrior's hand was warm on her arm, almost scorching through the rough fabric of her riding gown. *How did he retain such heat in this briskly cold country?* And unlike the gentle green gaze of the younger Sinclair who escorted her to the yard, this Sinclair man, with his broad chest and barbarian hair, had eyes that burned as fiercely as his skin. This man was no gentle spirit.

But his hand held her arm as though he held glass, and his ready assistance as she mounted her mare (they had permitted her to keep the white and gray palfrey she affectionately called "Sweetie," even though the mare could run faster than the autumn winds) made her wonder if there were more to this hard man than his outward appearance and demeanor suggested.

After she settled into the saddle, a brief rush of hope surged in her, that he would release the reins to mount his own destrier and she'd make her escape, ride Sweetie hard and fast south to England. The man was more shrewd than she'd expected. He held tight to the reins even as he swept himself atop his horse in one fluid move that showed both his agility and more leg than Aislynn had seen on a man before. His dusky green plaid wrap lifted with his movements, and his thickly muscled legs flexed to grip the horse with his thighs.

She turned her head away from the view, averting her eyes as a rich blush rose from her neck to her hairline. The man was her enemy. She should not rest her eyes on him so.

Fortunately, his back was to her as she struggled to regain her composure, and she hoped most of her color returned when the red giant shifted on his horse to address her and the rest of the traveling party.

"Are ye settled, lass?" His gentle voice also clashed with his fierce expression, asking her in a kindly manner. Not trusting her own voice, she nodded. His commanding green gaze then moved to the other men astride their horses.

"And ye, Marcus? Are ye ready?"

This time John grinned, and Aislynn couldn't hide her shock at how his entire being changed with that smile. No longer a vengeful warrior, John now appeared easy-going, almost cheerful, open and engaging.

Keeping her eyes cast downward, she looked shyly from John to his Sinclair men. This was it. They were off, the horses ambling past the postern gate, and Aislynn feared she might never again see her home. Who knew what circumstances she would encounter, what impediments to her safety, or even if King Edward would ever try to rescue a distant female relative from the Scots clutches?

Aislynn knew. She knew Longshanks as well, if not better, than most. He was not a man who trifled. Longshanks would leave her to rot in the Highland to focus on concerns he deemed more worthy of the crown's time. A lowly niece was not one of those concerns. Her uncle had abandoned her. Her sister had absconded without her. Her King had forgotten about her.

She risked a glance back at the Dumfries stronghold which had been her home for the last half-score of years, steeling herself so as not to weep as they exited the bailey.

Would she ever have a home again?

***

Their ride north was a sauntering pace, most likely out of consideration for her. Aislynn had to laugh inwardly. *What fools these Scotsmen were,* she thought with pretension. Having ridden some of the finest English thoroughbreds, this jaunt on a gentle mare was an easy ride.

Much of the Lowlands and the moors made for slow going regardless, heavy with mud and muck, and the horses bogged down as they crossed the landscape. When possible, they rode close to the trees, searching for firmer trail-ways north. She heard Marcus griping behind her in his deep Scots burr, complaining about the sluggish nature of their journey.

"Say what ye may of hoeing around the rocks o' the Highlands, 'tis a fair sight better than mucking through the moors." His voice rumbled like a growling dog's.

31

"Mmm," John mumbled in agreement, keeping his complaints to himself.

Their ride over the course of the day, while uneventful, had not met her expectations. Riding her own horse, enjoying the fresh Scottish air, she didn't feel much like a prisoner. John had been correct in that. The Sinclairs also permitted her to attend her personal needs on her own and didn't watch over her when they did take short breaks. At best, they made sure a man rode alongside her, and that was all. They seemed, at least to Aislynn, to think that guarding over a slight English lady didn't require much effort. She huffed to herself. Perchance their lax attention could work to her benefit.

Night fell in a slow curtain as the Sinclairs tied the horses to the trees and made camp under the stars. They dined on dried haddock and oatcakes and prepared to bed down on the clumps of new, cushioned grass under the leafy boughs of fresh spring trees.

Aislynn lay her cape on the lumpy grass, plumping it as much as possible to make a decent bed. 'Twas the first time she'd slept on the ground, and she was puzzled in how to best make it comfortable enough for sleep.

Behind her, a voice cleared to gain her attention, and she swiveled on her heels, looking up at John Sinclair, his hair a deep russet-brown halo in the moonlight. His plaid hung limply from his hand. Evidently, he had slipped on a pair of worn trews while her back was turned.

"Here," he said, extending the plaid to her. "Ye are nay used to the cool night air or camping on the ground. I dinna need it."

She took it with a pursed smile as thanks and lay the woolen garment across her shoulders. The earthy, heady male scent of the older Sinclair brother clung to the material. Though she may not have shown it, she was grateful for the extra layer.

Marcus followed his brother's lead and handed over his woolen plaid as well. She again nodded her thanks and lay on her cloak, wrapped in the warmth of the Sinclair plaids. Though her muscles ached from the day of riding, she didn't expect to fall asleep anytime soon.

Sleeping outside in the fresh air was a novel adventure for Aislynn – pampered as she had been with satin and linen bedding, sleeping in naught but her cloak was a strange experience. Even with the plaids offered by the Sinclair brothers, she spent the night shivering, slept little, and felt a groggy mess when she woke early the next morn.

A twittering bird flitted amongst the leaves above her head. She rubbed her eyes and peered around at the men still snoring in a loose circle around her. They seemed oblivious to the world, and Aislynn decided that now was the time to take advantage of their laziness. What kind of men were these Scots who didn't keep watch over their prisoner? *Fools,* she thought with disdain.

Moving slowly to avoid making any noise, she lay the borrowed plaids on the ground and gathered her cloak around her shoulders. Her eyes scanned over the campsite, hoping an oatcake or extra haddock was within easy reach, but no. Everything was packed away and too close to the men for her to risk breakfast. She hoped to find something to eat as she made her way back south.

The bird kept twittering as she lifted her skirts and roamed through the slender copse of trees, convincing herself that she escaped without notice. Surely the bird would have stopped singing had she disrupted it. Keeping her steps light, a slight smile crossed her face for the first time in months. Finally, *finally,* she was free.

But she was also lost.

***

Aislynn remembered to keep the rising sun to her left – while that may help her stay on a southward path, winding among the trees caused her to lose her sense of direction. Was she going more southwest? More southeast?

A crunching sound on fallen branches in the woods near her made her jump. She bit back a squeal of panic. Her eyes searched for the source of the sound, only to hear a voice directly behind her.

"Ye forgot something, lassie," John Sinclair said.

She whipped around to see the Highlander, shining brightly in the morning sunlight, holding out his plaid to her. Aislynn groaned inwardly, her chest tightening with nerves. *So, he was not as lazy as he appeared.*

"If ye are going to make a run for it, ye may need the plaid to keep warm at night."

Was he letting her escape? Somehow, she just couldn't believe he would do such a thing, act against his king's direct orders, but that didn't stop her from reaching out for the plaid. He gripped her wrist as she did so, yanking her close.

"But I canna let ye make a run for it, understand?"

"Because I am your prisoner," Aislynn grumbled under her breath, but John's keen ears heard her, nonetheless.

"Nay, ye are no' a prisoner," he began, but Aislynn cut him off with a hard look and sharp words.

"Really? What else would you call it? I recognize my uncles are responsible for the imprisonment of the Bruce's wife and daughter, and I am naught more than retribution! You are to hide me away, imprison me in a God-forsaken land, and keep me captive with little chance of ever seeing my home again!"

Her voice reached a panicked crescendo, and the twittering of the birds stopped. John loosened his grip on her arm but didn't let go.

"Is that what ye think? That we are going to take ye to the Highlands and throw ye into a dank dungeon until ye die of the bloody cough? What type of men do ye take us for? We are nay the manner of men to throw innocent lassies into a pit. And my King would nay condone such treatment of women." Anger erupted in his harsh voice.

Aislynn stopped struggling against his hold, her arm going limp in his grasp.

"Then, why am I here? Why are you taking me to the Highlands?" Her tone sounded as desperate as she felt.

"Ye truly canna guess?" He raised a darkly scarlet eyebrow and sighed. When she didn't answer, he shrugged. "What do ye think the loyal Scots want to do to a relative of the enemy? Not all men are as thoughtful as our King. And what of your own people? How would they welcome a lassie who'd spent most of her life in the enemy's lands? Think, lass."

He spoke aloud the words that haunted her mind since her sister and uncle left. She had no place, no home, no family anymore. Who could she rely on to protect and defend her? Where was she to go? Was the supposed King of Scotland truly providing her with an option? With hope?

"So, if you are not my warden, then what are you?"

John's long fingers scratched absently at his light beard as he considered.

"Nay a guard, but a guardian. A protector, if ye will. Sent to escort a British lass to the safety of the Highlands."

This time, Aislynn's aggravated eyebrows rose, but in disbelief. *Did he honestly expect her to believe that?*

"Ye dinna believe me? No' all men, or all kings for that matter, are set against ye." His fingers dropped from her arm to her hand, holding it as suited a man who was wooing a lady. His fingertips were warm and delicate against hers. "I am no' set against ye. I only want for your safety."

"And my freedom?" she asked with an edge to her voice. Sinclair only shrugged.

"Are any of us truly free?" His intense green eyes bore into her. "Ye can be free as long as I can stand your guard. Is that agreeable?"

What choice did she have? 'Twas a fair sight better than landing in a moldy Scottish dungeon.

"Aye. I can agree to that," she told him. He squeezed her hand and dropped it when the sounds of other men approaching crunched throughout the woods.

"John, have ye found the lassie yet? I canna believe ye lost her!" a voice taunted. Etan and Oggie crashed through the brush, followed by Marcus who cast a wry look at John. Sending a smug smile his brother's way, John put his arm around Aislynn's waist.

"If we are done with our promenade, we should continue our way north," John announced, swinging Aislynn toward the horses and giving his chagrined brother a wink.

Chapter Four: When We Must Guard Our Loyalties

To Aislynn, the air seemed to thin, become crisp and sharp in her lungs as they rode farther north. Even as summer was coming on, a dankness gripped the land. For as rocky as the land was, bogs, lochs, and fens littered the mountains and glens. After several days of gray drizzle, the clouds shed their modesty and permitted swaths of sunlight to reflect in a glittering landscape. She was truly in awe of the regal mountains, rich purple heather moorlands, and the reflecting lochs. The majestic vistas stole her breath away, and she began to understand why mayhap the Scots fought so fiercely for their land.

They traversed the base of lower mountains where the air still held a chill. No snow on the lower passes they rode through, but the peaks were crested with whitecaps. John noticed her head swiveling to and fro at the majesty surrounding her. He grinned, riding alongside her.

"The mountains are unlike anything else ye've seen, aye?"

Aislynn bit the inside of her lip, not missing the subtle boast of a man proud of his homeland.

"Yes. I've never seen such tall mountains. No more than a rolling hill in the Lowlands. I didn't know the land could rise in such a way."

"If ye look just there, past the break in the clouds?" He pointed toward a part in the skyline, where a snowy mountain peak was barely noticeable through the thick, grayish clouds. "'Tis Ben Nevis, thought to be the highest mountain in Scotland."

She leaned over her mare's neck, squinting into the distance.

"Oh! I can see it. Covered in snow?" Exuberance bloomed across her features, and her hazel eyes sparkled with flecks of green in the pale light at her find.

"Wait until ye see the Highland Glens, and the Sinclair land of Reay, where the mountains crash down into the sea, with sandy beaches betwixt. 'Tis unlike anything ye have seen in the Lowlands." He paused, inhaling with an air of pride. "And in England?" John continued, inquiring about her homeland. "More rolling hills?"

She shrugged, dismissing his statement. "I've lived most of my life in the Lowlands. If England has any mountains or hills, I don't recall them."

John stiffened slightly as he mulled over her words, finding himself a victim of his own assumptions. The lass was not the pretentious English princess that he, or all of Scotland for that matter, was led to believe.

"Ye are more of a Lowlander than *a sassenach* then, aye?"

"I've heard that word afore, *sassenach*. It means English?"

"Close. The truest translation is 'outsider' or 'one who doesna belong.' If ye were called that, mayhap 'twas nay accurate. If ye've lived in the Lowlands for most of your life, why do ye consider yourself English?"

Truly, the lass was an enigma. John rubbed his beard, considering. Why was she trying to escape, wanting to return to a place where she had few ties?

Aislynn pursed her lips before she answered. "I'm of English heritage, raised by a Duke, a distant niece of the King. Location, often, is less of a concern than people and their past. Their heritage. At least, that's what I've been taught."

"Perchance," John admitted, "but sometimes, mayhap more than ye ken, a location can change ye. That location, the land, can become one's heritage. 'Tis many a man in the Highlands who care less for their name than they do for the land upon which they live."

Aislynn was silent for a moment, pondering John's words. For so long, titles such as "King's niece" and "nobility" gave Aislynn her identity; the idea of taking her own identity from the land on which she lived was never a consideration. She told John as much.

"A novel concept, Mr. Sinclair. I shall have to think on it."

A satisfied smile passed John's lips – 'twould seem the lass was not so invested in her English heritage as they believed. Perchance she could be convinced to fall in love with the beauty of the Highlands, and a man who lived there.

***

They crossed through the mighty Grampian Mountain pass to the Highland Glens surrounded by more foothills and mountains, and Aislynn noticed the men had grown unusually quiet. For much of their journey, light-hearted banter kept the men's humor high, some of it even directed at her, designed to elicit a smile rather than a scowl. Truthfully, she pouted – as though being a captive was a minor childhood inconvenience – but she swore to herself she wouldn't let these men know just how much they entertained her. These Sinclair Scots were more engaging than any fool at her uncle's hall.

As they drew north, so far north it seemed impossible, brush gave way to grasses and the men seemed to sit taller in their saddles and pull closer to her own mount. Aislynn's hackles stood on end when she caught sight of how their eyes scanned their surroundings. Only a great simpleton wouldn't notice something was amiss, and she was no simpleton.

The Sinclair giant, John, rode near enough that she could reach out and touch him, should she so desire. Heat emanated off his skin – he radiated brighter than the sun itself – and he didn't look at her as he had for most of their excursion. His gaze was riveted on the fields and rocks unfolding northeast before them.

A shifting in the tall grasses to her left attracted her attention, and when she lifted a hand to point it out, John slapped the haunches of her horse, sending the animal, and Aislynn, into a gallop. She scrambled to grab the reins less she fell from the horse like a green rider. The red Sinclair clansmen rode beside her, guarding her from a small throng of men who rose from the grasses – tartan-clad spirits rising from the grave.

Aislynn's horse followed Marcus's around a small rise. From an outcrop of rock, a rigid Marcus Sinclair watched the events unfold as he stood guard for Aislynn. She leaned across the strong neck of her own mare, peering around Marcus.

John and the two other Sinclairs stood their ground against the strange clansmen who emerged from the marshy grass.

Their stained tunics and scruffy braies didn't speak well of these men, at least in Aislynn's estimation. Their fierce stance, however, indicated their readiness to fight, and the little hairs on the back of her neck stood stiff. These rough men didn't immediately attack – instead they took on warrior stances, swords and bows clenched in anticipation.

"What are ye doin' here, Sinclair? I thought ye had fled south with your brother to fight for your king," a heavyset man at the front of the group spoke with authority.

That easy smile of John's never left his face but grew into more of a smirk even as his eyes remained hard – green flint set in his face.

"Ooch, Duncan MacKay, ye havena changed. Ye and your lads stay behind while the men fight for *our* king."

"Nay, ye found an excuse to run off from a fight with neighboring clans. Are ye starting to take after your brother?"

"Are ye still trying to steal things that aren't yours?" Oggie taunted, puffing out his chest.

"If your Laird decides to leave Reay open by taking his kinsmen to fight for a lost cause, one where ye will all certainly die anyhow, what does it bother ye to lose the land? 'Twould be forfeited when your bloodline dies out. Better to have it under the control of the MacKays."

Several MacKay men had shuffled forward as Duncan spoke, fists balled and ready to fight.

"Your whole clan is comprised of cowards. Instead of fighting for your king, for the land ye have, you let other clans fight for ye while you try to steal their land. Ye and your kind are the lowest manner of men." John punctuated his accusation by spitting at Duncan's feet.

With his head still tipped forward, John wasn't expecting the left jab that made sharp contact with his jaw. His head swam for a moment, but that was long enough for two other MacKays to jump on him, their fists raining down like hammers on his face and midsection. Oggie and Etan tried to pull the men off, only to find themselves fighting three other MacKays who wanted a piece of the action.

***

Aislynn's interest rose at the conversation between the Sinclairs and these MacKay characters. They didn't seem to agree on the present politics of Scotland – perchance this clan could help her escape her present situation. While the Sinclair brothers had been naught but kind and considerate, she was an English noble in Scottish land, and she *needed* to find a way home.

Keeping her head low, she risked a glance at Marcus who seemed intently focused on the action with his clansmen. His hand had dropped her reins, clenching his own, ready to launch into action on his brother's behalf most likely.

She realized her attempt to flee earlier had been in haste. With no assistance and unsure of her exact location, of course she would be caught. Her stupidity at the impulsive action, even with John's compassion when he retrieved her, made her brain fevered with embarrassment. And though John told her his presence and their journey was more for her protection than imprisonment, her stupidity only extended so far. Aislynn knew what it really was, and this time, with a clan of people who didn't support Robert the Bruce to back her up, mayhap her escape attempt would be successful.

When she believed Marcus to be completely engrossed in the skirmish, so much so his own horse took a light step forward, she reciprocated by nudging her horse a step back. The mushy land covered any sound her horse made. When Marcus leaned farther over the horse's tense neck, she risked another step, awkwardly backing up her horse as slowly and silently as she could manage.

A sudden burst of angry shouting, and Marcus exploded toward the fray, briefly forgetting his obligation to Aislynn. He urged his steed at the skamash, and Aislynn didn't hesitate. She reined her mare around the rocky outcropping, aiming in the direction from which the MacKay men came. Her best chance was to find their keep before any of those dangerous men or, God-forbid, the Sinclairs, found her. Setting her heels into the mare's haunches, she rode northwest as fast as her mare could carry her.

At the same time, Marcus rode to the center of the fight, using the vantage of being horseback to kick the MacKays off his kinsmen. Sending one of the MacKays who was trying to bring Etan to the ground spiraling off with a sound kick to the head, Marcus yelled at Etan to return to Aislynn. The bruised and soiled lad obeyed without question, and Marcus took his place in the fight.

At first, the MacKays had the element of surprise and the force of numbers on their side. Soon they realized their fight against the Sinclairs, especially with one on horseback, would not end successfully. The Sinclairs fought as men possessed, as men defending their own land often do. As a last resort before they retreated deep into the tall grass, Duncan pulled his dirk from his belt and stabbed John in the shoulder, then disappeared into the overgrowth.

Between the hits to the head and abdomen, the furtive dagger strike from Duncan was enough to do him in. John collapsed into the mud.

***

She turned west when she reached the edge of the marsh, only to be flung from her horse and into the damp grass when her hoof stuck hard in the muck. Landing face first, Aislynn tasted a mouthful of muddy greens just as she had the wind knocked out of her. Before she was able to catch her breath and lift herself off the ground, an arm snaked under her waist and pulled her upright.

A dirty face with an even dirtier beard leaned in close to her. His breath, stinking of dried fish and decaying teeth, overwhelmed her, and she had to hold her breath so as not to vomit directly on the man's plaid.

"Weel, what do we 'ave 'ere?"

Aislynn's eyes widened with panic. Once again, she cursed her stupidity as she tried to come up with a response that may perchance save her from this grimy man. She had believed this clan would help her? She had the sense that she jumped from the heat of the stew pot and into the fire itself.

"Good sir," Aislynn started, hoping to appeal to the man's courtly sensibilities. "I am a British subject in need of assistance finding my way back to England. If ye could provide such assistance, my uncles would see you greatly rewarded." And appealing to his sense of financial renumeration couldn't hurt, either.

The man clucked his tongue, leaning near enough that his rough beard scratched against Aislynn's cheek and made her skin crawl all the more. She looked around with frantic eyes, hoping that someone else was traipsing through the grass who might be more reasonable than this reeking man with a leering gaze. Surely, if she could make it to the MacKay stronghold, their Laird or Chieftain might be more agreeable? They must certainly have to *smell* better than this man, if nothing else.

"Ooch weel, I dinna need renumeration as much as I need something else, lassie. An English lass? Do ye ken something, lassie? I've never had British quim afore."

British quim? What did that mean? That question was the only thought that managed to pass through her mind when the man clutched at her leg, yanking her roughly back down to the ground.

"Wait! What are you doing? Didn't you hear me?"

The man kept his heavy grip on her arm. "Ooch, I heard ye aright," he answered as he wrangled with her.

Angered at the man's presumption, Aislynn wasn't giving up without a fight. At this point, her mind swirled at the truth of John's statement regarding her protection. Resigning herself to needing his help, or the help of any Sinclair, she screamed for all she was worth, right into the man's ear, praying someone would find her before this man had his way.

The grimy man snapped his head back at her scream, cringing in pain and clasping a grimy hand over the offended appendage. Then, given the unfortunate situations she'd found herself in as of late, God and His Heavens decided to smile upon her. One moment she was grappling with the man, slipping in mud that seemed to coat everything, and the next he was landing on the ground next to her with a solid thump.

She lifted her beleaguered eyes to find young Etan atop his horse, a large stone in his grip and several cuts and bruises on his face. He threw his rock carelessly next to the unconscious man and reached his hand down to Aislynn.

He spoke as though he hadn't just caught her trying to run away. "Come. Hurry. John has need of ye."

Aislynn had started to rise and brush at the clumping mud on her kirtle, but something in his voice made her chest jump. He yanked his hand and her mare came around. Without hesitation, she grabbed Etan's hand as he helped her climb into her saddle. Gripping the reins with panicked fingers, she raced with Etan back to the scene of the skirmish.

Chapter Five: A Steady Hand

They found Oggie and Marcus at the rocky outcropping. John was slumped atop a smooth boulder, Marcus holding a dirty cloth against John's upper chest. Aislynn didn't wait on Etan to help her down. She slid off before the mare came to a full stop, rushing to John's side. Marcus's hard eyes watched her arrive, while Oggie's bruised expression was one of concern. When Aislynn got close enough, she understood Oggie's distress.

Marcus pulled the cloth from John's upper chest – right where his chest muscle met his shoulder. A river of blood coated John's tunic, still wet and pulsing from a rend near his shoulder. His head was a mess of bruises, cuts, and blood, matching Oggie's. Only Marcus seemed unmarked, at least on his face.

"We need ye to treat the wound, lassie," Marcus ordered, obviously trying to keep his anger at her disappearance controlled while he focused on John. "I ken many noble ladies are well versed in surgery, herbs, and the like. How are ye with a needle and thread?"

The bright ruddiness that was John paled under the shadow of his pain and injuries. Aislynn's brow furrowed, and she pressed her fingers through the rent in John's tunic. He moaned at the pressure of her fingers, letting his chin drop to his chest. She braced herself for the work ahead of her.

"Can you remove his tunic? I must see what we need to do to best treat the wound. And can you bring me my small leather bag? I have essentials there."

Marcus was not wrong in his assessment of her skills. Her ability to sew included tapestries, leather, cloth, and human skin. 'Twas not the first, or second, time she'd plied her skills on a wound. Etan retrieved her bag, and she dug through it to withdraw a small satchel and a parchment packet.

"Can you bring me some fresh water?" She kept her eyes on her patient as Oggie and Marcus helped relieve John of the tacky fabric, exposing his upper body to Aislynn's view.

***

The blood had soaked through the tunic and dripping downward to mar his broad chest and hard stomach, adding to the sodden red mess that spilled from his shoulder. In any other moment, one that didn't involve so much blood, she understood why John exuded such power. His chiseled muscles and a small patch of russet hair ran from his chest to the waistband of his braies, attracting her eyes in such a way that she found it difficult to concentrate. A heady flush consumed her as she regarded his body.

Stop it, Aislynn, she told herself, shifting her attention to his wound. She'd seen many a man's torso before, having sewn up the Earl's men's after their misadventures. Why did this Highland warrior affect her in such a deep and unabiding way?

As it was, John's wounds had weakened him, and that powerful strength sagged. She hoped he had more in him – sewing up his arm and treating his wounds would take even more out of the man.

Etan pulled a skin of water from his horse, handing it to Aislynn. She wet a clean-ish edge of John's tunic and used it to wipe away a bit of the tacky blood from the stab wound. Fresh blood pulsed from the gash, but at least she could see what she was doing.

She wiped at the wound again and pressed the fabric against his shoulder to staunch the flow until she finished threading the needle. Once she was ready, she lifted the fabric from the wound and pressed the needle against John's aggravated skin.

The men were silent as she toiled, only the sound of John's ragged breathing breaking the silence of the glen. She could tell he was trying not to move every time she stabbed his skin with the needlepoint, and she marveled at the strength it took to ignore such pain on top of pain.

Using her teeth to bite off the thread after each stitch, Aislynn stitched quickly and soon his wound was tightly bound together. Only a thin line of blood had seeped through, and it was already thickening into a scab. Satisfied his skin would hold, she then put a pinch of the herbs from her packet into her hand, added water, and mixed it with her finger. She applied the paste with a light touch, though John groaned at her efforts.

The heat from his body was unmistakable, and she at first feared that it may be a sign of infection. Considering the injury so recently occurred, Aislynn surmised it was something more, heat of the fight, of fighting off the pain. But such closeness and the fire he put off made her feel hot as well, though the afternoon air was cool.

A bandage was going to be a problem. She had nothing in her bags that would suffice, and she doubted any of the Sinclair men carried spare linen. She sighed, realizing what must be done. Lifting her skirts, she reached to her chemise and yanked, tearing away a long strip, confident that her chemise was also cleaner than anything the men might have – unquestionably cleaner than what remained of John's tunic.

She did this several times, noting the men kept their eyes averted out of modesty. Compared to the MacKay man in the brush, the Sinclairs were almost courtly in their manners, and she regretted trying to escape their custody.

When she had several strips ready, she wrapped one under the pit of his arm and pressed it to the poultice, covering the wound. John was able to help her move his arm slightly – otherwise she wasn't sure she could have shifted his muscular arm. It seemed to weigh nearly as much as she did.

The rest of the strips she fashioned into a type of sling. He might not use it long, or at all, but she was going to do everything in her power to treat him, whether he wanted it or not.

Finished with her work, she turned to Marcus, handing him John's soiled tunic. He took it with one bright red eyebrow raised.

"I don't know if you want to try and redress him. Best not with this. The tunic is filthy as it is. Do you have anything else, another tunic perchance?"

Marcus flicked his eyes from Aislynn to John, and reached around his shoulders, unwrapping his plaid from his own chest.

"Can he just wear this? The day grows late, and I would have us reach home afore we stop for the night. 'Twill do well to keep the chill off him, I think."

Aislynn nodded, taking the warm wool from his hand. Concern for his brother pained Marcus's features, and Aislynn softened her voice for him.

"Yes, 'Twill do fine. Thank you."

Wrapping the plaid around John's shoulders, she noticed his color was returning. He resembled more of a man and less of a corpse now that his wound was treated. After he was wrapped in the wool, she then applied a bit of the poultice to the injuries on his face and sat him up fully.

"Thank ye, lassie," John said in a tone so low she barely heard it.

"I am just glad I am here to treat you," she answered formally, trying not to let her pity show.

"I am fortunate to have a healer as fine and beautiful as ye."

Aislynn's head popped up to find a sideways grin on John's otherwise pained face. She pursed her lips, and John bobbed his head in a gesture of acknowledgment. *Or apology?* He was an enigma to her – his rough exterior coupled with his enticing words. *Why does he say such things?*

Flustered and huffing in response, Aislynn finished her ministrations, put her sewing tools away, and turned to the other men crowded around John.

"I think he will sit on a horse fine, if we go slow and don't have too far to go." She looked Marcus up and down, then shifted her gaze to Oggie and Etan. "I have a bit of poultice I can apply to your injuries, to speed healing and prevent pus."

Both men nodded, and she worked quickly to salve their wounds. Then she turned to Marcus.

"Do you have any injuries that need attending? If they knifed John's shoulder, mayhap they caught your leg or arm?"

Marcus pressed his hand against his stomach and hips exaggeratedly, then shook his head.

"I think I am well. Nay more than a few bruises, naught that your poultice can heal. If ye think John is well enough to ride, we should proceed."

This time, Marcus helped her onto her horse. Once she was settled, he paused, his hand resting lightly on her horse.

"I thank ye for treating my brother," he said in his own low voice, his eyes downcast. "I ken ye are no' happy to be with us, and I dinna blame ye for wanting to try to escape. But I hope ye see that we are no' here to hurt ye, and right now, I am grateful ye are here."

His open gratitude struck her heart and made her feel even worse about her escape attempt. Mayhap John wouldn't have been wounded had they not sent Etan to search for her. They'd been more than kind, and she had returned that kindness with folly and deceit.

Marcus's hand had shifted to her saddle, and she patted it comfortingly.

"I'm pleased I could be of assistance." She swallowed thickly before continuing. "I am sorry that I tried to leave again, especially if it caused his injury." She tipped her head toward John on his horse.

"Nay, I dinna think anything would have prevented Duncan's egregious attack on John. The MacKays are no' the most reputable of men." His eyes scanned the mud coating her gown. "As ye may have discovered for yourself."

"Yes, well." Words failed her, and she tipped her head again. "Should we depart?"

Marcus nodded in agreement. Then he grasped another smaller bladder of water from his saddle and held it to John's lips. He sucked encouragingly, and Aislynn figured it wasn't water. Realizing any words of caution would fall on deaf ears when it came to the Scots and their whiskey, she faced forward and waited.

The men made sure John was secure on his own horse, and once they were all mounted, Marcus slapped the haunches of her mare. Their bedraggled troupe continued their journey eastward. The Sinclairs of Reay stronghold was only a few hours off.

***

They moved slowly at first, so John could find the best way to ride one handed while still a bit dazed. The last thing they wanted was for the man to fall off his horse. He certainly didn't need any more injuries.

What they failed to realize was John Sinclair was not a man to be felled by a small prick of a MacKay needle. The dirk barely broke the skin, but still bled with shocking ferocity. 'Twas the shock of the blood loss that made John's head swoon. At first.

Once he sat and Aislynn pressed the cloth to his shoulder, another element entirely caused him to feel faint.

He had barely touched the lass in all their time together, and each time he did, 'twas for the sake of formality – to escort her to her chambers, to assist her onto her horse – chivalrous actions befitting a woman of her station. Each time his skin touched hers, a blazing heat overwhelmed him, a flame of desire that shot through his core whenever her gaze, that searing, dark whiskey gaze, caught him unawares. He found himself more drunk on her eyes than the actual breath of life drink in Marcus's pouch.

Then when she treated his injuries, the heat that built between them was enough to burn the world to ashes. He had removed his shirt, giving her a ready view of his muscular chest and his stomach as hard as the side of a barn. He didn't miss the assessment of his physique in her expression, one that was gone as fast as it appeared.

Trying not to smile, as it pained his busted lips, he knew in that moment she appreciated the body presented before her. Did she feel that same swell of desire toward him? Did the heat in her build, too? He hoped so, but knowing she saw herself as naught more than a captive, well, his hopes were as tenuous as the morning mist.

When she touched him, her slender fingers left trails of excitement that pushed away the pain of the fight and made his cock flex with need. He was relieved she hadn't needed to remove his braies to treat a wound. But with her touches, even the delicate care she used to sew up his arm, he felt deep in his bones that this woman, this lassie who should be his enemy, his prisoner, must instead be his woman. John would have it no other way.

And now here they were, continuing their ride home, and Marcus was the one riding closest to her. *Feckin' Marcus.* Marcus, who was uninjured and able to engage her in amusing conversation, made his charming impression, and a flash of anger toward his brother, unlike any emotion he'd experienced before, raged through John like a clawing, manacled beast. John needed to figure out a way to shine brighter than his younger, boyishly handsome brother.

***

Soon, the riders found a steady cadence and fell into a comfortable silence. Aislynn was sure they were reflecting on the unfortunate events of the afternoon, just as she was.

She had mistakenly believed that all Scots, particularly these Highlanders, were the same – that they backed the Bruce, despised the English, lived as barbarians. To see the difference between the Sinclairs and the MacKays was a shocking eye-opener. *How could the Sinclairs live on land adjacent to another clan they so hated? Was there anyone the Scots didn't want to fight?*

She reined her horse next to Marcus. John needed to focus on staying atop his steed and, she surmised by his hard face, was still too injured to answer her questions.

"Why are the MacKays so angered with you?" she ventured, hoping she wasn't asking something that they preferred to keep secret.

"Ooch, everyone in the northern Highlands seems to have trouble with the MacKays," Marcus answered openly. Evidently, 'twasn't any secret.

"Why is that? Isn't it difficult to be at war with neighboring clans?"

"Most clans have skirmished with other clans. 'Tis the history o' the Highlands, lass. Often alliances are made against other clans, or the bairns of Lairds or Chieftains will wed to unite clans."

She nodded, trying to understand what it would be like to live in such a warlike state. Having lived in the Lowlands while the English tried to establish their domain helped considerably.

"Why don't they support the Bruce?" That was the biggest question lingering in Aislynn's mind. From the English perspective in the Lowlands and England, they believed every Highland clan backed the Bruce. That some clans didn't came as a surprise to Aislynn.

Marcus cut a wary glance at Aislynn. The lass had just tried to escape, again. Did she think to obtain information about the clans and use it if she tried to escape again? She shook her head at his glance. She had been horribly unsuccessful in her most recent attempt and learned the hard way that even if a clan didn't support the Bruce, it didn't necessarily mean that clan supported the English. Some clans were only interested in their own fortunes. And he told her as much.

"Clans are only as strong as the men who lead them. Just as there are good men and bad men, there are good and bad clans. Some clans dinna care for the larger concerns of Scotland. They're solely concerned with how to improve their clan's lot. The MacKays have a long history of trying to take advantage. They've encroached on the land of many clans. And 'tis suggested they have familial ties to Moray, Comyn supporters."

"The Sutherlands, most often," Oggie interjected, having listened in on their conversation. "That clan is most often the recipient of MacKay's fighting ways."

"Aye," Marcus agreed. "If I recall, there is a blood feud betwixt those clans."

"Aye, 'tis. The Sutherland's Laird of Loch Naver had a gaggle of kids, and one of his sons tried to attack a group of MacKays and found the wrong end of a dirk. The Gunn and MacLeods, too, have had troubles with cattle-reiving," John added, starting to come out of his injured stupor.

Highland history was a wonderfully detailed distraction, and John's comment about the Sutherland lad losing his life to a dirk was not lost on Aislynn, nor was the MacKay association with Comyn and English sympathizers.

"Ooch, aye," Oggie nodded. "I've heard rumors that they also tried to invade on the Murray land to their south but were quickly run off. The Murrays had seen the havoc the MacKays wreaked and didna give them the chance."

"Ye seem to be a strong clan," Aislynn hoped flattery might endear her to her captors. "Why do the MacKays try if ye will just resist and push them back?"

Oggie, Marcus, and John shared a look. Etan wisely remained a quiet observer behind them.

"Tis the reason most clans share in the honor of the Highlands. When a King calls for an army, most able-bodied men flock to his banner, just as the Sinclairs did," Oggie explained.

"Tip of the spear, ye ken?" Marcus said. Aislynn didn't comprehend what he meant and knotted her brow as she shook her head.

"If ye want to go to battle, lassie," John breathed heavily as he tried to speak through his injuries, "then ye call for the Sinclairs and the

Douglases. They are the first to answer the call, the first to arrive, if possible, and the first into battle. They are the tip of the spear that strikes a blow to the enemy." He flicked his hazy green gaze to her. "No offense intended."

"None taken," she whispered, waiting to hear more.

"When the men leave, much of the clan lands are exposed," Oggie continued. "Honor of the Highlands demands respect for those lands, to nay invade or the like. But the MacKays have no honor, and they try to press their advantage while most of the Sinclair men are away."

"I'm sure our return was no' welcome, in light of their attempts to encroach on our land. They did no' expect us," Marcus surmised. "We can only hope our present chieftains in standing have kept a strong front to those good-for-nothing trespassers."

"Will they try to attack again, knowing you have returned?"

Once again, the men shared a look.

"Ooch, well. The Laird isn't here, just his brothers," John said.

"And 'tis only the three of us, so much as they know. I'm certain they will try again," Oggie answered sagely.

So much for safety, Aislynn thought as the conversation dropped to silence. They were tasked with protecting her. How could they do that when they barely managed to protect themselves?

Chapter Six: The Gateway to the Sinclairs of Reay

Caithness, Northern Highlands

Marcus rode alongside Aislynn as they crossed into the security of Sinclair land. He was chatting amicably of old family ties when a decrepit barn rose into their view. Once a great domicile, Aislynn presumed, the barn now boasted only a few weathered boards attached to wattle and daub and a crumbling stone foundation. Its height and imposing stature still remained intact. Ever curious, Aislynn pointed at the building.

"'Tis the gateway to the Sinclairs of Reay and the marker of Sinclair land," Marcus explained. "With the trouble the MacKays cause us, having a noble structure of Sinclair history right on the edge of our lands reminds us all of where we are."

John rode right behind them, listening in. "The MacKays may try to encroach on our lands," his words were garbled slightly under his swollen lip, "but they ken they can no' try too much. The ol' Sinclair marker barn stands to let them know where they are supposed to stop."

"Just a barn?" Aislynn inquired. It seemed rather silly that only a falling-down barn stopped an entire clan from invading, given what she had learned and seen earlier. "How does the barn stop them?"

"We value history, here, lass," John said.

"Aye," Marcus agreed. "That barn is older than time, built in the old ways, and has stood for centuries. Though the MacKays may try for the borderlands, they hesitate to encroach farther. There is a respect for such things."

"Built in the old way?" Unfamiliar with building construction, she was intrigued by the fact the ancient barn still stood amid squabbles over land rights and the heavy tang of salt air.

"Aye," John played with his lips to work his words out. His speech was a bit better than it'd been earlier in the day, but not much. "The first Vikings, Norsemen, used pegs and wedges, allowing the wood to move as it swelled or contracted with the weather. The markings, noting where each wedge is placed, can still be seen on several of the timbers."

"No iron pegs, ye ken?" Marcus lifted an eyebrow at Aislynn, then flicked his eyes to the sky. "No weakening or rust. The interior of the barn is just as strong today as 'twas when it was built."

"'Tis also believed that the strength of those early men protects the barn and the lands. Some stupid MacKays even think the barn's home to evil spirits, Sinclair spirits, aye? Methinks 'tis what keeps them from attacking farther in, at least around here." John tried to wink his blackened eye at Aislynn, and the painful effort tore at her insides.

"Don't flex your eyes like that, Mr. Sinclair. 'Twill do no good to your injuries," she cautioned in her best motherly voice.

John caught up to ride along her other side, giving her both a half-shrug with his uninjured arm and another painful wink. "'Tis a flesh wound, lassie. Naught more than that lunkhead on your other side and I gave each other as laddies."

Marcus feigned offense, splaying a heavy hand across his broad chest. "Speak for yourself, Johnnie. Ye always fought recklessly and took your hits. Ye earned every one o' them," Marcus taunted.

"At least I took my hits," John countered with a grin pulling at his busted lip, those earnest green eyes flashing. "Unlike ye, hiding behind Asper and I till the fighting was done."

"I didna see me hiding in this last fight. And look who walked away unscathed!" Marcus answered back.

Despite the dire nature of her predicament, Aislynn couldn't help but laugh at their brotherly banter. For all they were her wardens, they had been comical and engaging during the entire journey. Other than the encounter with the MacKays and her misguided escape attempt, which landed John in his current bloodied state and for which she had expected to be severely punished, the Sinclairs treated her in a way befitting a respected guest than a prisoner. Just as John had indicated when they first departed Dumfries.

And as much as she hated to admit it, she found the Sinclair brothers quite entertaining, and was flattered, even, at their attentions. A smile settled on her face more often than she cared to admit. Adding to that, the heat that ignited between them when she was treating John caused conflict within her. She didn't want to believe the men refined, yet their ardent attentions seemed to belie something more civilized, respectful.

But they were still her enemies, her guards, nothing more, she reminded herself – no matter their behaviors toward her. She may never see her family or her home again. That knowledge, as haunting as the deep purple shadows cast by the unyielding Sinclair barn, weighed on her. While she listened to their continued banter, humorous though it 'twas, her lips pulled down in an unwelcome frown.

**

Broch Reay loomed dark and foreboding in the moonlight. Their path guided them more northeast after they passed the barn, and Broch Reay clung close to the bay that spilled into the North Sea. An icy breeze sprung up as night took hold, and the heady scent of salt water clung to the air. The damp stone monolith of the Broch was cold and silent as they approached.

At the gatepost, an older Scot wrapped in the blue-green Sinclair plaid raised a hand to halt the riders. Oggie, in the lead, slowed his steed and called out to the man.

"Hark, 'tis Robbie Sinclair, aye? Calm yourself. 'Tis Oggie Sinclair, and I have the Laird's brothers with me."

Robbie jumped at Oggie as much as his creaking bones would permit. Oggie slid off his horse to clap the elderly man across his back.

"What are ye doing home?" Robbie asked, pounding Marcus on his back after he dismounted as well, and then did the same to Etan. "And who is this lass? And what is amiss with – is that John?"

The questions poured out, and Oggie wrapped his arm around Robbie's rounded shoulders.

"Come, man! Let us put up the horses. Then we shall find ale and a warm hearth, and I will tell ye all. 'Tis quite the adventure . . ." Oggie's voice drifted into the night as he and Robbie walked ahead. Marcus stayed with John and Aislynn and helped them both dismount from their saddles. He handed the reins off to a sandy-haired stable lad, and they made their way to the keep, Etan scrambling after them.

Brock Reay was a lesser stronghold, a lone stone tower with its back to the sea. The inner bailey was narrow and crowded and asleep. Under the hush of evening, they entered the keep, Aislynn on John's stronger side and Marcus on his injured left side, prepared to assist the man should his wounds prove debilitating.

But John's demeanor had improved as they rode – approaching home eased his pain and made his chest feel lighter. He was sure he would ache like Robbie's old bones when he woke in the morn. As for tonight, the joy of homecoming overcame everything else.

Few kinsmen loitered in the hall when they entered. Aislynn suggested that John find light refreshment afore she checked his wound, then find a warm bed right after. John's stomach growled at the mention of food. He didn't argue with her recommendation.

Robbie had awakened one of the kitchen maids who rushed to serve up steaming parritch from the pot over the hearth and a small platter of fruit and greens. She drizzled honey over the bowls of parritch and served them at a low table in the hall.

Oggie amused old Robbie with their traveling tales, introducing Aislynn while he spun his stories.

"The lass is English, aye, but she is under the strict protection of the Bruce, and the Sinclairs. Her safety and comfort are of the utmost importance," Oggie emphasized, wagging his bushy eyebrows at Robbie.

The older man looked at said lass, seated between John and Marcus, while Etan sat at the end of the table by himself. A sly grin tugged Robbie's lips to one side.

"'Twould seem the Bruce asked for more than that. The laddies seem quite taken with the English rose, mmm?" He rubbed his face with a wrinkled hand, and a deep chuckle shook Oggie's chest. Marcus sent a glare in his direction.

"Aye," Oggie answered, keeping his voice low. "I think they are in a bit of a competition for the lassie. But there is a complication." Oggie leaned in conspiratorially. "She thinks she is a prisoner. I dinna ken if either laddie can win her hand if she sees them as naught more than her captors."

Robbie kept his watery gaze on the trio who were intently focused on their sweetened parritch. He lifted one white eyebrow.

"Stranger things 'ave happened, aye?"

***

Once they had settled their appetites, Etan grasped John under his uninjured arm and helped him up to his quarters. Knowing Aislynn was assuredly watching, John wanted to throw Etan off and march with a swagger to his chambers.

The loss of blood and digressions of the day, however, demanded more from John than he wanted to give, and the staunch warrior swayed on his feet. Resigning himself to relying on Etan, John nodded goodnight to Marcus and Aislynn, trying to hold her gaze for a moment, before they set off for the steps winding up from the rear of the hall.

Etan, sensing John's frustration, remained close-mouthed as they made their way upstairs. For John, the steps away from Aislynn were more than just physical distance. Jumping into the fight with the MacKays and taking the brunt of the injuries of the day, while it may have shown what a powerful Highlander he was, did naught to grant him time with Aislynn.

Instead, his winsome brother was able to spread his charm about like leaves dancing off the trees in the autumn wind. Many a lass had fallen to that boyish charm, and John feared Aislynn might be among those numbers.

'Twas foolish for him to think the lass should fall for his brother's charms, especially as she still saw herself as a prisoner (one who just tried to escape again, into the MacKay land no less!), but he had to admit he was feeling defeated.

At first, when the king suggested the brothers try to wed the English rose, 'twas more folly and a chance to be aligned with royal blood and earn favor with the king. For John and his brother, that alone was enough to compete for.

Then he saw the lass and realized more was at stake. When she stepped into the King's study, every bit of air fled the room, and John's heart slammed in his chest. He didn't know if his brother experienced the same effects, and truth be told, John didn't care. When he escorted Aislynn to her chambers, he had hoped to impress her, show her a wild Highlander can be a civilized man.

His impassioned sentiments for the lass grew when his gaze fell on her noble form in her riding gown, the light catching her in a way that made her almost glow in the pale beams of the sun. If he had to pick a moment, one single moment where he knew deep in his heart, deep in his soul, that he wanted Aislynn for more than the riches of kings that came with her, 'twas that moment. And his stinking brother had been the one on her arm.

Etan and John reached the dim hallway leading to his chambers. Settling into a threadbare chair near the over-sized hearth, John watched as Etan stoked the fire to warm the night chill from the room, then departed. John slouched, trying to ignore the throbbing in his arm. He unwrapped the plaid from his shoulders and poked at the stitches. 'Twould be a rough night's sleep, not that he planned on sleeping much with his fervent thoughts continually returning to Aislynn.

And to his brother. The lad managed to chat up the lassie at every turn. Though John believed that he and Aislynn had shared a heat, a connection of body and mind as she treated his wounds, 'twas short -lived, and Marcus was once again on the prowl with the English lady.

Marcus wanted to win the English rose's hand just to win the wager with John. His younger brother was still young enough to be blind to the consequences of his actions. And as a young man, Marcus was not ready to be tied down, either through handfast or marriage. Yet here John was, losing the wager to his rakish younger brother. Worse, he worried he was losing the lass – the very lass who made his heart race and his loins throb.

John shook his head at the injustice of his present situation. Surely rest in a warm, soft bed would do wonders for his aching body, and in the morn, he could return to his wooing efforts tenfold. She may not be able to fall in love with a Highlander at all, and not in so short a time. He knew without a doubt that she couldn't feel any romantic emotions toward him, given her sense of imprisonment. Regardless, he must show the lass just who the better man of Clan Sinclair was. And in doing so, mayhap he would disabuse her of those captive thoughts.

He began to drowse before the hypnotizing dance of the flames when a hard knock at the door roused him.

***

Aislynn's eyes followed the injured Highlander as he exited, her heart reaching out to the broken man who'd shown her nothing but kindness. To be wounded so egregiously seemed unfair.

But unfairness was the way of the world, Aislynn knew. As evidenced by her current predicament.

Then Marcus escorted her to her own rooms upstairs, and she reflected on that very instance. The Sinclairs had truly been nothing but the most chivalrous of men, more than she deserved after her intrepid escapes and insulting assumptions. Over the course of their journey, Marcus had engaged her in light conversation, obviously trying to put her at ease. His easy smile and bright green eyes could soften the hardest of souls. Even as they walked toward her rooms, Marcus chatted in a lively fashion about life with the Sinclairs, though her mind continued to drift.

Yet, the young man was naught more than that, a young man. Aislynn understood well the passions of young men ran hot and fast. She had the sense that he was a charmer who already had several young women lined up to cater to any need.

His older brother, John, though just as attractive, was handsome in a harder, world-worn way. John Sinclair seemed more of a mind as Aislynn herself, one who knew exactly how unjust the world was. And when John looked at her with his smoldering green gaze, her breath caught in her chest.

She pondered as to why she reacted this way to a man who was supposed to be her captor. But was he? John called himself her protector. She probably needed one, truth be told, abandoned as she was by her own uncle, left to her own devices by the aging King Edward, followed by her escape misadventures. She huffed a light breath that blew tiny tendrils of hair off her forehead.

Truly, if she were anyone's prisoner, it was King Robert the Bruce who claimed that title. Aislynn was cast adrift with no options for her own security. If this russet Highlander was willing to step in as a guardian, who was she to complain?

Perchance remaining under the care of the Sinclairs was a benefit to her. But it still didn't explain why she felt dizzy every time her eyes met his.

***

Etan caught them in the hall, outside a chamber door. Aislynn expected Marcus to escort her in, but worried-looking Etan begged differently.

"Methinks John's wound is paining him. Milady, would ye be able to treat it properly now that we are home? Otherwise, I can send for the surgeon?"

Aislynn's heart raced at the mention of John's name and at the prospect of seeing him this night. She shook her head at Etan.

"No, I can treat him, but I will need supplies. Perchance you can obtain them for me?" Her face implored Etan, who nodded a bit too excitedly and was eager to be of use.

She gave him a list of supplies. Marcus then instructed the lad to retrieve Aislynn's items from the packs in the hall below. The young man ran off to carry out his task.

"Let me show ye to your chambers," Marcus told her. "Ye can let me know if ye need anything more. I can retrieve it for ye while ye care for John, unless ye require my assistance . . .?" His bright eyebrows rose high on his head at the question.

"No, I shall be fine, I'm certain." Her words dropped off as they entered what were to be her chambers at Broch Reay.

In her prisoner mindset, she had expected little more than a pallet in the corner of the hall or in the servant's quarters. Instead, the Sinclairs gave her a room that reflected a measure of respect – one fit for a high-born lady. 'Twas large, almost as large as the chambers she'd had with her Uncle Aymer, though the bedding and furnishings represented a much more simple and rustic lifestyle – plaids and coarse furs for bedding instead of satins and damasks, rough-hewn ash wood instead of polished oak.

Marcus kindled a fire in her small hearth as she continued to take account of her living quarters. The chambers only reinforced John's words from early in their journey, that she wasn't a prisoner. More than once during the ride north, she had fretted her chambers would be in the dungeons. All her conflicting ideas and the present reality in which she found herself confounded her further. She honestly didn't know what to make of it all.

"Do ye need anything in your rooms? Anything for tonight?"

Aislynn peeked into the wooden pitcher on the side table. It was dry, dusty. She blew on it, sending dust motes sailing in the firelight.

"Water, perchance? A clean cloth to go with it?"

Marcus nodded and held out his arm. "Shall we check in on John? I will retrieve the necessaries whilst ye are treating his arm. Etan must have brought your supplies to John's room by now."

Not quite – Etan had trouble finding some of the herbs in the kitchen, and he met them outside John's door.

Marcus gave the door a sharp rap, and John appeared in the doorway. Aislynn allowed her eyes to rove over his well-muscled, half-undressed form before averting them with mild modesty.

John's deep red hair stood straight up, and his face, swollen and bruised, seemed angered at being disturbed. His body, naked to the braies that hung low, very low on his hips, displayed a path of chiseled muscle highlighted by the light of the flames at the hearth. He resembled a creature of myth, dangerously attractive.

"What are ye doing here? Etan? Marcus?"

His tired eyes flicked among them all. Marcus pushed Aislynn toward the door as Etan handed Aislynn the sack of supplies.

"Etan mentioned your shoulder must be properly treated. Instead of waking the surgeon, Aislynn said she would see to your wound. Etan retrieved the items she requested. We are going to retrieve the rest of her belongings while she tends to ye. Don't let her escape, aye?" Marcus teased, laughing at his own sense of cleverness.

John and Aislynn gave him matching flat expressions. John thought the comment in bad taste; Aislynn's look tried to hide her embarrassment at her past rash actions.

"Mr. Sinclair, please have a seat here," Aislynn directed, pushing a stool close to the fire. Etan and Marcus left the door ajar as they departed, and John did as Aislynn ordered.

"John, lassie. Ye can call me John. Ye've seen me at my worst. No need to stand on ceremony."

Aislynn pursed her lips as she nodded and leaned into his shoulder to get a better look at her stitch work. For crude field stitching, she'd done a fair job. She pressed at the wound with her fingers to see if any pus pulsed forth. Only a thin line of blood bubbled, trying to emerge through the stitches.

She reached for the bowl of water on the table, dunked the clean linen, and dabbed at the wound gently to clear away any remaining dirt. Her movements worked over his whole shoulder, and he sighed heavily, relaxing his upper body against the strokes of the cloth. His muscles shifted under her hands as she moved the cloth around to his uninjured shoulder.

Uninjured, but not without its own scars. John's skin was a testament to his warrior upbringing, silvery bolts of scarring that freckled his back, crisscrossed his arms, and adorned his chest. This small stab to his shoulder appeared minor, a scratch, compare to several of the scars she delicately traced with her fingertips.

"Why do you have so many scars? Were you in an accident? Do you get stabbed often?"

John chuckled, his body shaking lightly. "Nay lassie. No' quite. I have two brothers, aye? And more cousins than I can count. Young lads, they like to fight, and I took my share of hits when I was younger."

"No stabbings?" Aislynn continued, enjoying the air of humor.

"Weel, one or two, mayhap."

"Your brothers?"

John's lips pulled at his scruffy cheek. "Nay, though I'm sure they wanted to often enough. We've always had conflict with the MacKays."

Aislynn's fingers left his skin to shake several herbs and ground powders into the bowl, mixing another paste. Her fingers pressed the paste (which smelled better than it looked, John had to admit) into the wound and around the stitches. She peered at the wound closely once more, making sure she didn't miss any part of the injury with the paste, then unfolded the strips of clean linen. She wrapped the strips under his arm and up over his shoulder several times, creating a tight binding.

"There," she said into the heady silence of the room. "I think that shall suffice. As long as pus doesn't set in, you should heal well."

Sitting up straight, John lifted his arm, testing both the bandage and his level of pain. When he did so, the firelight danced across his chest, and that searing heat between them returned. Her face blazed, and she couldn't tear her attention from his hardened chest, those muscles that shifted and flexed under a light smattering of doeskin hair that encouraged her eyes to roam over his tight belly to where it disappeared under his low-sitting braies.

Fire burned red under her skin; her entire being flared, entranced, and she adverted her eyes as though she were observing something improper, or dangerous.

When she flicked her eyes back and noted how he studied her, she knew this was something dangerous indeed.

The air between them cracked and sizzled as John's face moved very near to hers, so near she bathed in his warm breath on her face, in his earthy, manly scent. John's good right arm snaked around her waist, inclining his lips little by little until they all but brushed hers. The kiss was more of a breath than a touch yet sent spirals of dizzying sensations through her. Aislynn's mind spun, conflicting thoughts pouncing and invading. She wanted him to breach that tiny, tiny gap, press his lips upon hers in full, and quench that bubbling desire.

At the same time, her brain screamed that this man was her enemy, her captor. Those thoughts she too easily shoved to the side as she shivered breathlessly, waiting for John to fulfill the promise of his lips.

Then a cough from the doorway brought them both crashing down to earth.

"If ye are quite done, I must return the lass to her chambers. Her necessaries have been removed to her room." Marcus's wry tone left no doubt to either of them that he'd been observing for a while.

John stiffened, his arm dropping from her waist, and Aislynn stepped away. Her cheeks flamed brighter than the fire as she moved to follow Marcus.

"Please let me know in the morning how you fare?" she asked John as she crossed the threshold.

John remained where he sat on the stool, his wide, muscled back heaving with his own deep breathing. Without facing her, he lifted his hand in acknowledgment.

"Aye, lassie," his voice was hoarse. "I'm certain I'll be well by morn."

Aislynn gave a quick bow of her head to Marcus, whose curled lips mocked her at the compromising position she almost found herself in. With the flourish of a courtly gentleman, he held out his arm for her to grasp and walked her back to her room.

Once her doors were solidly barred against the Sinclairs, she let loose a shaky breath that she didn't realize she'd been holding. She pressed her head against a rough bedpost and tried to soothe herself in the serenity of her chambers.

She almost let a Sinclair man kiss her. Aislynn wasn't sure if she was more upset because she assumed she was betraying her own country, or because they didn't get to finish what they started.

***

John kept still by the fire until he heard the door clank shut, then stood with an anguishing groan. He feared rising afore they left, that both the lass and his brother might notice his hardened cockstand.

The lassie's fingers had played havoc with him as she tended his wound. From the moment her fingertips touched him, he wanted to pull her to his lap and let his lips have their way across her skin. Only out of a sheer force of will he didn't know he possessed did he sit motionless under her delicate ministrations.

When she completed her task and looked at him with those innocent eyes that belied something more, he nearly lost himself. Gathering her in his arm had been a mistake. He shouldn't have tried to press his longing on her when she was so vulnerable. Had his brother not offered his snide commentary from the doorway, John may have committed a sin which neither would have forgotten.

John strode to his water pitcher, cupped a splash into his palm, and doused his face and hair as best he could one-handed, hoping the cold water might extinguish his throbbing passion.

If he wanted to win the lass, and after tonight he knew without question that he did, then he needed treat her as the noble lady she was. Trying to steal a kiss like she was a willing milkmaid would nay endear the lass to him.

But he convinced himself as he found a comfortable sleeping position in his familiar bedding, at least he was closer to kissing the lass than his brother was – an added benefit of the moment he shared with Aislynn this eve. With those thoughts rolling around in his mind, John fell asleep with a half-curled smile on his face.

Chapter Seven: Indulgences

Broch Reay was in full bustle by the time Aislynn opened her heavy eyes the next morn. An early riser, she was struck at the lateness of the day, rays of sunshine penetrating the narrow window slit and casting long lines across her bedding. Why did no one wake her?

She made to sit up, and every muscle, at least it seemed to her, screamed in protest. What with the prolonged, hard ride north over nigh a fortnight, followed by the tension of John's injury and the lateness of her bedtime, she really shouldn't be surprised.

Now, in the bright light of the morning, she was able to better appraise her chambers. The short first impression of the night before, in the dark and while tired, did no justice to the room. Yes, more plain than her noble quarters with her uncle, but everything was clean, in its place, with minor luxuries she didn't expect, such as the delicate thistle etching along the trunk at the foot of the bed or the finely carved lines of her narrow table.

Reusing the cloth on the water table, she wiped sleep from her face, trying to wake up. Only then did she notice her brush and small box of personal desk items had been placed next to a wooden tray of food at the edge of the table – hard cheese, a flat piece of the oat-like bread the Sinclairs appeared to eat at every meal, a small pot of honey, and a cup of a dark liquid. *Did the servants place the items here while she slept the morning away? What did they think of her?* She lifted the metal cup and sniffed. Spiced mead. Taking a sip, she grabbed the hunk of cheese off the platter and walked toward the etched trunk.

Since she didn't see the rest of her belongings in the room, she assumed that whoever brought her food also put her gowns and necessities away. She took a large bite of cheese and placed her cup on the low stool next to her. Then she lifted the heavy lid of the trunk.

Not only were her items put away, someone had taken the time to place them in a neat, orderly fashion. She fingered the green, embroidered gown fastidiously folded on the top of the pile. Whoever cared for her garments did a better job than Aislynn herself may have done. Too often, she just threw her gowns across a chair or on top of her trunk, hoping either a house servant or a clothing fairy would take care of the cleaning for her.

What a spoiled life she had lived. In her tenuous position of guest/prisoner, Aislynn vowed to be more accountable for her own belongings. She mustn't rely on the charity of strangers to do a chore she should be doing. Here, in the Highlands, she was no longer spoiled nobility, and she resolved to adapt to her new position, whatever it might be.

Her stomach rumbled. She grasped her drink from the stool and returned to the table near the window slit to finish off the rest of the food. 'Twas possible this would be the only nourishment she would have until the evening meal.

Aislynn was shoving the last of the honeyed oatcake in her mouth when a knock sounded at her door.

"Come in," she mumbled around a mouthful of food, and two young women with matching pink cheeks entered.

"Hello, Missus," the sable-haired girl bowed as she spoke. "Milady has asked that we check on ye, and once ye awake, help ye wash and dress or whatever ye need."

"And she encourages ye to rest for the day after your long trip," the red-haired girl piped up. Her wine-hued hair and green eyes marked her as a Sinclair. "We will come retrieve ye for the eventide meal, so if ye need anything afore then, please tell us so we can retrieve it for ye."

"Ohh," Aislynn squeaked out, swallowing her mead to clear her throat. "I would love a wash. The meal and the clothes in the trunk, was that you two?"

Their heads bobbed together. Aislynn smiled. "Well, thank you. You two cared for my belongings better than I have. And thank you for the food. I was famished."

"Milady thought ye might be." Dimples played peek-a-boo on the brown-haired girl's cheeks as she spoke around a slight smile. "So ye would like to wash? Milady told us to have the men bring ye a tub, and we will fill it."

Aislynn's chest pinched at the thought of these dainty girls drawing her bath, but after days and days of travel, 'twas not an offer she would refuse. The young women appeared eager to please, so she nodded, and the red-haired girl launched out the door to accomplish her task.

"I can help ye set the rest of your room to rights and help ye undress after the water fills. Milady has several scents we can add to your bath. She recommends lavender and heather oils, but she has others. Rose or violet oil . . ."

"The lavender is fine." Aislynn was in no place to argue. She would defer to the lady of the keep. "What should I call you, if you are going to be assisting me so much this day?"

"Mary," the slight girl curtsied. "The other is Esther."

"Sisters?" Aislynn guessed. Mary nodded.

"Aye. I'm older." Mary's thin chest swelled with pride. An older sister herself, Aislynn felt an affability with the slender girl.

"Will you assist me in selecting a gown for today? I cannot spend the day in my shift, after all."

The girl's eyes lit up, and she rushed to the trunk, excited to help the mysterious English visitor with her wealth of fine clothing.

Perchance the Sinclairs are a welcoming sort, Aislynn thought. Thus far, she'd seen nothing to indicate she was nothing more than a guest, though how it was possible was beyond her mortal ken. *Didn't war mean prisoners? Perchance John was right.*

The Seduction of the Glen

***

Her luxuriating in a midday bath undoubtedly convinced Mary and Esther that Aislynn was nothing less than royalty. She'd never had a midday bath while living with the Earl – most baths were evening affairs she shared with her sister only a few times a year. And they involved shallow tubs with buckets of lukewarm water dumped over her head. A deep, narrow tub with heated water was a significant improvement, in Aislynn's estimation.

And the lady of the keep's recommendation for lavender and heather was a sage one. The past month after the capture of Auchinleck Castle, the absconding of her uncle, her implied position as a prisoner of war, then as a guest of the Sinclairs – 'twas enough to make anyone's head spin. While she sometimes had to pinch herself to make sure this strange reality wasn't a dream, knowing that this manner of kind treatment may end kept Aislynn rooted. At any moment, word from the Bruce could change her circumstances from this warm welcome to a dirty cell in the dungeon. Having one's life subject to the whims of a foreign King didn't make for any sense of security, no matter what John Sinclair promised.

But right now, scented bathwater reaching just under her breasts, her head and one leg perched along the tub's edge, Aislynn let herself forget those warring concerns of men. 'Twas just her and her warm bath, and she was more than ready for the rest of the world and its concerns to fall away.

Too soon, the water cooled and a light knock at her chamber door distracted her. The young Sinclair sisters returned with Etan, and using his muscle and several pails, they dumped the water from the window before Etan removed the narrow tub.

Mary and Esther remained behind, their nimble fingers helping her dress in one of her simpler gowns. Aislynn hoped to avoid stares and fit in as much as possible. The fact she was hidden away most of the day told her that the Sinclairs probably desired the same and contributed to that endeavor. And now she was to go below, and to Aislynn it felt a bit as if she were to be put on display – like stained glass or a fine gem.

Giggles and low "ohh!" sounds accompanied the girls' work and help to calm Aislynn's nerves. She shooed them to the side as she twisted her own still-damp tresses into a rough mesh coif.

"Are ye ready, milady?" Mary, evidently the more talkative of the two sisters, swept her arm at the door in a dramatic fashion. Aislynn's mouth tugged with amusement at Mary's flair, and she moved to the doorway, the Sinclair sisters in tow.

Trying to blend in, to not draw attention to herself, Aislynn realized as soon as they entered the hall, had been a silly notion. Marcus and John met her at the entryway and led her to the long table near the hearth. At the head of the expansive stone room, a stern blonde woman surveyed the hall from a heavy wooden chair covered in one of those large swaths of dark green and blue plaid. Two older Sinclair men sat on either side of her, providing the image of added strength to the woman's position. Of course, the Laird of the Reay Sinclairs was not present – he was still in Dumfries with the Bruce. His wife, this blonde, served as head of the clan in his absence, a strange but not completely unheard-of circumstance.

"Lady Haleigh Sinclair, may we present Aislynn de Valence, niece to the Earl of Pembroke and the King of England."

Aislynn curtsied, a natural movement she had learned at the same age she learned to walk. She started to rise, but when the lady didn't immediately acknowledge her, Aislynn peeked up from her hooded eyes. The woman's brow furrowed as her eyes flicked around the room, unsettled. Whether the lady was worried about an English interloper in her clan or had a wealth of other concerns weighing on her, Aislynn couldn't guess.

Finally, the woman spoke, keeping her gaze on those gathered in the hall. "Aye, lass. I welcome ye here. Welcome to the Sinclairs."

The woman's pinched voice was kind enough but distracted – she was overly focused on those in the hall. Not wanting to add to her worries, Aislynn simply curtsied deeper, then stood upright to be shepherded to her seat by the men at her sides.

As for an introduction to the leadership of the Sinclairs of Reay, 'twas unimpressive, which suited Aislynn just fine.

***

And if other kinsmen in the hall paid Aislynn any undue attention, she didn't notice. John and Marcus spent the meal with Etan and another eager-faced young lad tearing into roasted pheasant and sharing uproariously funny childhood stories.

Courtly bards had nothing on their storytelling. Aislynn tried to keep her face straight and stoic, representative of a woman of her class, but by God the Sinclair men told such wild tales that her cheeks and sides ached by the time they finished their meal. 'Twas unladylike to laugh in such a way, she knew. And by the end of supper, she didn't care.

"And ye, Etan, trailing after Marcus like he was Zeus incarnate!" John brought poor, pink-eared Etan into the joviality. "He was such a devil, having ye chase chickens about the yard, promising ye a ha'groat if ye caught one for supper!"

"Ooch, did Mistress Eva yell fit to raise the roof when ye burst into the kitchens, a lump of mud covered in loose chicken feathers!" Marcus bantered back, slapping the table as he laughed at the memory.

Several young women inched closer to the men, and many a solicitous eye fell on the chiseled features of young Marcus. Aislynn didn't miss that his own gaze roved over the milky swells of bosoms encircling him, appreciating the attentions, and once again, Aislynn presumed the lad had his choice of the Sinclair lassies.

While John garnered his own appreciated glances, he didn't return the favors, unlike Marcus whose young Scots blood raged with noticeable abandon. Instead, she found John's verdant look glowed in her direction, never straying from her shining face. Aislynn's own ears pinked at his interest, and they were both so preoccupied with each other, neither noticed when Marcus, Etan, and the other Sinclairs left the hall for the fresh Highland air of the yard.

Once the childhood stories came a close, Aislynn flicked her gaze to the lady of the keep. That stern expression hadn't left the poor woman, who bowed her head to the graying warrior next to her. Her dark blonde hair was pulled into a loose braid, rogue tendrils worrying her face. 'Twas as if the woman held the world upon her shoulders, and with the Laird gone and John assigned guard duty to an insignificant Englishwoman, Aislynn readily presumed that was not far from the truth.

"The Lady Haleigh?" Aislynn probed, curiosity nibbling at her without mercy. "I ken she is in command of the clan in the Laird's, and your, absence. The men with her, they are advisers?"

John nodded, leaning back to have his own look at the lady of the keep. "Aye. They are my brother's advisers, tacksmen, as well."

"And why aren't you standing in as Laird until your brother returns? Why is that duty on her still?"

Her question seemed to amuse him. His eyes crinkled and the edges of his lips turned up.

"Weel, 'twould seem that I should, aye? But I can give ye several reasons why. First, once I returned, I went to Haleigh to reassure her Asper was well and that if she needed me to stand in, I would without question. But for the past half-year, she and Reed and Fleck have governed the clan well enough. I dinna want my presence to suggest Asper was no' coming back, or that I wanted to usurp his position. We have enough infighting with the surrounding clans. Surely our clan doesn't need to arouse any suggestion of instability, no matter how inaccurate any rumor of such might be. 'Twould take verra little for the MacKays to try and press their advantage on our land more than they already have."

When John spoke, his words logical and his voice smooth, she easily forgot her presumptions that the Highland warriors were uneducated, lawless barbarians. He would do just as well conversing at the court of King Edward as he did sharing childhood tales in this remote Sinclair hall. Her imagination envisioned him in a satiny, embellished tunic and hose, cutting a suave figure at court, and she blushed at her fancies.

"Is that what she is worried about?" Aislynn asked. "About the MacKays?"

John gave her a one-shouldered shrug, and she wondered if his arm yet pained him. She hadn't treated it all day, but he was a grown man. If he needed her medical attentions, he could have called for her. But she still reminded herself to ask afore she quit the hall for her chambers.

"'Tis an everyday concern. We are well into spring, so they could be worrit about planting. With so many kinsmen in service to the King, few able-bodied remain to farm or hunt. Filling the larder is always a concern. We are fortunate to be so close to the sea and several lochs. Fish and mussels and the like are easy to catch or collect, even bairns or old men can do it."

"Close to the sea?" Aislynn's interest peaked again, distracting her from John's wound. "You are close enough to fish?" An excited light shone brightly from her eyes, which sparkled as dew on fallen acorns.

Studying her intently, John's light beard twitched into a full smile. "Have ye nay seen the shore afore? Surely ye have been to the sea?"

"Only from a far distance, and there's not much to see from the narrow window of a carriage."

"We will have to change that," John said in a low voice as he leaned across the table on his uninjured arm.

A nervous heat surged through her body at his smoldering nearness, and she sat back quickly, trying to calm her shaking. Every time he came close, she had a peculiar, visceral reaction, and she blinked, feeling lightheaded.

A need to question the comment he made when she treated his arm in the glen – if he indeed thought her beautiful – burgeoned in her mind but unease that he may ply her with more sweet words to make her head spin faster, and the sheer vanity in asking, prevented her.

She looked around the hall, anywhere but at the man across from her who gave rise to the most conflicting feelings. Standing to say her goodbyes for the night, she noted most of the Sinclairs had departed, including the lady and her advisers, and none had made a comment about her. Perchance she did manage to avoid unnecessary attention by the Sinclairs.

Well, most of the Sinclairs, she thought as she glanced over her shoulder. John tilted his head to watch her leave, his face a tapestry of intensity and desire. She had forgotten to ask him about his shoulder.

***

After Aislynn left, John pursued his brother, hoping to share in a draught of whiskey Marcus was assuredly drinking in the bailey.

Etan and the entertaining lassies laughed and chased each other in a mock child's play, hoping 'twould lead to much more adult activities. As he watched his brother enjoy a young man's antics, a sense of certainty came over John. Marcus may think his boyish charm would win the English rose, but the young woman was nobility, raised to consider the political implications of marriage, and a brash young Scotsman didn't fit with what that lassie wanted.

John, with his more worldly experience and toughened exterior, was a stronger choice for her, he assured himself. Winning the wager against Marcus, and settling the king's concerns with the de Valence lass, was guaranteed. The moment he shared with Aislynn when she checked his wound the night before only convinced him of it more. He bit his lip, trying to hide the grin at his own inflated self-confidence.

"Brother!" Marcus called out in an inebriated slur, lifting his whiskey cup. "Are ye coming here to drown your woes at our wager?"

John grabbed the stout metal mug from Marcus, opening his gullet to down the fiery liquid in one swallow. Marcus grimaced at John finishing off his drink, then slapped his brother on the back, laughing as John coughed.

"Ooch, such a good burn, aye?" Marcus teased.

"Water of life, brother," John choked out. It had been a while since he drank with his brother. "And ye think ye are the winner of the lass?"

Barking out a laugh, John swept his arm across the yard at the collection of blushing Scotswomen making puppy-eyes at Marcus.

"Ye are nay ready to give up the attentions of women to wed one. Ye are a rake of the highest order!"

"Ahh, but one woman of such value, to be wed to nobility?"

John shook his head, leaning against a low rock wall on the edge of the yard. "Weel, when I wed the lass, ye will be related to her by marriage. I am the older brother, ready to settle down. I shall win the lass."

"Ready to settle down? Have ye met us Sinclairs? Hell, it took Asper almost two score to wed! And he's still only handfast," Marcus sputtered his disbelief at John. "Ye are no more ready to settle down than I am."

Marcus's words resonated painfully with John. Was his brother right? Was it just the wager that made him think he was anxious to wed? Pretending to brush off his brother's words, John raised the cup to Marcus and handed it back.

"We will see when she makes her choice, *little* brother."

Marcus and the others hooted and laughed as John marched back to the keep, ready to sleep off the whiskey.

***

Instead of heading up to his chambers, the presence of Haleigh in the hall, her own goblet of drink clutched in hand, brought him up short.

"John," she breathed in her heady, slightly drunken voice. Keeping her face straight ahead, she gestured to the chair next to her, and he sat.

"I am glad ye have returned in relatively sound health." She emphasized the word "relatively." John huffed with good humor. When did he not return home with some manner of injury?

"Milady, how have ye fared whilst we've been gone? 'Twould seem ye have the clan well under control in Asper's absence."

She nodded at the compliment. "Thank ye, John. I appreciate that. Please do no' take any insult when I say that, while I am glad to have ye home, I would rather Asper had joined ye."

"Ye ken the Sinclairs are the tip of the Bruce's spear," he answered, his tone serious. "He could no' leave the Bruce's side. I was surprised he agreed to myself and Marcus leaving."

"This lass must be important if the Bruce was willing to have ye leave." Keeping her face straight, her shoulders shifted in question. "And I am to understand 'tis more to the lass and her presence here than just guarding a prisoner?"

"She is nay a prisoner." John's serious tone stressed. "She is an unwed English lass, abandoned by her Duke and uncle, and is related to the King of England. The Bruce sees a larger use for her than as a prisoner."

"Ahh," Haleigh rested her head against the back of the chair. "The marriage and politics game. Rumors tell the Bruce likes to play matchmaker. He hopes to wed her to an important clan, creating leverage with England." She sipped her goblet, thinking. "I dinna ken if 'twill work, but 'tis a far sight better than throwing the poor, pale thing into a miserable cell."

"I agree entirely."

"I'm sure ye do," Haleigh commented with a touch of humor. "And since your older brother was spoken for, Asper graciously offered ye as a fine substitute."

John ducked his head, the wager with his brother flitting through his mind. "Myself or Marcus, whichever of us suits."

"Ahh," she said again. "And ye hope ye suit better?"

He didn't answer but kept his head low and let her draw her own conclusions.

"Even though she may no' be well accepted into the clan? 'Twill be an uphill battle with some in the Sinclairs, to be sure. And what if the lass does no' want to be here? Will ye force her? And what if the English learn she is here? Will they attack to retrieve her?"

John kept his mouth shut – those were questions he had pushed from his mind, not wanting to focus on those undesirable possibilities.

"Weel, whomever she chooses, the man will be a fortunate one."

"Something seems to be weighing on your mind, something more than a fair English lass?" John tried to change the subject.

Haleigh looked to the ceiling, sighing with a long breath. *Aye, John was right. Something else aggrieved her.*

"Reed and Fleck, our clan would sink into chaos without them. Asper was clever to place them with me. I canna do this by myself." Self-doubt filled her voice. "We do have a larger problem. While most of our men are away following the King's banner, the same is no' true of other clans. I fear we canna rely on some of our neighbors if the English should press this far north."

John snorted, her implication understood. "The feckin' MacKays." Anger burned away any whiskey left in his body, though he doubted the English would ever make it to these far reaches of the North Highlands.

"Oggie told me ye encountered a small band of the degenerates on your way home," she pursed her lips when she paused. "And 'twas one of their own that caused your wound. That alone is enough to carry out vengeance."

"But there's more," John prompted.

Haleigh nodded. "They see us as exposed. And they are taking advantage of it. They have stolen crops, reived cattle, harassed our lasses, and ye are no' the only man they have sported with. I have tried to have Reed and Fleck meet with their chieftain, but he has ignored our requests. I fear we dinna have enough men to keep them at bay. I fear that to gain our country, we may lose our clan."

Shame consumed John in a ragged cloak. He should have risen to the role of clan leader regardless of any politicking or rumors they might encounter. To leave the weight of such concerns on the shoulders of a woman, a powerful woman with strong co-leaders, but a woman, nonetheless, spoke ignobly of his sense of responsibility. He'd been distracted by a wager for an English lass, and he was ashamed for it.

Haleigh cut her eyes sidelong to the dejected-looking man next to her, and a low laugh escaped.

"John, dinna chastise yourself. Ye've had other obligations, an injury notwithstanding, and I was no' forthcoming. But perchance ye can ride to the MacKays with your brother and other Sinclair men, a show of force, and let them know that under no uncertain terms will we continue to permit these behaviors, and we will take our retribution if they continue."

"I should have offered it from the start. Tomorrow we will come up with a plan and ride to the MacKays."

"I prefer to wait a day or two. It's been quiet, and I expect the MacKays are planning another attempt or ken ye are home and standing down. Let's have ye and your brother announced as advisers, a united front standing in for your brother. Then we may ken if the MacKays will continue their petty encroachments, or if they will recognize the import of the Sinclairs and respect our borders."

"I am at your disposal, milady." He rose, placing his hand lightly on her slender shoulder. "We will corral these rogue MacKays, and Asper will return in the fall for your wedding. That I can promise."

"From your lips to God's ears," she muttered, taking another sip.

***

The sisters woke Aislynn much earlier the following morning, appearing rather like matching dolls in their aprons. They helped her dress, fitting the tight sleeves of a gray-blue gown over her kirtle and helping her twist her hair into a netted, silver coif. After serving her breakfast, Aislynn mentioned she would enjoy a walk around the grounds, mayhap enjoy the fresh air?

Esther dropped her nervous eyes, finding the rushes on the floor interesting, and Mary frowned, worrying her hands in her skirts.

Aislynn stared at the young women. They didn't hide their emotions well.

"They'd rather I didn't leave my chambers," Aislynn concluded in a flat voice.

"Oh, nay!" Mary's face was suddenly animated, her eyes wide. "Ye can leave your chambers!"

"Oh, but not the keep."

This time Aislynn guessed correctly. Mary grew quiet.

"No' everyone is as excited to have a noble Englishwoman on our land," Mary explained in a low voice. "The lady and her men would rather we ease ye into the clan. Give our kinsmen time to get used to ye."

Aislynn bit the inside of her cheek. The sisters, and their message from the Lady of Reay Tower, were accurate in their consideration. Loyal and proud, the Scots of Clan Sinclair wouldn't receive a captured English noble with open arms. Taking the time to first become familiar to those in the keep, and then share that with those in the clan proper, may be a better approach. Haleigh Sinclair was quite astute.

Just how long am I going to be here?

Not for the first time, that disconcerting question crossed her mind. If she were a temporary guest, or a prisoner, having the clan accept her presence would be irrelevant. But to have it as a concern? A smoldering awareness crept over Aislynn.

Rumors from her uncle had whispered throughout the halls of Auchinleck Castle, that Robert the Bruce's entire family had been either dispatched or imprisoned, including his 12-year-old daughter, that the lass and the Bruce's wife had spent time in cages – *cages!* – for the past year. And time could only tell when those women would be released.

If this war with the Scots dragged on, so would her time here. Was she destined to spend the rest of her life in the remote Highlands? Was she truly a captive? A guest? A new resident? Again, she sensed her life was not her own. When would she make the decision regarding the course of her life?

Not this day, that was for certain.

"So, what am I expected to do?" Aislynn asked.

"If ye can write, I can bring ye quill, ink, and parchment. Or we have wool and thread for embroidery, if ye prefer." Mary was eager to be helpful, and Aislynn found it endearing. The girls resembled small animals just wanting to please.

"The sewing," she decided, trying to keep her spirits cheerful. "The light here is bright enough to make it easy."

The girls bobbed their heads and scrambled from the room, racing to meet Aislynn's request.

***

She had a fair hand and a strong eye for color; thus, sewing was a skill that came almost naturally to Aislynn. Unlike Agnes who wanted to spend most of her day outside with the animals, Aislynn found a quiet joy in the repetitive movements of the needle and fabric, the flicking of her fingers, the slippery feel of thread passing over her skin. Even amid the greatest upheaval, Aislynn found she delighted in sitting with her sewing and finding a modicum of peace in the chaos.

Keeping one eye on her embroidery, Aislynn's attention flitted around the room, to the window, appreciating the light and the view. And though she was engrossed in her project, 'twould have been nigh impossible to miss the noise in the yard. She ignored most of it, until a loud cheering forced her concentration from her threads to the window. The sounds below grew louder until she could ignore it no longer, and she set her sewing aside to assuage her curiosity.

What she saw below caused her to freeze in her spot. 'Twas a fight. Not just a mild pushing and shoving from young men, but a thorough fistfight, with solid punches landing hard against skin and bone, leaving bruises as badges of honor. Blood flew in spattered flecks onto the ground and surrounding onlookers. The combatants were both red-headed, which didn't cause Aislynn any surprise distress at first – she had well noted many of the Sinclair men had deep red or graying red hair. When one man pushed the other away to regain his feet, Aislynn gasped.

The combatants were John and Marcus! And as soon as her eyes caught sight of the blooming red splotch on John's shoulder, she cried out and reacted without thought.

Rushing from the room in a flurry of skirts, she ran as fast as she could down the spiral stone stairway and burst out the hall doors to the yard.

She went unnoticed by the crowd, which craned forward to get the best view of the fight as possible. Aislynn elbowed her way through the throng of clansmen and women to throw herself at the fighting men.

"John!" she screamed to make herself heard above the din. John had managed to shove Marcus to the ground, grappling at the young man's shoulders.

"John! Your stitches! Your shoulder!" she screamed again, grabbing at his other arm to pull him off his brother.

He shifted his chest around to face her, a huge smile plastered on his face. Aislynn's brow furrowed. *Why was he smiling?* She looked down at Marcus, who had a similar grin on his face. The lines on her forehead thickened.

"Lass! What are ye doing down here?" John seemed more concerned over her sudden appearance than at his fight with his brother.

"What are you doing?" she hollered at them both.

"Weel, fighting," John said as he climbed off Marcus. "I think 'twould be obvious."

His eyes flicked around the crowd that had quieted and now stared at the finely clothed English stranger in their midst. "Ye should nay be here, lass," he said in a low voice.

He reached his hand out to Marcus who grasped it, pulling himself out of the dirt.

Aislynn ignored his statement. "You shouldn't be here! You can't be fighting! Look at your shoulder!"

She waved her hand at his stained tunic, and he shrugged it off for a better look. His bare, bruised chest was inches from her face, and she adverted her eyes, scandalized. *To be half naked in public view!*

He poked at his stitches. Marcus leaned in close to gawk as well.

"Aye, I did a fair bit of damage to your stitching, brother," Marcus bragged.

Aislynn pushed her modesty aside and placed her hands upon John's chest, pressing at the wound. The stitches had pulled from the skin in jagged flaps. If the original wound was bad, this was so much worse.

"Ugh," she groaned heavily.

She had skill with a needle, but to repair the wound now would truly test her abilities. Reaching under her skirts, not caring who watched, she ripped a long strip from the hem of her kirtle and wrapped it around the now-gaping wound.

"Why were ye fighting?" Her attention was on the injury, so she didn't see the look the men exchanged.

"We're brothers," Marcus said glibly. "We like to fight."

Several onlookers laughed at Marcus's reply, and Aislynn realized she had a large audience of Highlanders watching her. *The Sinclair clan,* she lamented.

If John and his family had intended to keep her hidden for a while, she had ruined that plan. Clan Sinclair knew an Englishwoman, a wealthy one from her dress, lived in their midst. No wonder John said she shouldn't be here.

"I couldn't let you ruin your shoulder more," she explained, worry etching more lines in her face. She kept her eyes focused on John's naked shoulder, trying to avoid the stares from the clansmen watching. John elbowed his brother in the gut.

"Ooch, the fight is over, my fine kinsmen. Let's get back to our work," Marcus announced. Several groans of discontent followed, and the crowd dispersed.

"Lass, let us retire to the keep," John said, ushering Aislynn inside with his good arm.

So much for keeping the lass a secret, he thought grimly as they made their way to her chambers to treat his arm. They had wanted to keep knowledge of her concealed for as long as possible, fearing what the MacKays, the English, or the Sinclairs would do with that knowledge.

All of the Highlands will ken the presence of an English lass with the Sinclair clan now, he grumbled to himself.

Chapter Eight: Assimilation

After a heated discussion between John, Reed, Fleck, Marcus, and Haleigh, 'twas finally decided that Aislynn needn't hide any longer. Her presence was known; keeping her to her chambers or secreted inside the tower served no further purpose. Haleigh and her Sinclair advisers did recommend that the kinsmen keep a keen eye on the lass. If she took it into her head to try another escape or communicate with the English, they wanted to nip those spurious ideas before they took root.

Otherwise, Aislynn was given free rein of the Sinclair lands, even assigned specific chores so she might feel a sense of purpose and contribute to the clan. Haleigh and the Sinclair men hoped 'twould encourage the lass to assimilate to the Highlands – the odds were she'd be living with them for quite a while.

The ability to walk about the Sinclair lands provided a sense of freedom Aislynn sorely lacked for much of her life. Like Haleigh, Aislynn also came to the realization that she would probably live in these Highlands for years until she was exchanged or ransomed. This knowledge seemed to relieve a weight, as though she shrugged a heavy mantle from her shoulders.

And the Highlands, she surmised, were not a poor choice of place to spend one's time. Whenever she worked in the kitchens and had time to step out into the pale sunshine to retrieve vegetables from the gardens or water from the well, the shockingly fresh air and scented breezes gave her pause. Often, she smuggled moments away and walked up the low rise that gave her views to the waving green glens to the east and west and the shimmery blue horizon to the north. *The sea,* she guessed, and inhaled the sweet and salty wind that caught loose tendrils of her hair and made them dance. The idea of an unending expanse of water was beyond anything she dreamt of in her imagination, and she pined to see it up close.

The more time she spent in admiration of this place that seemed more fantasy than real, the less she missed the controlled, limited existence she'd lived as an English noble – and hardly a noble at that. Her life at English court was valued only in a possible marriage she would make to improve the King's alliances or to meet his needs. Everyday being told what to do, what to wear, how to speak! Aislynn didn't miss that contrived life. She didn't miss the pretense of power or the petty squabbles among men or the stifled, enclosed chambers that reeked of dirty rushes and ashy hearths.

'Twas easy to accept such a beautiful, open, raw space as these far Highlands. If this was her prison, then perchance capture wasn't as dire as she first presumed.

The only thing she did miss from her previous life was Agnes. In this pristine place, sad reminders of her sister still passed through her mind, even though those memories came less frequently and didn't ache as deeply. The fact that Agnes had left Aislynn meant her sister could be anywhere – England, the Lowlands of Scotland, even here in the Highlands, or scuttling around in the Holy Roman Empire for all Aislynn knew. Since she'd left Auchinleck Castle in Dumfries over a month ago, Aislynn had resigned herself more and more that she wouldn't see Agnes again soon, if ever.

Losing her sister was a hard lump to swallow, although the serene beauty of the land made swallowing it much easier. Here, in these Highlands, Aislynn decided, she wanted to make the best of her new life, accept it, make this unsullied land her home, and if the time came to return to England, well, she would have to deal with that choice when it came.

She desperately hoped to be granted the option to choose. She'd already been forced to leave so many homes, she dreaded having to lose another, especially one as lovely and tranquil as this.

Meanwhile, there were chores to be done.

***

To that end, the dainty sisters Mary and Esther showed her several labors that the women of the tower were employed in. Though Aislynn preferred sewing, she knew that manner of labor was considered less essential (unless she was repairing clothing, but she had not yet been asked to do so) and welcomed an assignment to other chores. As typical for the rest of the Sinclairs, her work was determined by the day of the week, and she spent the next several days with her sleeves rolled up and sweat on her brow.

Pleased to find she would spend much of her time in the kitchens, Aislynn lamented that this was not one of those days. Today, she cursed her bad luck. 'Twas the great laundry day, and no one in all of Scotland or England fancied those labors.

Boiling clothes topped Aislynn's list of the worst of the chores. She hated it at Dumfries, even with the luxury of having many stout men at the ready to tote water. The fires roaring with a vengeance and the oppressive heat made laundry even worse. Here at Reay, with most men away fighting for the Bruce, Aislynn was recruited to yoke buckets from Reay Burn to the grassy area behind the kitchens. Not her favorite chore by far, but she didn't have to do the more arduous work on the linens with the tallow soap and washing paddle, so she tried to find joy in the short, pretty walk in the fresh air.

The women she worked with seemed pleasant enough, smiling with thin lips as Aislynn brought water to the boiling pots. A few younger women waved and told her "good day" when they passed each other in the yard. The rest appeared to ignore her, which suited Aislynn fine. Acceptance would come with time.

***

Those waves and smiles turned out to be masks. Aislynn didn't realize just how unaccepted, how disliked she was as an outsider by many of the Sinclairs until a cold mass struck her head with a hard and painful *thunk*, followed by harsh words from somewhere behind her.

"*Sassenach witch.*"

Stunned, she dropped her pail on her feet and reached her hand around to the back of her head. A mess of mud and muck clung to her hair through her mesh coif and part of her neck, dripping uncomfortably under the collar of her gown. Her skin stung where the mud hit, and when she pulled her hand away, clumps of the smelly yuck coated her hand. Mud from the dirty laundry water. The sour odor of the muck told her 'twas more than mud mixed with yard dirt.

She stood sickened and horrified in the middle of the yard, sniffing her hand. Her cheeks flamed a deep red and an embarrassed heat overcame her. Once she gained control of her tear-filled eyes, she swept her gaze around the bailey. To Aislynn, it appeared that those gathered in the yard were either openly staring or pointing and laughing at her stupefied discomfort.

And she froze where she stood, one hand dangling at her side, the other held before her face, covered in muck. Should she run to the tower and hide? Try to see who threw the offending mud? Stay rooted where she was and cry?

Never had she experienced such embarrassment. And as she stood there in the center of the inner yard, mud and debris dripping down the back of her gown and hot tears burning her eyes, she wanted nothing more than for the ground to open up and swallow her into the nether.

"Come with me, lassie," a voice behind her commanded. Aislynn turned obediently, as though she lacked any choice in the matter, to find the lady of the keep, Haleigh Sinclair, standing behind her.

The woman threaded Aislynn's elbow through hers, dragging Aislynn from her center stage of humiliation in the yard. They returned to the shadowy sanctuary of the broch, mounting the steps in a slow march to what seemed like the very top of the tower.

The lady of the keep held open a chamber door and Aislynn entered. Afternoon light filled the room, and from the window slits, Aislynn spied where the North Sea met the land, the thunderous crashing of the sea testing the will of the shore. Aislynn turned, facing the woman who rescued her.

Haleigh Sinclair was a woman who exuded power and grace. Her face, striking with strong features, was framed by fiery blondish hair she pulled back in a loose braid that fell midway between her defined shoulders.

The only flaw the striking woman had was in her soft, doe-colored eyes. Aislynn had not looked at the woman directly on the night she met her, and thus hadn't noticed. Haleigh's right eye didn't match her left, but almost floated to the side as she spoke. The result was an unnerving gaze whenever Haleigh's eyes roved over Aislynn. Every so often the eye would catch itself, move back into place, only to float away again.

Aislynn did her best not to stare – how rude would that be, considering this kind woman rescued her from the yard? – but the strange eye coupled with the woman's strong features was difficult to dismiss. Aislynn fought to keep her own gaze on the woman's left eye, so as not to offend.

"Let's start here," Haleigh said in a soft voice. "We should get that muddy gown off ye."

Treating Aislynn as though she were a child, Haleigh reached down to the hem of the fine bliaut and lifted it up and over Aislynn's head, trying to keep the muddy section of the gown from spreading any farther.

"Sit here," the woman gestured at a stool near a delicate table. Aislynn, shivering in her creamy kirtle, sat.

As Haleigh scrubbed at Aislynn's stained gown, her eyes flicked between her task and the English lass's face. She did her best to put the *sassenach* at ease.

"We Sinclair's are normally no' so rude, lassie. I apologize on behalf of my kinsmen."

Aislynn chewed on her bottom lip, appreciative of the woman's extension of an olive branch. She couldn't hold the actions of a few against this woman or the whole of her clan. Aislynn had just experienced what oft happens with that manner of thinking; she was hardly in a position to do the same.

"'Tis difficult enough to be an outsider in a new place, aye? To also be from another country, one 'tis nay well liked, weel, that only makes it worse, I imagine."

The delicate lilt of Haleigh's voice was soothing, a gentle cadence of a stream over the rocks. Aislynn's shoulders relaxed and the knot in her stomach loosened the more the woman spoke.

"Here, I will have a laundress in the kitchens work more at this stain. 'Tis nay large, thankfully, and your hair will well cover any that remains, but the laundress can oft work miracles."

The reminder of the laundry work made Aislynn's head sag. Haleigh set the dress at the foot of the bed, then grasped Aislynn's cold hand. Haleigh's hand was like her voice, soft and warm.

"Let's tackle that hair, coif, and kirtle, now shall we?"

Aislynn nodded silently, biting back tears that threatened to fall at the woman's kindness. They removed the stained kirtle to find the chemise unmarked. Haleigh's fingertips were tender as they worked through Aislynn's matted hair, extracting the clumpy mesh coif, pulling pebbles and chunks of dried mud from her hair. She used her fingers for a comb, brushing through the larger clumps, then dipped a cloth in a nearby scented bowl and scrubbed at Aislynn's hair to remove the rest of the muck. Haleigh hummed under her breath as she worked.

Having been handed over from one man's hands to another, this quiet moment among women was welcome, needed, *craved*. Even with the Earl, 'twas a dearth of women in the household; other than the maids, 'twas solely Aislynn and her sister.

Her thoughts went to simpler times when she played the mother role to Agnes, treating her sister's hair with the same care that Haleigh gave her own tresses. The memories were agonizing, a knife in Aislynn's heart. Though she'd managed to push those emotions aside, Aislynn worried for her sister, missed her desperately, and this woman's kind nature brought these tamped down emotions to the fore.

Aislynn herself felt like a child under Haleigh's ministrations, and now the tears fell. Her mother had died while she and Agnes were little, and she held few memories of what it was to be spoiled with a mother's love. Maids and servants had been kind enough, but never a replacement, and never with a mother's touch. The humming, that sound of contentment in one's work not unlike a purring cat, reached as tendrils of care and love long absent from her world.

"There," Haleigh fingers kneaded at Aislynn's shoulders and neck when she finished, relaxing Aislynn further. She fairly melted into the Sinclair woman. "I think ye may need a bath to really get the rest out, but for now, ye'll suffice."

She leaned around to face Aislynn, wiping the slow tears from her cheeks.

"Thank you," Aislynn whispered, eyes downcast. Haleigh patted Aislynn's cheek.

"Ooch, lassie. Ye deserve better. I can only hope my help here shows ye no' all the Sinclairs are unruly barbarians."

A light smile tugged at Aislynn's lips before she could stop it.

"Nay. Most of you, here in the tower, have been nothing but kind."

Haleigh gave a one-shouldered shrug. "Makes sense. Those of us in the broch, we ken why ye are here. The rest of the clan, though, they dinna ken ye are a guest, a noble guest of honor. For many, it can be hard to see beyond their limited experiences, aye? And anyone different from them, no matter how small that difference is, causes feelings of fear, and from that hatred. The fact ye are English –" here she tipped her head and clicked her tongue, "just makes that fear and hatred easier to rise and deeper to abide."

Her words were truth, that Aislynn well knew. The fears Haleigh described were not limited to Highlanders, but to men in general. History was rife with disasters resulting from fear and hatred.

"So, now I have an idea."

Haleigh's voice grew light, excited. Aislynn lifted her quizzical eyes to Haleigh's strange, dancing ones. Haleigh took both Aislynn's hands in hers to help her rise. Clad only in a chemise, Aislynn felt even more like a child under a mother's gaze.

"Let's find ye clothes more fitted to the Highlands. Your gowns are fine, dinna mistake me, but these trappings have no' use for every day. We in the Highlands dinna stand on such finery. If ye are going to live with us, become a Highlander, ye should dress as one, aye?"

Become a Highlander?

Haleigh led her to the ornate trunk pressed against the wall near the bed. Lifting the lid, Haleigh dug through the contents and removed a swath of fabric with a flourish and a smile.

"Here! 'Tis perfect. Lass, 'ere in the Highlands, we wear woolen kirtles and an *arasaid* if there's a chill in the air. Do ye have a brooch or the like? 'Tis still cool in the evenings and ye may want to wear a plaid."

The pale, wide-armed kirtle that swayed in Haleigh's hand paled in comparison to the brightly striped wool cloak that she held aloft. 'Twas similar to the plaid wraps that Aislynn had seen the men wear, only with one set of dark blue stripes woven into a beige field. And when Haleigh lay it on the bed, Aislynn noted 'twasn't a cloak in the traditional or English sense, but a long swath of striped wool that draped around the head or shoulders as the wearer saw fit.

Haleigh tossed the light wool kirtle to Aislynn, who shimmied it over her head. Once her head popped through the neckline, Haleigh tugged it down, so it brushed near her ankles. The fabric was a more natural pale blue gray, resembling the sea she had seen from the distance – a sharp contrast to Aislynn's hunter greens and deep browns she oft wore.

Her attentions, though, focused on the large wool fabric draped over the bed. After Haleigh finished tugging at the gown, she pulled the wrap off the bed and, with a talented flip of her wrist, flapped the plaid around Aislynn's shoulders.

"Hold this, if ye please," Haleigh asked.

Aislynn replaced Haleigh's grip at her neck while the woman returned to the trunk to resume her rummaging. Popping up like a squirrel who just found a beloved nut, Haleigh held a shiny object in her palm and a look of triumph on her face.

"Ah-ha! I kenned it to be in here!"

Handing over her open palm, Haleigh extended the object to Aislynn. The object, a large silver circlet with a stag's head at one end of the penannular that came to a sharp point, barely fit into the palm of her hand.

"Tis a Scots brooch, to fasten the plaid, aye?"

Without waiting for Aislynn to respond, her fingers worked their magic once more, effortlessly fastening the wool under Aislynn's chin with the silver jewelry.

"Ooch!" Haleigh cried, clapping her hands together. "We shall braid your hair, and ye will look like a proper Highland lass!"

Haleigh's excitement was infectious. Tears and embarrassment forgotten, Aislynn sat back on the stool where Haleigh directed her, allowing herself to fall again under the spell of Haleigh's talented hands. She pulled the top part of Aislynn's hair back, braiding with deft fingers. A fuzzy strip of leather served to secure the bottom of the braid. The rest of Aislynn's hair was left to fall about her shoulders, a shining compliment to the woolly plaid.

She touched a hand to her loose locks and looked down at herself. Such a difference compared her stuffy English dress! Where her gowns were confining, the Scots kirtle was freeing. Where her gown made her stand out, these colors would help her fit in with the rest of the Sinclairs. Even her hair was free, not contained by a delicate coif. 'Twas as if she stepped from the harsh reality into a dream, and she understood why the Highlanders fought so fiercely for their land. If she didn't know better, she almost believed 'twas a fairy-land.

"Come, see yourself in the silver."

Haleigh hefted an oblong silver platter into her arms, angling it at Aislynn. When she stood right before the platter, Aislynn saw her reflection in the highly polished surface, and she gasped.

What she saw in the reflection was not Aislynn de Valence, niece of the Earl of Pembroke and the King of England. She didn't recognize herself. *If the King of Scotland wanted to hide me away, he couldn't have found a better way!* With her hair in a loose braid, and soft waves of freed locks falling over the immense plaid wrap, she appeared a full Highland woman. Her fingers danced over her clothing and hair as she marveled at her reflection.

"Aye, lassie, ye look fine, indeed," Haleigh commented lightly as she set the silver aside, "but we dinna want ye to grow vain."

Haleigh's face softened, and she took both of Aislynn's hands in hers again.

"Well, lassie. Ye have no' said much. What are ye thinking about all of this?"

Aislynn studied Haleigh's face, her strange eye, and wondered just how much she was fishing for. Did she want Aislynn's opinions on the entire experience of arriving in the Sinclair's land? Or did she solely mean the dress? Aislynn split the difference.

"The Highlands are unlike any place I've seen. Most of the people have been kind," she swallowed thinking of John, Marcus, Etan, and the other Sinclairs who'd been honorable, even amiable, "but this, 'tis far beyond anything I expected when I learned I was to be sent here. Thank you for your kindness."

Haleigh waved her off. "We pride ourselves on a tradition of Highland hospitality. I just regret that ye were nay exposed to it earlier today. Ye handled it verra weel, if I do say so myself. That behavior, though," her eyes flashed, her floating eye shifting into focus, "will be handled without delay."

As they spoke, a faint din from below drew Haleigh's attention, and she glanced out the window where the brightness of day painted long slashes on the floor.

"'Tis such a pleasure to have longer days as summer comes, but I find I lose track of my obligations far too easily. Come, let us attend the kitchens. The men will soon return with bellies calling for vittles."

Haleigh took Aislynn's hand a final time, escorting the lass downstairs, *back to the lair,* Aislynn thought. But this time, she was dressed for the fight and had an ally at her back.

***

Having a job in the kitchens for the afternoon also helped relieve Aislynn's humiliation over the thrown-mud incident. No one in the kitchens looked at her with anything other than appreciation for her hard work, no side-long glances or snide remarks. 'Twas evident Haleigh made her opinions regarding any errant behaviors clear, and Aislynn took comfort that her assailant likely was not working on the evening meal.

The diminutive cook and all-around chatelaine, Mistress Eva Sinclair as she insisted on being called, graciously carved time out of her preparations to show Aislynn how to prepare bannocks, the dry-looking biscuit made of oats that she had eaten most days since landing in King Robert's lap. Patting them onto the baking stone, Mistress Eva Sinclair showed her how to flip them at the right time, until they were golden brown and not over cooked, lauding both Aislynn's quick learning and the joy of warm bannocks freshly made.

Platters were laden with all manner of meat, fruits, and cheese. Much of the fish was pulled straight from the shallows of the Reay inlet, and fresh fish was readily available to the clan throughout the year. Aislynn hefted a wooden platter larger than her head onto her shoulder, as she had seen the other kitchen lasses do, and followed them into the main hall. The last vision she had of the kitchen before exiting was Haleigh watching her with that fiercely strange gaze, smiling widely at how well a simple change of dress changed one's whole outlook.

The men stomped in, loud and calling for mead, heather ale, and whiskey. Aislynn dropped her platter on an empty table, then raced back to the kitchen to gather pitchers to place before the men. As she departed, Haleigh told her to find her place in the hall and eat. Only too eager to oblige, Aislynn grasped two of the largest pitchers she could manage, set them on tables in the hall, then found her place at the same table where she'd sat previous evenings.

When she looked up, she found John and Marcus sitting across from her, mouths hanging agape. Her brows knitted at their comical, shared expressions.

"What ails you, brothers Sinclair?"

They exchanged a brief look, then Marcus snapped his jaw shut so his teeth clacked together.

"Weel, 'tis ye, Aislynn," John's voice held a note of wonder. Aislynn reached her hand to her mouth, covering the grin that blossomed there.

"And what of me?" she asked behind her hand, playing coy.

She'd not played the coquette before, never having the chance under Pembroke's rule. Although with John and Marcus, 'twas a behavior that felt surprisingly natural. The jovial character of these men contributed much to it.

John's eyes flicked down her dress, what he noticed of it where she sat – her graceful neck and enticing bust – then back up to her face which was shining at his attentions.

"Your gowns? Ye are dressed, uh, weel, like –" he stumbled over his words. Aislynn dropped her hand, laughing out loud.

"Like a Highlander?"

"Aye!" John and Marcus exclaimed together.

Now her smile reached her eyes, joyous, an emotion she didn't expect to feel after her unpleasantness earlier. *What a strange day it had been!* But most of these Sinclairs made her feel welcome, comfortable, wanted. *Desired*, she added, peering at John, then shook the thought away.

"I stained my gown earlier," Aislynn hedged around the event. "Haleigh was kind enough to assist me in finding more appropriate clothing for your clan lands. She did well, *aye?*"

She mimicked their dialect, and John's deep, explosive laugh drew more attention than she cared for. Her cheeks bloomed in crimson, and her eyes flicked around at the smiling faces that wanted to laugh along with John.

"Ooch, lassie," John continued. "We will make a proper Highland lass of ye yet."

The Seduction of the Glen

***

Though his words were light-hearted and bantering, they were nothing more than a cover for the deep yearning that welled up when he first caught her maneuvering the tables with her arms full of food. He didn't recognize her for a moment, wondering who the doe-haired Highlands lass was, until Marcus elbowed him.

"'Is that Aislynn, the English lass, in an *arasaid?*"

They both kept their gazes on the young woman, wonder-struck and mystified at what prompted the staunch niece of the English King to adopt their Highland dress. Her kirtle clung to her curves in an enticing flow, the dusky blue flattered her coloring, and her *arasaid* hung from her shoulders in a proud cape, gathered at her neck with a familiar-styled brooch. The stag emblem, an animal their grandfather adopted as their clan herald, was etched into the hilt of the penannular. The brooch had long been a family heirloom; Aislynn's Highland dress must be a gift from Haleigh. *Does she ken the import of the brooch?* John pondered briefly.

He quickly dismissed the question, as he had larger concerns at hand. 'Twas fortunate he could sit down, otherwise his hard member would be obvious, visible beneath his trews, and that wouldn't give Aislynn the right impression *at all.*

Throughout the evening meal, John ate little, unable to tear his attention from the fair English rose wearing Highland petals. Her hair, escaping from a braid to flow lose about her shoulders, softened her features, tiny wisps framing her face. His blood hammered in his veins and vitals, his stomach, previously ravenous, forgotten. Every time she looked up from her meal and caught his eyes, the pounding intensified. And when she rose to leave, the men at the table stood respectfully, but with disappointment, the meal a now less invigorating experience.

The rest of the men demolished their food and imbibed to their fill, then departed to finish their chores or find their entertainments where they were wont. Even Marcus left with several of the younger men, probably to find a sport to prove their prowess.

John dwelt with patience, a trait with which he was becoming intimate. The numbers in the hall thinned, as did the sounds of the kitchen. When he was certain most of the work was done, he bounded outside from the main hall around to the kitchen door at the rear of the tower.

Standing to the side of the door, he again bided his time, inhaling the heady salty air. The distant sounds of the crashing waves from the incoming tide lulled him into such a relaxed state he nearly missed jumping to the side when the door to the kitchen burst open and one of the kitchen maids tossed a bucket of filthy water into the dirt, splattering his legs with droplets of mud and dirty water.

"Ooch, John Sinclair! I did no' see ye there in the dark!" The lass threw a startled hand to her mouth.

"Of course, ye did no', lassie. 'Tis past dusk and I wasna paying attention. Is the English lass still within?" he ventured.

The maid dropped her hand, allowing her knowing smile to taunt him.

"Aye. Shall I retrieve her for ye?"

"Kindly, if ye will."

The lass nodded in the way young women do when they know where a man's affections lie, keeping that mocking smile plastered on her face. She didn't leave the door.

"Aislynn!" she called over her shoulder. "Mr. John Sinclair would like a word with ye."

"Weel, ye did no' have to announce it to the entire kitchen," John grumbled as the maid laughed at his discomfiture.

"Nay, I did no'," she laughed.

John rolled his eyes to the heavens and rubbed his hand over his beard stubble. 'Twas naught a secret in this keep?

***

Aislynn peeked out the doorway. "John! What do you need from me?" she asked.

Oh, what a question! If she only kenned . . . His perverse mind flitted over how he wanted to answer the question, then cleared his throat. He made to speak and noticed the maid still in audience near the door. John peered around Aislynn at her, glowering.

"If ye please, lassie? Some privacy?"

The maid paused a moment to let her smile linger, then slowly retreated, closing the door behind her.

"John?" Aislynn asked, her face a mask of confusion. "Did you want a word?"

And so much more, his brain reeled again.

"Aye, if ye would walk with me?"

Aislynn flicked her gaze back at the kitchen door.

"I will be a gentleman, I promise," he said as he held his arm out to her. "From the sounds, the kitchens will no' miss ye."

A curl of a smile tugged at her cheek.

"Where are we walking?"

John didn't answer but let his own scruffy lips twitch into a smile. His teeth shone stark white in the moonlight as he held out his hand in invitation. Aislynn eyed it warily, as though he were offering her a snake rather than his hand. She pulled her *arasaid* against a breeze that swept at the plaid, then with a sudden move, as though she were afraid she would change her mind, Aislynn gripped his hand. His smile widened, relaxing the hardened features of his face.

"Come with me, lass."

***

John flipped the torch from its scone on the wall of the keep, and threading his fingers through Aislynn's, moved surefooted across the stony grass.

He led her away from Broch Reay into the breeze that carried the clean smell of salt on its back. After a short distance, the grasses thinned, giving way to dirt and sand. When they were close to their destination, John shortened his steps to walk alongside her and watch her face as she took in the view.

When she looked up from her footing, Aislynn stopped short and a breathtaking gasp escaped her lips.

They stood at the spot where the sand formed a beach, a gentle curve of light against the black expanse that seemed never-ending. The bay and sea beyond were black glass in the night, a mirror to the heavens and its stars that reflected the soul of the universe. 'Twas as if the water spoke to her own soul, challenging every idea she'd had before while inviting her to open herself to a world she'd never known. Who could cast their eyes upon such greatness, such depth, and not feel as if the very fundament under their feet shifted, changing the course of their lives?

And John knew this. Though he'd grown up on the rocky shores of the North Sea, few had viewed the largess of the water and not be changed. He saw it mirrored in their eyes, how they held their shoulders, the way their breath caught. And he saw this same change in Aislynn.

The silence was both heavy and welcome, spinning out to the night as they stood at the edge of the sandy beach, taking in the view. John's view, however, included Aislynn, watching as her eyes scanned the bay.

The sand swerved into a fat crescent facing north into the sea. To the east and west of the sandy crescent, the rough-edged mountains dropped from the skies directly into the sea, enclosing the shore and the narrow bay. Moonlit, gentle black waves kissed the shoreline before slinking back to the sea. 'Twas a private haven.

Aislynn finally pulled her eyes from the marvel to look questioningly at John.

"This place," she whispered, not wanting to break the serenity of the moment, "'Tis like it is looking into my soul."

"Aye," John agreed in a quiet voice. "Some places speak to us in a language only our hearts speak and change us. I feel changed every time I come here. On some days, ye can see whales in the distance or seals coming to the far shores."

"Such beauty," Aislynn's voice was full of reverence. "I have a bit of jealousy for your childhood, having this place so close. I could stay here forever." Her voice took on a dreamy quality.

John didn't miss his opportunity. When she turned to him again, he grasped her other hand, tugging her to face him directly. He stepped to her, blocking the robust sea breeze that whipped up as night enveloped the land in a sleepy embrace.

"Ye could," he whispered so low Aislynn thought she misheard him. "Ye can remain here, if ye wish."

Before Aislynn fully understood the enormity of his words, his lips captured hers in a bold kiss, finishing the moment they shared that first night at Reay. While his injury may have held him back then, now he was certain of himself and what he wanted with Aislynn. 'Twas more than a wager with his brother or a promise to a king – the flush of wonder that beamed from her as she gazed upon the cove clinched his heart as surely as her tender care and engaging temperament had over the past month. He poured that emotion, that desire, that passion for her into his kiss.

And she returned it, her own lips giving tentative movements even as John's need pressed her further. Releasing her hands, he slipped his arms around her waist, drawing her as close to him as their clothing allowed, his cockstand that surged be damned. She would know his desire for her.

***

Aislynn's mind spun out of control. John's intense gazes, the heat of his hand as he held hers, the dance of his lips against her mouth, were the culmination of their growing passion for one another. Aislynn couldn't deny her feelings, as much as she wanted to, as much as she believed she should. An English prisoner shouldn't have romantic inclinations for her Scottish captor – it went against everything she was taught, everything she thought she believed.

The more time she spent with John Sinclair, the tighter her chest became when she thought of him, and she shivered with anticipation when she knew she would see him. Her fingers burned whenever she touched his naked skin, and she longed to touch him more.

It was wrong, more than wrong – the man who presently skimmed his lips over hers and captivated her senses was supposed to be her enemy. Yet, from the moment he halted her pathetic escape in the wood a month ago, an undeniable magnetism built between them.

She clutched at his tunic, twining the material in her fingers, clinging to him as the kiss deepened. His hands slipped low, gripping her skirts, and her mind crashed down to where she was and who she was with. Aislynn wanted to shove him away, protest his actions, but her body didn't let her. She wanted him just as much as his lips showed he wanted her.

Instead, she pulled her head back, the excitement of their kiss glistening in her eyes.

"John," she said, his name carrying on the sea breeze like a prayer.

"Aye," he croaked. "My apologies, lass. I'm afraid I may have behaved inappropriately."

He moved a half-step back, trying to calm the raging storm inside him. Aislynn's hand remained on his chest. He glanced at her fingers – perchance he'd not behaved as inappropriately as he thought.

"I fear this is wrong," she told him honestly.

She couldn't tell him she didn't want him. 'Twould have been a lie. But given their positions on opposite sides of this war, how could it be anything but wrong?

"Why do ye think that? How is what we feel for each other wrong?"

"I'm little more than a captive here . . ." she started. John shook his head in a desperate gesture, his wild hair dancing in the wind.

"Nay, lass. Ye need to see that is no' the case. Aye, ye were sent here, and ye need to stay for your safety. Yet, have ye fared any better at the hands of your uncle? And is this place so terrible? That ye canna see yourself living here, mayhap as a Sinclair yourself? There are worse things than a change in location."

"A change in alliances?" She broached the subject head on. "'Tis more than a change in location. As a Sinclair? Do ye think the Sinclairs will ever accept a niece of the English King as one of their own?"

The memory of the mud attack from earlier caused her head to throb as if the mud were still there. She rubbed her hand across the back of her neck at the phantom sensation.

"I accept ye. Haleigh accepts ye. Your maids accept ye. The clan will eventually."

He sounded as if he were pleading with her. She shifted her eyes to the black night sea, trying to calm the roiling tempest inside her.

"And what of my choice?" She didn't look at him as she spoke. "I was given no choice to be here."

John inhaled deeply. 'Twas a question for which he had no good answer. An honest one would have to suffice.

"Do any of us truly have choices in our lives?" he asked. "Did I have a choice to follow my brother, the Laird, to the banner of Robert the Bruce? Not unless I wanted my own clan to take my head. And then to be sent home, the guardian of the enemy? Of that I had nay choice. The King commanded, and I followed."

He paused and tugged at her hand, so she faced him. His eyes reflected the depths of the sea, and Aislynn lost herself in those dark, forest-green pools. Her breath caught under the force of his gaze.

"We do have few choices in our lives, as small as they may seem. I choose that ye would remain here, by my side. Since I have met ye, my mind has nay been my own. I am drunk with thoughts of ye. I would spend the rest of my life drunk on ye. I would wed ye, given the chance. But 'tis your choice."

He gathered her in his arms, holding her to his chest so the warmth of his heat and the steady cadence of his heart reflected against her skin. His body served as a barricade against the sharp breeze. John was making a promise to her no one, not even her sister, had made before. He was hers, if she made that choice.

"You have caught me by surprise," she spoke into the wind. "I was not prepared for such a change in my circumstances. And here you were, suddenly in my life, offering your protection, looking at me in such a way that I feel the world shift under my feet. I find my heart responding to you of its own volition, no matter how oft my head tells me 'tis impossible."

She turned her shining face up to his. "With you, I feel everything is possible. Can you be patient while I consider? I shall need a day or two to consider your offer."

John didn't respond, only tightened his muscular arms, enclosing her in his warm embrace as they cast their gazes to the night sea.

Chapter Nine: The Only Acceptable Form of Lying

The next morning, John awoke full of pride and expectation. He was confident today Aislynn would accept his offer to wed. Asper and the King would be pleased with a union that aligned Scotland with England, if this war ever ended, and as an added perk, win the wager over his brother.

He scratched at his beard, the smile on his face hurting his cheeks. Brushing his fingers through his wild hair, he pulled on a pair of old braies and a tunic. 'Twas not too early, and 'twas a fair chance Marcus may be awake, poking about his work. The early plantings needed attending, and late spring crops of kale, turnips, and carrots must be sown as the weather had finally turned. The next several days promised to be a flurry of activity.

The pledge John made to Haleigh to meet with the MacKays also hung over his head. He hadn't been able to gather the men yesterday to ride out, busy as they were with so many kinsmen gone, so he vowed to assemble the men as soon as their commitment to sowing seeds abated. His mind had been too caught up over Aislynn, 'twas time to rise to his responsibilities. Not that he blamed himself.

His first task of the day was to find Marcus and collect his winnings. Pulling on his boots, he whistled to himself, his spirits as bright as his hair in the sunlight.

'Twas at the second place he checked where he found Marcus, beyond the stables and knee deep in muck, a large hoe snapping against the earth. Several women and older men followed suit, preparing the land to supply the clan with enough food for the year.

"Are ye here to finally work, ye layabout?" Marcus taunted, not lifting his head. "A dandy such as yourself needs a bit of mud to make ye a man this day."

"Ooch, brother, 'tis nay mud 'twill make me a man. And I'll grab a hoe as soon as I am done with ye here."

Marcus raised his head, and his hair poking out from the dirt made Marcus resemble a bright porpentine. John bit back a laugh at his brother. No need to add insult to losing the wager as well.

"But ye, Marcus, ye'll have a lot more work on your plate."

"Ooch, too good for work, do ye think ye are?" Marcus looked back at the clefts he left in the thick dirt. He was pleased at the color of the soil – a rich, dark womb of the earth, ready to bring forth life in the form of food.

"Nay, but in payment for the loss of a wager. Ye owe me a day's work."

Marcus threw down the hoe, his bright green eyes raging in disbelief.

"Nay! Ye did no' win the lass!"

"Ooch, but I did. We sealed it with a kiss yester eve. I took her to the sea, and we got caught up in the night air. I asked her to stay."

Marcus straightened and raised an eyebrow. "But has she answered ye, yet?"

"I expect her answer today. She will say aye, to stay in the Highlands and wed me. Ye may think ye a charmer, but your boyish charms are no match against the honest, resolved interest of a real man. The lassie kens who truly wants her."

Huffing in protest, Marcus bent to retrieve his tool, then hacked at the dirt with much less precision than he had earlier. John imagined he saw the steam erupting from Marcus's ears at losing. While the wager had become nothing to John and the lass was the only true prize, Marcus was young enough to still feel vexed at losing a bet.

"Alright!" Marcus finally admitted. "Ye win the lass. What chores do I need to finish for ye?"

John was holding a finger to his lips, pretending to ponder the list, when a flash of skirts appeared from the side of the stable.

"Win the lass?" Aislynn screeched, unable to contain her mortification at being nothing more than a prize in a wager.

She had approached the stables to retrieve the rest of the milk pails when she overheard the men talking, and the word "wager" piqued her interest. Though eavesdropping was surely low-born behavior, Aislynn couldn't help herself, and the voices *were* loud.

Then, the more the men talked, the angrier she grew until she burst like a water-logged dam. Marcus and John faced her, faces pale in a mix of panic and dismay.

"Is that how little ye think of me? Why ye conversed with me, feigned to 'protect' me? Out of a crass wager to see who would win the simple-minded lass?"

Pails forgotten, her fists balled as she spoke, as if she'd strike each man physically if she thought it would bring any resolve to bear. She had been the butt of a cruel joke, and she didn't know how to control her anger.

"Lassie. Aislynn," John spoke, taking a mincing step closer, "'tis nay like that at all."

"Are you saying I was *not* the prize in a wager? That I am mishearing your conversation?"

John inhaled deeply and pinched the bridge of his nose, convinced no answer would calm her storm. "Aislynn, we set the wager afore we even met ye, a stupid agreement between brothers . . ."

"Yes, stupid is the word I was looking for."

"But my actions last night were not an attempt to win a wager. Since I've met ye --"

"No." She held up her hand. Her mounting rage flushed across her face.

She'd been made a fool of enough over the last several days. A victim of a mudslinging and being made to feel a deep emotional connection to this crude Highlander, only to learn 'twas nothing more than a prank, 'twas too much for her. Never before had she felt more alone than she did in this singular moment standing among the Sinclairs. The one person in this strange land she believed to safeguard her was instead using her emotions for sport.

The day before, the humiliation at being hit with a ball of muck froze her in her spot. Today, she dealt with her humiliation in the opposite way. Hiking up her skirts, she turned and ran for the keep, wanting to hide from the world.

Marcus and John exchanged a shameful glance. Heads bowed, from beneath their hooded lids, they watched the lass run off. John now had a larger battle for the lass's hand than he had in the wager with Marcus, and he groaned inwardly at her exit.

"I'll take care of your sowing and your animals, man," Marcus said in a stoic voice. "Godspeed with Aislynn."

John clapped his brother on his back. He looked up to the windows of the tower, at Aislynn's chamber. The prospect of knocking on her door and asking for forgiveness for his boyish behavior loomed darkly. But, as with any unpleasant deed, 'twas best to get it done with sooner.

At least he knew where to find her. Most likely she threw herself on her bed, crying a river of tears, and 'twas his fault. He groaned to himself again before making his way to Aislynn.

***

"Mistress Eva Sinclair?" John popped his head into the kitchens, his eyes searching as he spoke. "Have ye seen the English lassie anywhere?"

"Ooch, is she nay about the keep? She left 'ere just a short time ago."

John scratched at his beard. "And she didna return this way? Just now?"

Mistress Eva shook her head, focusing her attentions at squeezing cheese curdles. John was dismissed.

When he finally figured out what to say in apology, he had knocked at Aislynn's door. He waited patiently for her to answer, and when she didn't, John tried the handle. The door swung open to an empty room. Puzzled, John left the hallway, trying to surmise where she was hiding herself. The kitchens seemed the next logical choice. Evidently, he was wrong. Where was she then?

He went outside to the gardens behind the kitchens. One of Aislynn's maids marched across the yard, a pail of water that probably weighed more than the lassie clutched in both hands.

"Esther," he called out, his mind starting to race. Where could Aislynn be if not in her chambers? The barns? The gardens? "Have ye seen Aislynn about?"

Esther splashed past him, shaking her head. John's hand worked from his beard to the back of his head, his fingers worrying at his neck. His eyes flicked to the northern horizon and slowly panned west. If she were upset, she may run to the shore, to lose her cares in the rushing sights and sounds of the water. 'Twas a common enough desire – John himself had sought refuge in that peaceful cove in the past. And she had wanted to see the astounding view in the daytime . . .

But 'twas the westerly view that caused a flare of panic in his chest. What if she decided the wager was the tipping point? What if she ran off, again trying to return home, or God-forbid, ran to the MacKays to seek refuge?

He didn't want to believe she would try the MacKays after what happened with their previous interlude. Yet, she was visibly upset, and perchance her thoughts were not fully balanced. A loss of home and family was dire enough, to believe she lost a love, weel, John conceded, 'twas enough to drive anyone to the brink of madness.

Haleigh stepped out of the kitchens, wiping the sweat of her efforts from her brow with a dusky cloth.

"Lady Sinclair," he called with an air of respect. Haleigh's face rose at his voice.

"John, how are ye this morn?"

"Haleigh, have ye seen Aislynn pass by ye this morn? Just now?"

She reached the cloth around the back of her neck as she shook her head. "Nay. I thought her to be in the kitchens with Mistress Eva Sinclair. Is she nay out planting?" Her quizzical eyebrows rose and curiosity sharpened her eyes. Her right eye came into hard focus.

"Ye do no' think she's outside, helping with the planting?" That panicking sensation surged in him again. Something more was going on. Haleigh exhaled forcibly.

"John, not everyone is pleased with Aislynn's presence here, a constant reminder of our conflict with the English and the overriding fear that the English will attack to retrieve her. I must tell ye, yesterday, she was assisting with the laundry when some of the clan made their discontent known. Someone, I dinna ken who as of yet, lobbed a handful of yard muck at her head. It stained her clothes, and we spent the afternoon cleaning her hair and gowns."

He recalled Aislynn's Highland dress the night before and realization hit him like a strike to the face. She wanted to fit in, to find acceptance, and learning of John's wager with his brother didn't help. He rubbed his hand against his scruffy beard.

"Weel, this morning didna help either. Marcus and I, we had a bit of a wager going on who'd win the lass's favor, and she may have overheard my bragging about winning."

The loud smack sound was as shocking as the force of her palm on his face. Haleigh's ferocious glare bit him to the core, and John found himself cowering as a red mark in the shape of Haleigh's hand bloomed on his cheek.

"Ooch, ye and your brothers! Always up to no good! Look where it has led ye!" Her reprimand fell short of John's own self-chastisement. Haleigh closed her eyes to compose herself. When she opened them, that unnerving, offset gaze has softened. "And now the lass is missing?"

John tipped his head north. "Aye. I think she may have escaped to the shore. Or, if she truly believed as though she had no other choice, I fear she may have tried to flee."

Haleigh snorted. "I am rather surprised she had not tried afore now."

John was silent, but his thin lips behind the red shadow of his beard gave him away.

"Ooch, so she *had* tried afore. More than once?"

John nodded.

"Weel, get your brother and Etan, and perchance Oggie or Reed, and have them help ye search for the lass. Try the cove as ye head west. She can no' have gotten too far, and ye should be able to overtake her afore she reaches the MacKay lands."

"Unless they are on our land already," John said under his breath as he bowed and raced off, hollering for Marcus.

***

John wrangled Marcus, Etan, and Oggie without haste, and the men rode northwest in a blur of plaid and dust. Rain had held back for the past few days, a surprising spring dry spell, and any broken grass stalks would be easy to track.

Though no tracks seemed to lead to the bay, the chance she managed to follow the trail and leave naught behind was not dismissed. The shore was close enough to check as they worked their way west. As the grass thinned into the creeping sand, Aislynn was nowhere to be found. No footprints disturbed the smooth crests of the sand, and the men wasted no time changing their direction.

West, toward the MacKays, 'twas.

The great barn rose in the distance. John and Marcus exchanged a knowing look, recalling their conversations with Aislynn when they had first arrived. The behemoth of crumbling stone and wood beckoned. The odds that the lass made her way to the notorious barn dawned on them. Would she have sought succor in the barn? They pushed the horses harder, sweat flinging from both men and beasts into the wind.

"Could she have come this far?" Etan asked. "Surely, we would have overcome her by now, if she were on foot."

Frustrated, John nodded as he slowed his horse. The others followed, and they reared up to the front of the barn. Etan was correct. Even if the lass ran the entire way, she couldn't have made it to the barn already, could she?

They dismounted, hobbling the horses, and a sound from the west of the barn caught their attention. Racing around the corner, they expected to see the lass resting against the ancient stone.

Instead, they found Duncan MacKay and several of his men loitering in the barnyard. MacKays' own horses grazed to the west while the men dallied in the grass. *On Sinclair lands.*

The MacKays snapped their heads up as the Sinclairs halted at the front of the barn. Anger rose to match the fear of Aislynn's safety, and John reached behind his head and released his broadsword, the metal scraping against the leather scabbard. Duncan MacKay left his mark last time, and John vowed to fight the man to the death if he had a hand in Aislynn's disappearance.

"Ooch, what a surprise to find ye here, Duncan." The fury in Oggie's voice was unmistakable. "On Sinclair land."

"Ye havena been on this side of your land for a long time," Duncan growled back. "Ye may want to say that we've a claim to it, since we are able to guard it."

"Only because your men will no' fight for the king!" Etan cried.

Duncan shrugged, spitting into the grass. "'Tis nay my problem."

"The barn is a Sinclair barn. Ye have no claim to it or our lands, regardless if we are here or no'," Oggie announced.

As they spoke, John and Marcus scanned the landscape, searching for Aislynn who didn't appear to be with the MacKays.

"This time there are more of us, old man," Duncan taunted. "Do ye want to try and oppose us again?"

John didn't hesitate. At the MacKay's words, John launched forward, bringing his sword down on Duncan. The man stumbled to the side, out of the sword's reach, and another MacKay leapt forward to take the brunt of the attack with his own sword. The glen echoed with the sound of swords unsheathing, and the Sinclairs pressed into the fray.

The MacKays did outnumber the Sinclairs, and John realized that fighting the MacKays wouldn't accomplish the goal of finding Aislynn. If the MacKays had taken her to their keep, killing these men wouldn't give them the answers they needed.

When Duncan stepped aside, John caught Marcus's eye. His brother stood stock-still as John shook his head, and Marcus understood the silent message. He fell back, waving at Etan and Oggie to do the same, just as John dropped his sword arm.

Duncan MacKay noticed the change in the Sinclairs and twisted his wrist, bringing the hilt of the sword down on John's head instead of the blade, knocking him senseless.

Marcus and his men rushed their horses, riding back to Reay as if their lives depended on it. As for John, perchance his life did. If the MacKays had Aislynn, who knew what they would do with her that may bring the English this far north. John had to make his way into their keep to learn of her presence.

John expected Marcus to return with a significantly larger coterie of men and make a deal for his return, and Aislynn's.

So much for meeting with Laird Malcolm MacKay and presenting a united front. John was certain this was *not* what Haleigh and his brother's advisers had intended.

***

The space in the undercroft storage beneath the stair was tight. Dirty, too, and stuffy, and Aislynn was certain she'd heard several mice scrambling under the crate next to her. But it was hidden and dark and the only place in Broch Reay that came to her mind where she could be alone with her misery. She'd expected John to search her chambers right after she ran off, and she wasn't in the state of mind to see him.

The longer she wept her worries away in her cramped hidey-hole, the more she believed that perchance she had reacted too rashly.

Throughout her life, she and Agnes had made their own sisterly wagers over events both great and small. Could she fault John and Marcus for making a wager before they knew her? When 'twas likely they wagered over any manner of event? Would he have expressed himself any differently if he'd not made the wager? Mayhap she should have let him say his peace instead of running off like a child.

Wiping her eyes on her *arasaid*, she let her tears run out. No, his words of love weren't tainted by his wager, that she knew in her heart. The heat they shared when they were alone together was real, as was the way her breath caught when he cast his intense gaze at her, making the rest of the world drop away until she was the only person in the room.

No, those moments can't be feigned.

The weight of everything over the past month needed a catharsis, and her weeping under the stairs was just that.

She'd reacted rashly. Now she needed to find John, listen to his words that she wasn't willing to hear earlier, apologize for her own imprudent behavior, and hope the direction her heart wanted her to follow wasn't untrue. She'd spent more than enough time hiding from the Sinclairs.

What she didn't expect was the tumult of chaos that welcomed her when she emerged from her hiding spot.

What now?

Mistress Eva Sinclair stood over a haggard-looking kitchen maid, commanding her to boil water faster, as if such a thing were possible. A stressful undercurrent was unmistakable, like thick smoke from a wildfire, and Aislynn approached Mistress Eva with caution.

"Mistress Eva Sinclair, is something amiss?" Aislynn's hesitant voice barely rose above the din within the keep.

The chatelaine dropped the metal spoon she clutched to her bosom, covering her open mouth with her hand.

Chapter Ten: When What was Lost is Found

"Milady!" Mistress Eva gasped. "What are ye doing here?"

"I thought you may need help in the kitchens. I understand I've been absent most of the morn, and for that I apologize."

"Nay, milady. I mean, what are ye doing here? At Reay?"

Aislynn's face creased with confusion. Where else could she be?

"I'm here, asking to help in the kitchens," she answered. *Was Mistress Eva becoming simple-minded? It oft happened when people aged . . .*

"Come with me." She grabbed Aislynn's arm. "Keep your eye on that pot!" Mistress Eva yelled over her shoulder as she dragged Aislynn through the hall into the yard.

Men of all ages and in every manner of dress were preparing their horses and strapping on their weapons, and a sinking sensation rocked Aislynn to her core. She had a strong idea that she was the reason for this woeful flurry.

Mistress Eva Sinclair called for Haleigh, who broke into a run when she saw Aislynn.

"Lady Aislynn! What are ye doing here?"

Aislynn's brow knitted further. *Why did they keep asking her that?* "I never left. I apologize. I had a bit of a spat with John, and I tucked myself away –"

"All day?" Haleigh screeched.

"Well, just the morn. I didn't realize –"

"Never ye mind. Marcus!" she hollered as she spun away.

The short-haired brother of John met her halfway. His bushy eyebrows reached his hairline when he followed the direction of Haleigh's finger, pointing at Aislynn. A moue of irritation followed, darkening his bright visage, and a bubble of fear rose in Aislynn's chest. Something very wrong occurred in her absence, because of her hiding, and that's when she noted John's wild thatch of deep red was nowhere to be found.

Something happened to John!

"Where's John?" Aislynn screamed into the yard, and Haleigh returned.

"The MacKays have him. He let himself be taken in hopes of finding ye there. Now we must retrieve him."

Aislynn's eyes roved over the men collected who prepared to go to battle for their Laird's brother. None looked in her direction, intentionally ignoring her. Their blame was obvious in their absolute disregard for her presence. Panic met the fear rising in her chest. The Sinclairs would never accept her if anything happened to John. Handfuls of mud would be the least of her worries.

And what of John? More than she had realized, she didn't want anything to happen to John – her heart clinched at the thought of any harm coming to him, especially since she needed to tell him . . . *Oh, John! What have I done?*

Pressing the awakening panic to the side, she searched her mind for a solution. She was the niece of a King and an Earl – politicking was in her blood, or at least she supposed it was.

Frustrated, she picked at her dusty arasaid as she wracked her brain, and the plaid cloth helped her conceive a scheme. Something, anything, to save John. She wasn't a Sinclair, or even a Scot – she was *English*.

"Haleigh! I have an idea!"

The lady of the keep tried hard to hide her irritation at the foreign lass who caused so much disruption in her short time in her clan, but the woman's floating eye gave her away, twitching fore and aft. Aislynn was surprised Haleigh listened to her at all.

"Aislynn, please. The men will go armed to retrieve John. 'Tis the best way to deal with men such as the MacKays."

"No! No, it isn't!" Aislynn held her plaid upright. "I have an idea that should work, given what ye have told me about the loyalties of the MacKays. Give me just two or three men, ones who can hide their clan?" Aislynn touched her hair for emphasis. "And I will need to change. I canna wear this."

Aislynn grabbed Haleigh as they made their way into the keep, explaining her plan as they went.

***

John blinked his eyes open, the back end of a horse and the ground in his view. His head ached mildly, but 'twas manageable. As he bounced along across the back of the horse, he considered the best way to find Aislynn and kept his ears tuned to the MacKays' conversation.

"Duncan, do ye think bringing the Sinclair to the keep is the best way? What do ye plan with the man?" A young, black-haired MacKay asked the older Highlander.

"'Tis no' my decision. The Laird will decide what to do with him."

"He will just let the man go. The Laird may want land, but he doesna want direct conflict. 'Tis a waste of time," Hager MacKay, a young warrior himself, commented.

Duncan often made huge mistakes, overreacted, and the Laird had to fix those problems, and the men knew this. Why Duncan was still a tacksman for Laird Malcolm MacKay remained a mystery to most of the MacKay warriors.

"So why are we bringing him with us?" the black-haired youth, Raphael, asked again.

Duncan waved him away. "Rafe, we need to send a message to the Sinclairs. Ye are too young to understand. Dinna worry your little head."

Rafe MacKay pursed his lips and fell back, and Hager just shook his head. *Dinna bother to ask,* was the message he sent. Rebuked, Rafe did as Hager indicated.

His eyes flicked to the man wobbling on the back of Josiah's horse. The Sinclair's dazed, green eyes parted, looking around, and Rafe caught his gaze. Not for the first time, a fiery malcontent burned deep inside Rafe about his clan. They didn't follow the Bruce or support Scottish independence; they preyed on the neighboring clans that did, and Rafe's conscience battled itself. And any loyalty to his clan was losing.

Not that his Laird wanted to listen to a young man like himself, but if he had the opportunity to speak on behalf of the Sinclair, Rafe decided to defend the man and encourage the MacKays to send him off unscathed.

***

Aislynn rode at the front of the three-man entourage, each wearing earth-colored bonnets and tunics, not a plaid among them. Aislynn made sure their leather belts were simple, adorned only with plain swords at their sides. Nothing of the men could scream Sinclair, or even Scots, if her plan were to work.

Readied for confrontation, Aislynn had also changed her own clothes, wearing her gilt-edged green riding dress instead of the Sinclair *arasaid*. With Haleigh's help, she wove her hair into a fine, silvery mesh coif high atop her head. She tugged at the tight sleeves of her kirtle. Aislynn looked to be a proper English lady, a paragon of English nobility.

Which was exactly what they needed. Aislynn convinced Haleigh, Reed, and Fleck that, with the MacKays' problematic loyalties, she would pretend to be a representative of the King of England wanting to take one of the Bruce's Sinclairs as a prisoner for England. A small bit of coin jingled in her purse – several groats and a few sixpence – in addition to a faked missive with a promise of more from the Earl of Pembroke if the Sinclair arrived in one piece.

In the back of her mind, she fretted at her believability – would she be able to pull off this guise? Were the MacKays the type of men to believe the words of a woman, even if she did presume to speak on behalf of the King of England? She sent up a silent prayer 'twould work. The jingling of her purse put in her mind Haleigh's words that, the more coin one has, the fewer questions are asked.

They had to hope the MacKays wouldn't look too closely at the English lady's escorts, and that Laird MacKay was foolish enough to believe a forged letter and an English lass. And that John caught on and was clever enough to keep his own mouth shut when he saw her.

Because if they didn't, then the Sinclairs must ride in, swords drawn, and fight for their man. The potential needless loss of blood weighed heavily on her shoulders as they approached the gate of the MacKay keep.

**

Aislynn and her entourage were welcomed at the gates with expressions of awe and curiosity. Priding herself on the striking image she presented, Aislynn then prayed again, this time that she'd have the strength to carry it through. She hardened her shoulders and face, taking on a visage she'd seen her uncle employ whenever he lowered himself to deal with errant Scots in Dumfries – a look that was hard, angry, and determined.

Leaving the Sinclair men astride their steeds in the yard, a young MacKay sentry escorted her into the main hall. The Laird Malcolm MacKay took a bony knee at her fine skirts. *At least he knew the station of the woman before him.* Appearing resigned, Aislynn waved the man to his feet, biting her lip at the smile that threatened their success.

"Lady de Valence," Laird MacKay said in his booming voice when they were introduced, "to what do we owe this honor?"

Aislynn cleared her throat, readying it for the lies that needed to slip with ease past her tongue.

"My men have it on good authority that your men absconded with a Sinclair. One of the red-headed brothers?"

The Laird leveled his eyes at Aislynn, unresponsive.

"If you do have the brother of the Laird Sinclair, perchance I could offer you an exchange? The Earl of Pembroke shall very much enjoy having one of the Bruce's most loyal men in his gaol. And he is willing to pay."

At this, she pulled the satin purse from her belt, making sure it jingled. The Laird's watery eyes alighted at the sound. Aislynn suddenly felt more secure in her malfeasance.

"And how do you manage to be here, this far north? A lady, with so small an escort?"

"Those men are only part of my entourage." She surprised herself at how smoothly the lies fell from her lips as she dodged the question. "And after the Bruce secured Dumfries, my uncle, the Earl, sent members of his household across Scotland to avoid detection. This morsel of a man, though, is too ripe a reward not to work my way back to my uncle."

The Laird scratched at the patchy growth of beard on his chin. Several MacKay kinsmen had formed a loose circle around them, excited to be a part of such an interesting development with the English.

"I get the reward coin, and one of my enemies is sent away to the English?"

Aislynn inclined her head. Her shining purse dangled like a ripe apple from her right hand, and a flat smile wore on her face. Beneath her laces, however, she held her breath. 'Twas the moment of decision, to measure the success of their subterfuge.

Laird MacKay snatched the purse from her hand. Duncan's return with the Sinclair brother had gnawed at Malcolm, and this lady's arrival eliminated his problem of what they should do with the man. This English lass provided the perfect opportunity to turn his problem over to someone else and keep his conscience clean. The Sinclairs could take their ire over the missing brother up with the English.

Waving his hand at the MacKay next to him, the Laird sent for the prisoner. John soon appeared, a crust of blood on his handsome forehead but otherwise hale. And confused. He squinted his eyes at Aislynn, who moved her head imperceptibly to one side. John took her cue, kept his mouth sealed, and kept his head bowed.

Seeing John once again injured by these men, Aislynn struggled to retain her composure. Her chest throbbed at the sight of John laid low, and she feared her face belied her heart. She wanted to run to him, apologize for her over-reaction, spill the confines of her heart, but she had to remain hard and stoic. All was lost if the Laird caught any sign of emotion from her.

"Please bring the prisoner outside to my horses," she commanded with as much authority as she could muster. "My men and I will take him from there."

The MacKays jumped at her orders, shuffling John, who feigned to struggle, out to the bailey. One of the Sinclair men, under the guise as an

English escort, helped the MacKay toss John over the rear of the horse that stomped in protest. The disguised Sinclair calmed the beast, then mounted.

"Cease, John!" the man muttered under his breath. "Ye can stop. Dinna draw too much attention to yourself!"

John immediately stilled, letting his body curve around the haunches of the horse.

Aislynn had also mounted, and tipping her head at the Laird who stood on the steps of his keep, swung her horse around and led her entourage past the post-tern gate, south.

A broad smile swept across her face as they rode out. Their ploy worked – it almost seemed too easy – and John was now back with his own people.

Well, his own people and Aislynn.

***

Once they were well away from the MacKays, they reigned in the horses, helping John to his feet and removing his bindings.

His eyes took in Aislynn, who resembled English royalty in green finery. She held her station well; even John was hard-pressed to think her anything other than a noblewoman working with the King of England.

The other Sinclairs yanked off their bonnets, brown and blonde hair catching in what was left of the sunlight. John grinned as he hugged his men – not a redhead among them. While Aislynn's plan was well thought out, without question, the inherent danger to her and his men struck John with force. The fact that Aislynn helped him escape was also not lost on him. *Perchance she forgave him for his stupid wager with Marcus?* His mind spun as he considered how bold and dangerous her actions were.

"What were ye thinking, lass?" John's face blazed as crimson as his hair. She ignored his question, instead pressing her fingers against this shoulder.

"'Tis neatly healed, is what I think," she said with authority. "It doesn't appear your fighting today damaged it further. I don't believe we must concern ourselves with your shoulder. Your head, rather . . ."

Aislynn's fingers reached for the wound on his head, and John grabbed her wrist in a tight grip. Fury emanated from his entire being. She

116

saw it in his hard features and stiff stance and felt it in the heat of his skin, but he didn't want to hurt her. Aislynn lay her hand atop his panting chest.

"John," she kept her voice soft, calming his inner torment, "your men were with me the entire time. This was a sight better of a plan than having what remained of your clan ride in, swords drawn, to spill blood. What would that solve? This way, we retrieved you without a single blade in view, and now we are headed home."

Headed home. Her words echoed in his mind. Did that mean she was going to stay with him? They had much to discuss, and that wouldn't happen here, in the glen below MacKay lands, with an audience of Sinclairs.

John released his fierce grip and let his fingers entwine with hers.

"Thank ye," he told her, then swept his eyes to his men. "Thank all of ye."

An older Sinclair man, Angus, peered to the north, squinting.

"While this reunion is tender and all, I suggest we make haste. If the MacKays decide to follow, we want to be well away from their lands. 'Twould no' do for them to see us turn east."

'Twas sage advice, and they mounted and rode east, staying far south until they reached the safety of Sinclair lands near dusk, then shifting north.

They couldn't wait to get to Broch Reay and end this miserable excuse of a day.

Chapter Eleven: Questions We Must Consider

The matching expressions of relief on Haleigh and Fleck's faces when they returned were the only welcome the small party needed.

If a select few of the Sinclairs present in the bailey glared at Aislynn as she dismounted in her full English gown, she did her best to ignore them. Right now she wanted to check John's head – the man was a mass of bruises and scars (*was there any part of him that wasn't injured?* she thought, then blushed at the notion of what parts she hadn't seen that were intact).

And she wanted to change out of the tight bindings of her bliaut. A few short days in the more casual Highland dress spoiled Aislynn. As exquisite as her formal gowns may be, the freedom of wool and linen without laces or stays, and the ease of blending in with the Sinclairs, fit Aislynn's new life. Though the rich green dress may have served its purpose, she was ready to shed it like an old, unnecessary second skin.

What was impossible to ignore was the way John's fiery gaze kept shifting in her direction, as if he didn't want to lose sight of her. And she hoped his gaze was out of desire to be with her, not out of anger at her actions, either running off this morning or entering the lion's den this afternoon.

Her question would soon be answered. As they entered the main hall, John clapped her elbow and leaned close to her ear.

"After this, meet me in my chambers. I must have a word with ye," he growled.

***

The Sinclair sisters squeaked in unison at Aislynn's reappearance and didn't wait for any orders. They rushed Aislynn up the curved steps, Esther pulling and Mary pushing, ready to relieve Aislynn of her gown and wipe the dirt of the day from her skin.

Though Aislynn was not in the best mood, fretting as she was over her upcoming meeting with John, a glow of happy nostalgia bloomed in her chest at their eager ministrations. A long time had passed since Agnes had been so eager to be with Aislynn, and more than a month since they last saw each other. These Highland girls could be the younger sisters she lacked, and Aislynn sorely missed this type of sisterly camaraderie. Their cheer over her return was infectious.

All too soon, she was cleaned up and in a fresh kirtle, and a knock sounded at Aislynn's chamber door. Her heart plummeted to her feet, the moment of truth like the sword of Damocles swinging above her head. Etan stood at the door, whispered something to Esther, who responded, and then held his arm to Aislynn.

"John Sinclair will see ye now, milady."

Her stomach rumbled, and she swooned as she stood. Lack of food and drink only made her fretting worse. She feared she would faint at the man's feet.

They walked the short distance to John's chambers where Etan shoved the door open without knocking.

John faced the hearth, leaning his muscular frame against the stones. His whole body seemed rigid. He wore only a set of braies, clean and loosely gathered at his waist. His broad, scarred back was as hard as the stones upon which he leaned, strong and set and marked with time. Glancing over his shoulder at Etan, John nodded once, and Etan left

Aislynn in the center of the room, tugging the heavy door closed behind him.

She realized she was in the room, again alone with a half-naked man. Surely, this was most inappropriate.

She opened her mouth to tell him so when John rushed at her, enclosing her in a steel grip that both frightened and excited her, and slammed his mouth onto hers.

***

They crushed against each other, John's hands exploring every curve of her backside as his tongue darted between her lips, touching hers in a shocking sensation that rocked her to her core. Aislynn couldn't deny her body's reaction to John's every touch. Without thinking, she ground her hips into his hard member that probed and throbbed against the thin barrier of her skirt.

He clenched the swell of her buttocks in a firm grip, and a guttural, animal moan escaped his lips. John pulled his head from hers, an unyielding expression on his impassioned face.

Aislynn remained flush against him and lifted one slender hand from his massive shoulder to trail her fingers along her scorched lips. Her emotions whirled, and she swayed on her feet. Had John's strong arms not held her in place, she might have melted onto the floor. Her knees were weak enough from his attentions as it was.

Just as suddenly as he grabbed her to him, John moved a hands breadth away – still inappropriately close but not touching her with the intimacy that made her body tremble.

"My apologies, lassie," he croaked out in a voice that sounded pained.

Every muscle on his bare torso seemed tight, clenched. The flush of heat on his skin cast his entire body in a coppery glow. He was like a burning fire – she didn't doubt that he would consume her. And she knew she would let him.

"But what were ye thinking?" he finished.

"This whole day," she whispered in response, "'tis my fault. You never would have encountered the MacKays had I not hidden myself away for so long."

John inhaled deeply, bringing himself up to his full height that dwarfed the room. Every muscle rippled, a reminder of his strength and power he held at bay. His usually bright features were dark and hostile, and Aislynn feared that his anger at her actions may explode. The long flow of hair atop his head was slicked back, so unlike his typical, wild thatch of hair. Cropped sides flowed in a deep russet line to his close-cropped beard that did nothing to hide his clenched jaw or pursed lips. His intense green eyes were hooded, unreadable – as blackish green as the glen in a storm. She cowered from him, the bed post at her back.

An elevated heat erupted between them as their eyes rested on one another, a singular focus that made the rest of the room fall away. Their chests rose and fell in a matching cadence. Her body was like a tuning fork, humming under John's ardent admiration while his gaze roved over her face and down her body. Aislynn clutched her hand to her chest, trying to calm her racing heart as she leaned harder into the post.

John's face broke at the sight of Aislynn recoiling in fear. His hard features hid the roiling emotions he'd had from the start of this day: rage, aye, but also fear, frustration, and admittedly, shame. And those hard features undoubtedly appeared fearsome to a delicate English rose. He reached for her hand. She didn't move and allowed him to enclose it in his warm grasp. John saw this as hopeful.

"Dinna fear me, lass." He kept his voice low, measured. 'Twould be too easy to let his voice rise in anger. "This day is nay your fault."

"If I hadn't eavesdropped, or if I just ran to my chambers . . ."

Her voice drifted off as the tears she'd held back finally won the battle of wills, rolling down her cheeks and glistening in the firelight. John stepped closer and caressed her face with his large, calloused hand, wiping away her tears with his thumb.

"Nay, ye only reacted to my stupid behavior. I'm a grown man, too old to be making foolish wagers at the expense of a lass who is on her own in a strange land. Who thinks herself a prisoner, stolen from her home. I vowed to protect you, to be your guardian, and I ended up being the one who harmed ye the most. Marcus, he's young. Of course, he'd make such wagers, but ye deserved more from me."

Aislynn held her breath as he spoke, and her heart raced in her chest. She'd taken so much of the blame for the day on herself, his admission took her by surprise. *How could he think this was his fault?*

"Mr. Sinclair," she began, and he shook his head at her words. *So, we are back to that?*

"I'm still John to ye, Aislynn. Naught has changed for me since last night."

That tumultuous green gaze bore into her soul and sparked a fire in her chest. His words struck her heart deep and hard. She'd not expected his feelings to remain after her childish reaction and the ensuing catastrophe. She certainly didn't feel as though she deserved more. In fact, she felt small and afraid.

"John," she corrected in her trembling voice, "you are not obligated to me, especially since you've seen the trouble I can cause. You have no responsibility to me."

She hated those words, hated saying them, even thinking them. She wanted John in a way she'd never known before, but not out of obligation. 'Twas too painful for her to bear – more painful than if she lost him.

"Ye are correct, lassie. I don't. To my brother, or my king, mayhap, I have an obligation. But ye are just a strange lassie who fell into my lap."

He agreed with her? A bolt of pain wrenched her chest. Before her mind wrapped around the harshness of his words, he yanked on her hand, pulling her close to his heated, naked chest once more. *How was he so hot all the time?*

"And fell into my heart," he whispered into her ear, his breath tickling against the loose tresses on her face. "Because of that, because ye have become so entrenched in my heart, become part of me, I *am* obliged to ye, no matter what ye may think. Ye are a part of me, the air I breathe, the beatings of my heart, 'tis ye. I dinna ken how ye did such a thing, as ornery as ye can be, but here we are."

His words left her breathless, her mind reeling. How did he manage to make her feel so nervous and excited at the same time?

And as much as she didn't want to admit it, from their first moment alone in the woods, she'd shared something enigmatic, a connection to this Highland warrior which was as unexplainable as it was ferocious.

"You're not the only one with an obligation, John," she said, lifting her exquisite face to his. "I could not ignore your injuries, disregard your banter, or leave you to the MacKays. If anything had happened to you, 'twould have killed my own heart just as if one of their swords plunged into my chest. I don't know how or why I feel this way for a rogue Highlander, and my head tells me I shouldn't, but my heart calls to yours, and I can't ignore that call."

John had no answer, but the throbbing passion and sheer want that rushed through him dictated his actions. Her pale, delicate beauty stood out, even in the dim light of the evening, and his eyes soaked in her comely face, her heaving breasts, her moonlit skin. And she held the same desires and emotions as he? Unable to stop himself, he captured her lips again, a bit less forceful this time, yet full of the love and longing he felt for her.

Their lips and tongue parried and danced – their panting as they kissed filled the room. One of John's hands reached around to the fullness of her buttocks, pressing her impossibly closer and lifting her slightly. His other hand traced a line of fire from her cheek, down her neck to her chest where the swells of her breasts heaved against the thin fabric of her delicate gown. His large hand covered her soft globe, caressing and kneading it lightly.

A burst of excitement stemmed from her core and across her fondled breasts to every extension of her body. Her fingertips dug into his broad shoulders as she clung to him with desperate passion. The savage intensity of their kissing and grasping was a divine ecstasy that drove the horrors of the world away. In this moment of skin against skin, clans, injuries, and fears fell away. 'Twas only John and Aislynn as they lost themselves in each other.

***

Until a light knock at the door interrupted their impassioned moment, and John growled as he lifted his head from her reddened lips.

"Feckin' knocks at the door interrupting me again!" he huffed under his breath. In two long strides he reached the door and flung it open.

Poor Esther stood at the doorway, cringing behind the platter she held aloft. The mead in her pitcher sloshed and spilled, splattering on the floor. John was immediately contrite.

"My apologies, Esther. I was no' expecting ye." He lifted the pitcher from her shaking hand and tried to cool his fearsome ardor that had frightened the poor girl. "Let me take these from ye. 'Twill be all for this eve."

Esther didn't wait for him to close the door and turned, fleeing for the stairs as quickly as her tiny feet could climb the chilled stone.

John chuckled as he shut the chamber door with his foot, barring them once again against the world. Only this time, they had nourishment for their rumbling stomachs. Again, the inappropriateness of being secluded in his chambers flitted across Aislynn's mind.

John placed the platter and pitcher on the hardy table by the window and tore off a hunk of bread, offering it to Aislynn. She didn't hesitate and grabbed the bread, chewing and swallowing as if she hadn't eaten in months. It certainly felt that way. The day had been far too long indeed.

A slender smile remained on John's face as he watched her eat. He took a large bite of the hard cheese and poured mead into the short goblets on the platter. They washed down their food with the heady drink, wiping at their mouths and taking account of their circumstances.

"So, what now?" Aislynn asked.

John held a nugget of cheese to her lips, and she snatched it from his hand, following it with her remaining sliver of bread. He took her free hand again and sat on the stool near the table. When he looked up at her, his eyes were as clear as glass. That fearsome storm in his eyes was gone.

"I want to wed ye, Aislynn. Not for your connections to nobility or because the King of Scotland shall be pleased, but because I canna live my life without ye. I want ye in my life, by my side, in my bed."

The brashness of his words caused a deep crimson to bloom on her milky cheeks, and he chuckled again.

"Will ye wed me, Aislynn?"

'Twas as if the air was sucked out of the room. Here in his chambers, the answer seemed obvious. Her body cleaved to his, clinging to him like the sea clung to the shore. Nevertheless, she was English nobility, a captured prisoner at the mercy of the Scottish King, and unwanted in this northern land. And if she were ever found, or returned to England, she would be charged with high treason and hung. Could she give up her heritage, her Englishness, perchance even her sister or her very freedom, and stay with John?

But her heritage abandoned her; the Scottish King wanted her safety, and she wasn't certain if she would ever see her sister again anyways. Truly, in her estimation, she'd naught to lose and everything to gain with John. As for any charges of treason, she'd have to trust that John, the Sinclairs, and King Robert himself would guard her against such an end. Aislynn had the sense that John understood the depth of these concerns as well as she did.

She wiggled her fingertips into the soft hair of his lightly bearded cheek. He nuzzled his handsome face against her hand, and she was lost.

"Yes," she spoke, her voice barely above a whisper, as if she feared the power of her own answer. "I will wed you, John Sinclair."

The dark hardness that had shrouded him since they returned to Broch Reay fled, softening his features and relaxing his muscles.

"In the Highlands, we have several options," John told her, his eyes closed as he rested his face against her palm. "We could wed right away, tonight even, clandestine-like. But I have the sense ye may want witnesses so the marriage can no' be called into question?"

One russet eyebrow rose above his eye that peeked open, just as a shy smirk pulled at her lips. He knew well what she was about. If an exchange of prisoners ever occurred, or the English tried to retrieve her, 'twould be much easier for Aislynn to abide in the Highlands with John if the wedding was witnessed and recorded by a priest.

"So, we will need witnesses at the verra least. If ye want a priest, we may need to wait until our own Father Richard returns. He likes to make his rounds to the villages when the weather is fair. I dinna ken when he will return."

Aislynn hadn't any idea that she might need to make this decision – with a priest or without? To wed now or later? In haste or with leisure? Which would be best?

"Or," John continued, "we can wait until later this year. My brother, Asper, is handfast – betrothed-like, aye? – to Haleigh to give her validity in his absence. They will be wed when Asper returns before the snow falls. 'Tis already approved by King Robert. The Bruce hopes he will be able to travel with Asper and attend the event. But that all remains to be seen, depending on the state of Scotland and our war with England."

Aislynn was silent, taking in the information, when John threaded his arms around her waist and pulled her onto his lap. Again, she was pressed against his mostly naked form, her bare legs skimming his as her skirts hiked up like a wanton, and her flaming blush returned. John kissed her nose and grinned at her embarrassed modesty.

"I would ask that we no' wait," he said.

Chapter Twelve: Decisions, Decisions

"John, are ye certain ye want to take this on? Ye barely ken the lass!"

Reed's strained voice revealed the depth of his concern over John's ill-conceived venture. Hastily wedding a lass from the Highlands was one thing, wedding an English noble and hostage was quite another. His concern was one shared by most of those gathered. "Mayhap your ale has gone too far to your head this time?"

Shooting Reed an angry glare, John returned his attention to Haleigh, who tapped the toe of her shoe as she considered.

John hadn't lied to her – that Haleigh knew without a doubt. The man was impulsive, true, but unlike his younger brother, he had the wisdom of age that tempered a fair amount of his impulsiveness.

When they first arrived back at Reay, John and Marcus shared with her the desires of King Robert the Bruce and their task under the dictates of Laird Asper. A foolish request, Haleigh had believed, and one she still considered impetuous and downright mad. Though capturing the Englishwoman's heart had appeared to be a significant challenge, the competition between John and Marcus had actually made that task easier, as they both laved attention on the lass.

But to vow his life to a woman who may well bring the ire of the Sinclair clan or worse, English soldiers to their doorstep, gave Haleigh pause. She doubted they could trust this Englishwoman, kind enough that she had been, or that she would ever truly fit in with the clan. Would a wedding to the Laird's brother change any of that? Was this asking too much of one man? Was it asking too much of her and the Sinclairs? Haleigh lacked any strong answers to these thorny questions.

John remained unmoved by these potential complications. His focus, his concern, was for the English rose, and from his words, Haleigh couldn't deny his passion for Aislynn.

And who was she to go against the dictates of her Laird or King? 'Twas something to be said of wedding in haste. Haleigh had been mocked for her allegiance to Asper, who took his own time to ask her to wed. Her finger flicked to the edge of her eye.

No' that I had streams of men asking for my hand, she sighed. Far too many in her own clan judged her unfairly, assuming her strange eye was an omen or something worse, devilish even. For all her Highland beauty, that one flaw caused so much judgment and sadness in her life. Asper saw past it, saw only her beauty, only *her,* and was worth the wait.

Haleigh viewed Aislynn's Englishness as she did her own eye. A flaw, to be sure, but not insurmountable. Not a hindrance to love and acceptance.

"Does she ken that she could be found guilty of treason against her king if they believe her to have embraced this marriage fully?" Haleigh asked.

John pursed his lips, inclining his head. Just how far a treason accusation might go, he wondered if Aislynn considered that. At her core, she was betraying her king and country, and she well knew it. That alone was enough of an offense to find herself swinging from the end of a rope.

"When do ye want to wed?" she continued, shutting down any further grievances from either Reed or Fleck.

The smile that slipped across John's cheeks brightened the study, his face like the sunrise, full of light, crimson and corals. And so reminiscent of his brother, it tore at Haleigh's heart. She couldn't deny anyone such joy. 'Twas too little of it in this world.

***

A larger argument arose when the discussion turned to who should witness the marriage. The priest could bless it when he returned – they didn't need to have him present. The more witnesses, the better, was Haleigh's opinion, which she shared with the men. Fleck agreed.

"The clan may well be more accepting of the lassie if they watch her wed our man's brother. To be so aligned with the clan and the Laird, 'twould serve her, John, and the clan well."

For Haleigh and Fleck, 'twas obvious. Not so for Reed, who thought keeping such nuptials private would do well to conceal the lass's location.

"If the MacKays learn that the same English woman who absconded with John, supposedly to take him to her King, is now marrying the Laird's brother, then they will have more incentive to reive against us, or worse."

Reed stood as he protested, rising to his full height, when John's words cut through the argument.

"Why don't we ask the bride in question?" One quizzical eyebrow rose as he spoke. "'Tis her wedding, after all."

John reclined against the stone wall, his plaid falling casually across his hips, his arms crossed. He seemed well-nigh bored at the conversation, as if their discussion was moot. Whatever Aislynn decided was what he wanted.

"Ye speak true, John," Haleigh conceded in a hasty tone. "Aislynn is the bride, and the wedding should reflect her desires."

"What she desires is me," John joked. "But she should choose what her wedding will be."

John didn't speak flippantly. The word *choose* was important to him, as 'twas important to Aislynn. He hadn't forgotten her lamentations the night he took her to the shoreline, and he vowed to do everything in his power to give her the ability to choose whenever 'twas in his power.

***

After he departed the study, John searched for Aislynn and found her in her chambers. Sitting in a pale shaft of light, which rapidly dimmed as foreboding clouds gathered to unleash a deluge of long-expected rain, Aislynn leaned in on a tapestry loom, working as fast as her fingers would allow before she lost her light. Her eyes narrowed in a deep squint, her fingertips feeling for the needle she plied with ease.

John admired her work for a moment before he spoke and disturbed her domestic reverie. Aislynn had adopted their Highland dress for her everyday clothing. The deep blues and thin lines of green in the plaid flattered her own earthy tones, and her skin shimmered against the bold colors. He imagined her as a woodland fairy, one that brought an impossible magic into his life.

He rested his now-healed shoulder against the doorway and cleared his throat. Without pausing her fingers, Aislynn lifted her eyes to the Highlander at the door, her Highlander. The thought of him in that manner sent a shiver of delight down her spine.

"Weel, I have told Haleigh, Reed, and Fleck of our plans. Since this union has the blessing of King Robert, 'twas little they could say against it. The largest quarrel was over what type of wedding we should have, and who should be our witnesses."

John stepped into the room and squatted on the dry rush mat where she was seated. His heavy hands rested atop her knees in a touch that was both intimate and comfortable.

"Ye have no' told me yet what manner of wedding ye desire. What do ye want, milady?" he asked her. "'Tis your choice."

Joyous satisfaction pursed her lips and crinkled her eyes. *He remembered,* she thought with delight. Such power there was in choosing one's own destiny. Even in something as simple as choosing how to wed was empowering. She dropped her hands from her sewing and lay them on his as he explained their wedding day options.

"I should think that if we speak our vows in full view of your clan, perchance they shall be more accepting of me?" Aislynn suggested.

Though she tried to sound confident, her hesitant voice bespoke her worries of living with a Highland clan that despised her. She reached one hand to the back of her neck, recalling the sensation of cold, smelly muck thrown at her head.

"I could nay agree with ye more. We can say our vows in the yard, before the Sinclairs and God, then partake in some food and music. Fleck's kin is renowned for their piping. Would that please ye, lassie?"

John rose on his knees as he spoke, the sharp lines of his face a breath away from hers.

"Yes, that sounds lovely."

"Ye must eat quickly though," he told her in a husky tone that sent chills up her spine, "and I willna let ye enjoy the pipers for too long. Because as soon as I can, I plan on whisking ye up to my chamber, removing every last piece of your clothing, and loving ye for the rest of the night."

Aislynn's heart slammed against her chest at his unabashed statement of lovemaking. She tried to take a breath, but John's lips found the soft curve of her neck, and she exhaled in a shivering breath. He clasped the back of her head in his hand as his tongue explored every hollow of her neck and along her shoulder.

John's own ragged breath escaped with a sigh, and he struggled to keep his fierce ardor under control. He wanted to rip her kirtle from her skin, throw her on the bedding and take her hard. He had to shift his hips where he knelt, his cockstand evident and throbbing, asking for release.

"We should wed soon," John said in a choked voice. "I dinna think I can wait, and I willna take ye afore ye are wed." He shook his head to reclaim control of himself, his casual smile returning to his face. He lifted her hand and kissed it formally. "Ye are English nobility, after all. We must stand on principle."

Aislynn barked out a laugh. Since she'd arrived in the Highlands, she'd felt far removed from her English lineage, and not just geographically. Though he spoke the truth, to have him on his knees and kissing her hand as though she sat on a throne struck her as funny.

John bowed after he stood, and Aislynn played along, dismissing him with a giggle and a wave of her hand.

Chapter Thirteen: An Unwelcome Wedding

The happy couple and their troupe initially wanted to wait out the rain, but as the long days passed gray and wet, the more irritable and impatient they grew. Finally, Marcus marched to Haleigh and her advisers to complain.

"God's Bones make them wed already. John canna contain himself, full of sour and hunger as he is. Make them wed in the downpour so he can bed the lass. A bit of rain never hurt a Highlander."

Haleigh raised her slender eyebrows at Marcus, her strange eye slipping to the right as she regarded her brother-by-law. So, John was reaching his breaking point, wanting to bed his English treasure and taking his ire out on his brother. Had the entire situation not focused on the seemingly traitorous nature of John wedding a captive British noble, she might have pushed the wedding, rain or no.

She had to admit she was dragging her feet – Reed and Fleck, too. While the wedding would assuredly happen, Haleigh desired more harmony in the clan regarding the lass. Time was a great salve, and perchance, with enough time, the clan may discard their staunch hatred of the lass and welcome her.

'Twas not to be. The long-suffering Marcus standing before her was testament to that. A soggy wedding in the rain 'twould be.

Haleigh flicked her eyes to Reed.

"Are ye ready to preside o'er a wedding, Reed?"

The grizzled man rubbed at his graying beard, pretending to consider but really hiding his smile. He may not like the English lass or the complications she brought with her, but the old man loved presiding over a celebration. Those events happened so rarely that the Highlanders, Reed especially, reveled in them.

"Ye wish them to wed in this rain?"

Haleigh shrugged. "We'll all be fair *drookit,* aye, but happy is the bride that rain falls on, just as God's blessings. We've been in worse."

"'Tis about time," Marcus mumbled as he exited.

Soon, John would plow the lass's furrow, and his amiable demeanor would return.

***

Admittedly, 'twas not the wedding Aislynn imagined for herself when she was a child.

Growing up as the niece of both an Earl and the King, Aislynn expected a host of pageantry – posting of the banns, a flurry of finely-gowned women in the castle preparing her wedding garb of gold and silver, a glorious bride in the church as she stood before a priest with her dashingly handsome future husband. The King himself would be in attendance with her uncle the Earl, presiding over her wedding just as much as the priest did.

Aye, 'twas a wedding every young girl dreamed of in her youth. Then age and experience showed those childhood dreams to be naught but smoke and lies.

The rain alone disheartened the event, forming every space into muddy pools covered by the damp, gray cape of the sky. Aislynn kept her head tucked deep under her plaid to hide from the downpour, which did nothing to stop the hem of her kirtle turning black with mud.

She wore a simple kirtle, dainty ribbons adding a splash of color to the dun-blue fabric. Her *arasaid*, with the hood pulled up to protect her once-exquisitely coiffed hair from the rain, hid any hint of a wedding gown. Only Haleigh's gift of the stag-emblazoned brooch at her neck sparkled in the din, her one piece of real finery on her most significant of days.

The sole part of her wedding day that met the expectations of her girlish dreams was the strong, handsome warrior by her side. At least she had the dashing future husband.

The man in question, sodden as he was by the rain, was still a vision of Highland majesty in Aislynn's eyes. His plaid matched her *arasaid*, draped over his tunic to ward off the rain. Droplets rolled across the tartan, the deep blues and greens an ever-duskier hue when damp. Bare-legged, his heavy leather boots shone a dark brown, resembling wet earth, and matched the belt he wore around his waist that held his sporran and his broadsword.

He exuded a sense of strength absent in most men, particularly the foppish Englishmen at court. Even John's wet hair, a dark clay color in the rain, lay lightly over his neck, not waterlogged and weighted like the hair and hoods of the Sinclairs who remained in the yard.

Which was nearly empty.

Aislynn stopped in her tracks, stunned at the lack of audience. Her heart hammered a painful staccato in her chest. John drew up short next to her, sweeping his understanding gaze from her stricken face to the yard. He leaned down to her, his breath tickling her cheek.

"Ye are beautiful, my lass, even in the rain," he whispered. "Ye are like a goddess from antiquity. I want to focus on ye this day, and nay anything else. Can ye keep your eyes and attentions on me? Watch my face and see it shine with love for ye?"

The pain in her chest seemed to split into two. How could she ignore his plea for her own ego that desired an audience for her wedding? Already her nuptials were nothing as she expected. Why should her attendees? Aislynn hurt eyes searched John's endearing face, and she smiled at him. In the fickle weather, with everything darkened gray or the color of earthy clay, his green eyes yet sparkled, much like the grass covered in rain drops. He was the embodiment of the Highlands. How could she set her eyes anywhere but on him?

Resigned to try to forget the crowd, she tucked her arm more tightly into his, and they entered the yard.

When Haleigh and Fleck first led the couple from the rear of the tower, a sort of sodden march to the front steps where they would make their vows to each other, a decent collection of the Sinclair kinsmen and women huddled in the muddy bailey. Their hard eyes, however, glared as they watched an English lass wed the man who essentially was second in line for the leadership of their clan. Many a father of a young Sinclair lass was personally insulted by the wedding and left the yard.

The Sinclairs had every right to be cautious – Aislynn readily understood. She tried not to look, to keep her attention on John, but she couldn't help herself. The disdain in their eyes shocked her – a spectacle of malcontent. John must have noticed their unhappy expressions as well, for he patted her hand in consolation as they finally reached the steps. Aislynn was certain 'twas the longest, wettest wedding march in the history of weddings.

And during the entire walk to the hall doors, panic had attached to Aislynn's chest like a plump, sucking leech. She feared that another onslaught of thrown mud would ruin her wedding day – more than the rain already had.

No one reached for the muck on the ground, fortunately, and Aislynn let loose a heavy breath of relief.

Which only lasted until she and John were situated at the top of the stair, with Haleigh, Marcus, and several others flocking the steps as witnesses. When Aislynn dared to peek around the edge of her hood, she was horrified as she watched the remaining Sinclairs witnessing in the yard turn on the slippery mud and leave.

She may be marrying the Laird's brother, but they wouldn't accept her as one of their own.

Would they ever?

***

Dazed by the fact she was actually standing with John, pledging her life and body to this man, Aislynn hardly registered her words or those left in attendance. From the moment Fleck joined their hands, the entire event was a blur. Her quivering knees threatened to give way, and only John's earnest gaze kept her on her feet. She returned his favor, her own eyes never wavering from his handsome, open face, and was only brought back to the real world when John's lips, warm in the cool rain, pressed against hers in an aggressive gesture of passion and declaration. Aislynn was his – she chose him – and he wanted everyone in his clan to know it.

The rest of the day then passed in another rush. She tried to focus on something, anything, but her eyes were for John alone and everything else was on the edge, obscured into a haze of colors and sounds.

She was sure others spoke to her, gave the couple well-wishes, cheered and drank to them. Aislynn, though, didn't recall any of it. By the time John carried her from the half-empty hall amid the jeers of his kinsmen, the day was gone as quickly as it had arrived, a fog of excitement and rain.

***

At John's chamber door, he pressed the iron bar down with one hand and kicked the massive door wide, his grasp on Aislynn in his arms never faltering. Sweeping her over the threshold, John eased her to her feet near the blazing fire that chased away any dank air in his chambers. The hem of her kirtle was still damp and muddy, holding the chill of the day, and Aislynn was grateful John noticed and endeavored to warm her.

While she held herself close to the fire, John unclasped her brooch, placing it delicately on the narrow table. Pulling the careworn *arasaid* from her shoulders, he grabbed a fresh plaid hanging off a chair and rubbed her arms and back to expel the wet and cold that clung to her skin.

John then shifted behind her, his lips replacing the cloth across the back of her neck. His lips swept aside curly damp tendrils of hair that had escaped her mesh coif. Warmth mixed with cold and shivers exploded throughout her body, this time from the enticing tingle of John's lips and the nervous sensations he aroused, not the weather. His hands gripped her upper arms, a powerful hold that kept her still as his lips continued their leisurely path from the back of one ear to the other.

Aislynn's knees weakened, and she wanted to melt into the solid heat John radiated behind her. At the same time, he stepped close, pressing the length of his body against her back, supporting her. His breath was warm on her chilled skin. His lips slipped around her shoulder as his finger tugged the edge of her kirtle down her arm.

"Ye are beautiful, a light in the darkness, my wife."

His whispers were as light as his touch, and her heart thrummed in her chest and pounded in her ears. He made her feel as though she drank too much ale, body and mind swirling at his words and touches.

"When I first saw ye in Dumfries," he said as his tongue played against her neck in between his words, "Ye were so fierce, so defiant looking. Your strength, 'twas the first thing that attracted me to ye."

"John . . ." Aislynn tried to speak, but her mind couldn't form the words she wanted to say.

"And when ye tried to flee as we rode north, 'twas an act that took such courage, such determination," he loosed the laces at the back of her gown and dropped her kirtle from her breast, cupping it, his warm palm tingling against her innocent skin. "'Twas the next thing about ye that I admired."

She reached her hand up to cup his, holding it tightly against her breast, encouraging him to continue. He flicked his thumb over her nipple which rose at his attentions.

"Then the day I saw ye in our Highland garb, just as fierce and determined, but wearing Sinclair colors . . . 'Twas the moment."

He spun her around, and her hand caught on his taut chest. John's eyes raked boldly over her, inviting her to peer into his soul as he opened his heart. His husky voice overflowed with emotion and desire, the same green flame of desire that lit in his darkened eyes.

"'Twas the moment I lost my heart to ye." His voice was hoarse and husky as he spoke. "The moment I decided that, though ye may still see me as an enemy, a captor, I did no' care. I would offer myself to ye and hope ye would take care with my heart."

Aislynn didn't know whether to cry at his emotional speech or throw herself at him.

She decided on the latter, thrusting her lips against his, returning his words of love with an eager, impassioned kiss.

***

John interrupted the kiss long enough to yank his tunic over his head. She lay her hands on his bare chest, relishing the heat he exuded. He found her lips again, his tongue searching and exploring her lips, jaw, neck. Lifting her once more in his strong arms, he carried her to the bed, shedding her tartan wrap as he moved her.

He then stood next to the bed, pulled his boots off his muscled legs, and placed his hands at the belt that held the waist of his plaid, waiting.

"Are ye ready for me, lass? I'll willingly show myself to ye first. I want to put ye at ease, please ye as much as I can."

He tipped his head to the side, awaiting her answer. Aislynn's breath caught in her chest as she silently nodded *yes*.

With a quick flick of his hands, his belted plaid joined his tunic and boots on the floor. Her eyes widened at his fullness, a new and thrilling vision. He stood strong and powerful, letting her take him all in. His defined stomach with its doeskin smattering of fur narrowed to his member that thrust out as strong and powerful as the man. A sense of nervous yearning surged through her – fear of the unknown and a fervent excitement to be familiar with him, every part of him.

Aislynn's one breast remained exposed above the edge of her kirtle. When John joined her on the bed, placing his lips on the pale globe that begged for his attention, he worked her gown over her hips and off her legs. Soon she was just as bare as he. John lifted his head, taking a long moment to let his eyes rake a hungry gaze over her own milky skin, lean limbs, the soft swell of her hips, the mound of her womanhood.

Her heart fluttered and spasmed when he reached his hand over her full, young breasts, down her smooth belly to her woman's mound that buzzed with the same exhilaration she felt everywhere else.

Aislynn then did the same, trailing her fingers across his firm chest, pausing at his pulsing manhood. It seemed to her that John's breath caught, in much the same way hers had. She lifted her face, and the intensity of his eyes burned into her like green lightening. Everything in this moment was heightened, elevated, as if their chamber was no longer in the fundament of the world, instead floating amongst the clouds.

Her hand splayed against his member, and John groaned deep in his chest, rolling her under him to ravish her mouth again. Aislynn returned his ardor, clasping her hands in the thickness of his hair. He moved his hips between her thighs, the tip of his member vibrating at her most private part.

She sensed his hesitation, most likely in consideration of the pain of a virgin's first love, and she loved him for it. Pulling his head to hers, she braced her hands against his back, crushing her to him as hard as possible, urging him on.

John groaned again. Unsure of how to encourage him more, to let him know she was ready for what he had to offer, she wiggled her hips, shifting under him, and 'twas all John needed.

"Oh, lass," he moaned as he pressed slowly.

Aislynn marveled with wonder at the strange sensation of being filled, of having something inside her, then clenched at the brief pain once he was fully immersed.

Aislynn puffed out her breath, trying to adjust, and John sucked in her breaths. He waited patiently, kissing her lips, her jawline, twining his fingers in her wavy tresses.

"Aislynn," he asked in a haggard voice. Again, she didn't say a word, but returned his kisses and shifted in invitation. They were joined as one now, and she wanted John to show her what that meant in full.

John began to move above her in slow, delicate moves. Aislynn began to relax, her body accepting him, instinctively knowing what to do even if she didn't. With the pain fading to the background, the excitement of being with John, having this most intimate moment, of clinging to him and riding with him, shivering yearning threaded through her.

This was the sensation that John elicited whenever he cast those stormy green eyes at her, when she thought of his bare, hard chest and his kisses on her lips and neck. Flames of passion burned between them, bringing them to new heights of ecstasy.

Then John's breathing changed, grew harsher, and he called out her name between gritted teeth. With one final, hard thrust, his whole body clenched above her, and she held to him even more tightly, filled with strange sensations that shook her to her core.

When his storm of passion ended, he fell upon her chest like a wounded animal, nestling his face into the curve of her shoulder as he tried to catch his breath.

***

Their bodily passions may have been sated, but their desire for each other still raged as fiercely as the fire in the hearth. Their lips caught and played and sought every crevice of skin not huddled under the covers.

John's face was buried in the alabaster curve of her neck, and his mumbled words vibrated on her skin when he spoke.

"What did you say?" Aislynn asked, threading her fingers through his abundant vermilion locks to pull his head away.

His eyes were half-closed, a sly, satisfied smile playing on his lips.

"I said, are ye well, Mistress Sinclair?"

Aislynn's heart caught in her chest at the words. For her entire life, her titles had included Lady de Valence, King's niece, or the Earl's niece and ward. To hear herself referred to as Mistress, oft seen as a lowly title, took her by surprise. And paired with the Scots name of Sinclair! A light sweat broke out on her brow, even as her skin cooled from her interlude with John.

He must have noticed her disquiet, because he rose on his forearms to gaze into her eyes – grass meeting whiskey. Aislynn shifted her gaze in response, unsure how to respond. She struggled to voice these deep thoughts.

"Ye are nay regretting your decision, are ye?"

His halting voice made Aislynn's conflicted heart tug again. He took a risk with his clan in marrying her, and she didn't want to cause him any further strife – especially in thinking that perchance she now regretted her decision to wed him.

And it was her decision. John had made that abundantly clear. Wager or no, she was the one who said yes. 'Twas the first time in her life where she felt that she had a modicum of control. Would she begrudge him that just for the strange sound of her new title on his lips?

Her hand wove through his hair to the scruff of beard on his cheek, holding his face. He nuzzled her palm in an endearing gesture.

"No, my love," she answered honestly. "Just the words. Mistress Sinclair. Sounds strange to me. I have to grow accustomed to them."

"I love the sound of that name on your lips. *Mistress Sinclair,*" he whispered against her mouth, kissing her deeply.

***

John tucked the plaids around Aislynn, nestling her close to his chest. She fit her shoulder right under his arm and lay her head on his heart. The steady tattoo was calming and intimate, a sound she'd only ever heard with him. A comfortable silence fell over them – the only real sound was the popping of the fire and, every so often, the spatter of rain when it surged.

"Asper should return soon, and he and Haleigh will be formally wed."

Aislynn wondered why he was sharing this news. Was he trying to prepare her for another large Sinclair event? The entire clan would surely come out for the Laird's wedding. She tried not to have a bitter response to that thought.

"Haleigh seems excited over her upcoming nuptials," she commented.

"We had hoped the Bruce might accompany him, but the King needs to keep the English and feckin' lowlanders in line."

Aislynn was silent, waiting. 'Twas more he needed to say to her – she sensed it in his tone of voice.

"Once they are wed and celebrate their nuptials, he will make sure the Sinclair borders are secure. Then we will return to Dumfries, or to wherever the King has removed himself."

We.

John was going with him. Aislynn's emotions caught in her chest, and momentarily her breath escaped her. They had just found each other, she newly married into a clan that didn't accept her, and soon he must leave?

John had known better than Aislynn that their time together as a wedded couple would be short. Laird Asper planned to return in summer for his highly anticipated wedding ceremony to Haleigh. Once they celebrated their union, Asper was to return to King Robert's side with his brothers in tow.

Aislynn had a short time to learn as much as she could of her new husband and the land of which he was so proud. She didn't respond right away, only pressed her naked skin impossibly closer to his and prayed that his clan would be more accepting of her by then. Or at least no longer see her as the enemy.

"I will miss you, John Sinclair." Her whisper against his skin was weighted with sentiment. 'Twas more than that – her words barely scratched the surface of how desperately she wanted him to stay and how passionately she would miss him when he departed. He clasped her body in his arms, holding her tight.

"But do not talk of leaving tonight," she continued. "Tonight, I am your wife, you are my husband, and we have the whole of our lives to spend together."

Chapter Fourteen: Understanding Our Place in the World

"Come with me, lass."

Aislynn looked up from her sewing. She'd just sat down at her tapestry, expecting to labor most of the day. What did John have for her this time? A halting smile spread across her lips. He'd spent the past several days surprising her – a gentle touch, a clandestine kiss, a handful of fresh grasses and damp flowers tied with thread that she had placed atop the hearth in the room she now shared with her towering Highlander. Setting her needle aside, she rose and took his outstretched hand.

"Where are we going?"

He didn't answer, but his smiling eyes told her an adventure was afoot.

Exiting the tower, they headed west in the damp air. The rain of the earlier days had receded to a steady drizzle during the night; the stone monolith of Broch Reay dripped with crystal remnants of the weather.

Dewy grasses wet the hem of Aislynn's skirts, and she was grateful for the protection of her *arasaid*. The usefulness of the garment became readily apparent to Aislynn as she pulled the hooded section over her head while they walked. John, too, wore his plaid over his shoulders, but let his russet locks dampen almost black in the mist. She watched his strides, the plaid he wore falling just above his knees, his powerful, bare legs unyielding to water droplets collecting on his calves.

Even in the dull light of the day, grasses, flowers, and bush leaves glistened in a myriad of colors, celebrating their Highland bath. Aislynn tried to look everywhere at once while they walked.

"Ye said ye wanted to see more of the Sinclair lands. Reay Burn to the east, ye've seen on laundry day. Sandside Burn to the west has better fishing."

Aislynn's mind went back to the night before, to the succulent trout they'd consumed at the evening meal. The clan boasted an abundance of fresh and dried fish, which Aislynn mistakenly assumed they fished out from the sea.

Reay Burn had a rocky shore, one that made for slippery foot holds. At Sandside Burn, the grasses of the glen rushed into the water, and the ground nearby was soft and mushy.

John led her to firmer ground, where gritty stones emerged from the grassy cover into the water and formed tiny pools. He crouched low on the stones and Aislynn followed, her eyes searching where he pointed.

In the pools, thin green moss clung to rock, waving gently with the water. Teeny fish, some no larger than Aislynn's fingernail, swam to the moss, biting and spitting. Aislynn squealed at their antics.

"The cove on the sea has one or two similar pools with verra bright fish or seaweeds," John smiled at her as he spoke, "but they are deeper in the water, and the waves can wash ashore with force. This way we stay, weel, a bit drier, and ye can still see wee fishies."

He held her waist as she lowered her head, trying to see as much of the fish pools as possible. His hand warmed her against the chill of the day, and Aislynn rather liked the pressure of his fingers holding her so she didn't fall into the shallow pools.

One fish, frightened by the giants watching from above, splashed out of the water to change direction and swim away. Aislynn jerked back as the cool droplets caught on her hands, and she landed in John's welcome embrace.

"I think we scared the fish," she observed. John helped her to her feet, holding her hand while she minced her way over the stones back to the grassy bank.

He escorted her to a slender tree, its leaves still dripping with crystal raindrops that hung like jewels on a royal necklace. A few dull red crossbills flitted from the stalks of grass to the tree branches, their gentle twitters filling the air with sweet music. Again, the land of the Sinclairs was a landscape of dreams.

"Thank you for sharing these places with me. Your Highlands are truly a place of beauty."

"Our Highlands," John corrected, pressing his scruffy, bearded lips against her dewy skin, leaving a trail of heat as he worked his way down her cheek to the soft curve of her jaw.

***

"And 'tis only beautiful as long as my wife is here," John told her between kisses.

The heat between them ignited the air as lightening does in a storm, sizzling against their skin as his lips searched for hers, capturing them with his teeth and pressing his tongue against the soft pliability of her lips. Their tongues met, and his kisses grew aggressive, needy. She returned his ardor, and they fell into the grass on the knoll, scrambling out of their plaids at the base of the rowan seedling.

They tore at each other's clothes, frantic to have skin touch skin, to become one. They couldn't come together fast enough, and when John grew frustrated with trying to remove her kirtle, he gave up and threw her skirts over her hips.

Their plaids served as dry bedding while the rain drops from the tree and grass splattered against them, sizzling, it seemed, on their burning skin. John found her open and ready. In a heated, almost frenzied movement, he slid inside her as she pressed closer, trying to take him in as deep as her body allowed.

Their zealous movements were those of star-crossed lovers, of a passionate embrace before a saddened departure, or of a long-awaited return to a lover's arms. 'Twas a joining of heat, a raw act of possession, as if they could not get enough of each other. Never enough of each other.

Desire surged in them, fierce and immediate. Aislynn threw her head back, biting down on her full lip to hold back the cries she wanted to yield. She abandoned herself in a whirl of dizzying sensation. In the moment that she held back no longer, her body vibrated with liquid flames, and John unleashed himself in his own moment of fire, passion, and love.

Together, they lay on the plaid in crumpled, exhausted satisfaction, while their need for each other continued to grow every time they joined. 'Twas never enough.

***

John thought he heard a rustle in the bushes and lifted his naked torso from Aislynn's heaving breasts. He searched the damp landscape but didn't see anything of concern. 'Twas probably a small animal scampering in the underbrush while the rain held back.

Adjusting himself to remain wrapped around Aislynn, his eyes fell on the bold stag brooch stabbed into her plaid. He lifted the brooch to admire it.

"Do ye ken of this brooch, lass?" he asked. Aislynn shook her head, turning her attention to the jewel.

"My grandfather, always the faithful man and Scot," John explained, "adopted the stag as the emblem of the Sinclairs. The stag is the King of the forest, protector of every little creature who calls the woods home. My grandfather saw the Sinclairs as the guardians of Scotland, and stags made their appearances within our land. No' just the actual animal, but in tapestries, parchments, jewels, even etched into my father's trunk."

"A protector, eh?" Aislynn's eyebrow, slender as a bird's wing, lifted on her brow.

John's chest vibrated against her in a low chuckle.

"Do you believe like your grandfather? About the Sinclairs and the stag?"

John's lips dotted quick kisses across her face and hair.

"I dinna ken about other Sinclairs, but for me, aye. I take my position as protector seriously."

Aislynn struggled not to laugh as a thought bubbled in her head. "The protector of the woods? The woods?"

He took her hint, reminding him of her first escape attempt, and this time a full laugh burst from him. Capturing her mouth with his, he kissed Aislynn deeply before answering.

"Your protector of the woods," he teased back.

Aislynn lifted her hand and trailed a finger over the delicate lines of the brooch. "So whose brooch is this? Was it a gift to Haleigh?"

John's finger followed Aislynn's across the brooch.

"Aye, in a way. 'Twas my grandfather's, who gifted it to my father, the first-born. Then he gave it to Asper, his first-born. Asper didn't want to worry that he may lose it on a military campaign, so he gifted it to Haleigh."

Aislynn pulled back, confusion lining her face.

"'Tis an heirloom! Why did she gift it to me? Perchance I misunderstood. She obviously only lent it to me. I shall return it as soon as I return to the keep."

"Nay, she would no' have handed the heirloom to ye unless she had good reason. She must have seen something in ye."

Aislynn sat up, her rich, earthy hair falling to cover her breasts. To John, she was more heavenly and beautiful than Eve in the holy garden. Aislynn held the heavy brooch in the palm of her hand.

"She gave it to me on the day someone threw mud at me," she told him. John propped himself up on his elbow and nodded.

"Aye, she told me of the event the day ye went missing."

"That day, she took me to her chambers, washed my clothes and brushed the dirt from my hair, as though I was her child, and dressed me in Highland clothing. She said she wanted me to feel welcome, to feel like I fit in."

John placed his hand atop the brooch in her hand, clasping them both in his immense grasp.

"Then the stag was her way of offering ye acceptance. I pray ye do feel welcome. Ye are where ye belong. And like the stag, I will guard ye to my dying day."

Wrapping his arms around her, he pressed her backside into his chest, encircling her with as much of his body as possible. Aislynn's fingers played against the russet hairs on his forearms.

"I did no' know what it was to live afore ye," his voice in her ear was heavy with emotion. "I can never get enough of ye. I just had ye, and I want ye more."

Aislynn blinked, her eyes misty at the depth of John's words. That someone lived for her, loved her with such honest passion, struck harder than a hammer in Aislynn's breast. Who was this man to love her with such staunch conviction, a stranger, an enemy no less?

Her own heart swelled with urgent realization that she, too, loved him with that same depth. Her world, this extraordinary new life in the Highlands, would come to a crashing end if anything happened to him. She closed her hand around the brooch, clutching it tightly as though she held John's heart in her hand, and didn't let go.

"I love you, John Sinclair," she told him, breathlessly.

"And I love ye, Aislynn Sinclair."

***

Adjusting their clothes, they left the sanctuary of the tree, following the nearly invisible trail east. John held her hand tightly as they made their way back to Reay Tower. Her eyes scanned the landscape as they walked home. Inasmuch as he promised to show her more of the exquisite Sinclair lands, the fact few kinsmen worked or even fished at the burn was not lost on Aislynn.

"Did you bring me here to keep me away from other Sinclairs?"

She didn't hesitate to broach the topic, uncomfortable though it may be. Wedding a strange man in a land far from home was difficult, true, she recognized John's predicament. As the brother of the Laird, many a lass assuredly pined for John and his brother. As a man in a position of power, many in his clan wanted him to wed into another powerful clan to form alliances.

John's decision to take an English bride, one with connections to the English King, didn't sit well with his clan. That Aislynn well understood. After the strained reception of the Sinclairs at the wedding feast and her self-imposed seclusion in the keep, she'd have to be suffering from a head injury not to notice.

Aislynn wasn't sure why she thought that marrying John meant she'd be miraculously accepted by his clan. 'Twas a foolish notion at best. Her countrymen would no sooner welcome a Scots Highlander if she brought him to her uncle's court. Acceptance by this fiercely loyal Highland clan would take time – a long time.

"No' quite," John's normally powerful voice had a tremor to it. "I will no' lie, 'twas part of my ploy. 'Twill take time for the clan to welcome ye. Scots have long memories, aye?" He lifted her hands to his lips, kissing her damp skin to soften the blow of his words. "Ye asked to see more of the land, to learn more of our Highlands. I would show ye all."

"Even the little fishies by the sea?" Aislynn teased to lighten the mood.

John's eyes squinted when he smiled. "Even the wee fishies, lass."

***

Hager MacKay waited until the couple was long gone, then crept away from the marshy burn. He wanted to run back to Clan MacKay and report what he had just seen to his Laird.

Instead, he walked slowly, picking his way over the stones that erupted from the earth like quills from the hedgehog – contemplating. 'Twas important he made certain, with no doubt possible, that the lassie who lay in the muddy grass with the Sinclair brother was the very same lassie who had claimed to be an English noblewoman paying ransom for a high-born Scot.

The man was John Sinclair, Hager had no question about that. Wildly long deep red hair that fell casually across his head but was clipped by his ears, the scars from the injuries on his head and on his shoulder shining pink and silver against the Sinclair's skin (and Hager saw too much of that man as he pumped into the lass, more than he cared to see of any man).

And though Hager enjoyed watching a good swiving, his attention remained singularly focused on the lass under the Sinclair man.

When he first encountered the two by the burn, his intention was to observe, be a voyeur to their supposedly private moment, perchance catch a good glimpse of milky, feminine skin. However, his brain screeched to a halt when he heard the lassie speak. No one in the Highlands spoke in such proper, high-born English. Their light voices reflected their soft words of love, and he'd nay heard anyone this close to the North Sea speak with such dulcet British tones.

Her voice intrigued him, since he'd only heard that accent once before – when the English noblewoman arrived to retrieve John Sinclair.

His view of the lassie was obscured by the swiving of that same man, but her smooth brown tresses and delicate milky skin screamed English. Dressed as a Scotswoman, mayhap she could fair blend in if she kept her mouth shut. But hearing her speak, 'twas the nail in the lassie's coffin.

After careful consideration during his deliberate walk home, he decided his first instinct was the correct one. Clan MacKay had been made the fool by a vapid English lass and the pridefully loyal, King's arse-sniffing Sinclairs.

Fury boiled in Hager as he approached *Loch na Moine* east of his own Laird's keep, then his pace increased until his legs were pumping full force, every stone catching on his leather boots. By the time he entered the postern gate to the inner yard, he was breathing painfully and bawling for his Laird at the top of his lungs.

Chapter Fifteen: When Truths Come to Light

"What has ye yelling in such a way?" huffed Duncan as he greeted Hager in the yard.

Hager didn't acknowledge the portly kinsman, bypassing him to careen headlong up the steps of the stronghold. The MacKay man was singularly focused.

While he needed to share this shocking development with his Laird, Hager also dreaded being the bearer of unfortunate news. Messengers oft suffered a long, violent history. Hager hoped the Laird, once he heard what Hager had to say, wouldn't take his anger out on the messenger.

Because Malcolm MacKay would be angry indeed.

***

The Laird himself reclined in a threadbare chair by the hearth, the ale he drank spinning his head splendidly. The older he became, the more he needed a drink by the fire, especially on rainy days like these when his knees ached and ached and refused to bend.

His name echoed from the hall. Malcolm sighed inwardly, wondering what manner of trouble his kinsmen were up to this time. He lifted his hands from where they cradled his slowly expanding lower belly and gripped the arms of the chair, using it to support his sore knees as he rose on struggling legs.

Several MacKay men also rushed the hall, following a panicked-looking Hager leading the troupe. *What now?* Malcolm gruffed to himself.

Since the Sinclair brothers had returned, for a reason still unclear to Malcolm, they had to reduce their encroachments on Sinclair land. With so many Highlanders joining the King's banner, borderlands of clans were in flux, and Malcolm willingly took advantage of said flux. The MacKay land started to stretch farther than it had in years, and part of that stretch was into Sinclair lands. Of that, Malcolm was proud. Pride came easily to him.

The look on Hager's face immediately caused that sense of pride to drop to the pit of his wame. The MacKays had concerned themselves with little and feared even less. Why did the man look as though he'd seen a ghost?

"We have a problem," Hager began without preamble. He scanned the hall, noting several of his kinsmen waiting for his news, with Duncan and Rafe standing near the door, watching with mild interest.

Malcolm tugged at his tunic, which pulled taut across his belly, waiting to hear about this *problem*. What manner of problem did Hager think they had? Did a neighboring clan try to reclaim their borders?

"What is it?" Malcolm didn't try to hide his bored voice.

"The Englishwoman? She's nay English. She's *Scots*." Hager paused, letting his words take hold. Malcolm raised a steel-gray eyebrow.

"Ye dinna make sense, Hager." Malcolm squinted his eyes, trying to recall an Englishwoman. "Och, ye mean the English King's lass? I met the woman. She spoke, dressed, and behaved English. I'd wager my life on her connections to British nobility. Ye dinna ken what ye are saying."

Hager ground his teeth together, speaking through a clenched jaw. "Then ye would forfeit your life. The same lass was by the burn, layin' under John Sinclair, nay an hour ago."

The rumbling previously echoing in the hall halted abruptly as every man present took in the news. Malcolm tensed, forgetting any aching in his legs. Hager's words made no sense. What was a noble Englishwoman doing with Sinclair, both of whom were supposed to be well on their way south?

"John Sinclair? The Sinclair brother who's supposed to be a captive of the English? She gave me English coin!"

"Weel, she's a Scot now. He called her wife."

A shadow passed over Malcolm's face – the bored expression of annoyance replaced by a slow progression of splotchy red anger.

"Wife? We were tricked? By so simple a ploy? By a woman? And Sinclair is wed to the Englishwoman? Here in the Highlands?" The ground under Malcolm's feet shifted. How had he been tricked so? Had he been taken in by her pale, refined charms accompanied with a bag of coin and left his faculties behind? His mind reeled as he struggled to make sense of this news.

"Och, John is nay with the English? He's on his own lands?"

"Aye, and they both looked verra pleased with the entire outcome of events."

Then Malcolm dared ask the question that piqued the minds of the men gathered in the hall.

"Why were they swiving in the rain?"

Exasperated, Hager flung up his hands. "I dinna ken for certain, but I think I heard that lass say something about seeing all of the Sinclair lands. 'Twas senseless lover's blather to me."

Try as he might, Malcolm was unable to control the raging fury burning inside him. Taken by a lass. An English lass aligned with their weak neighboring clan, no less. Malcolm had been made the fool, and that was not something he was going to take lightly. Nay, vengeance would be at hand for such a ruse.

He scratched absently at his black and gray beard, struggling to puzzle out their next actions. Such trespass was unforgivable and must be met with retribution. Malcolm masked his inner anger with deceptive calm until an idea formed in his head.

"The lass said she wants to see the Sinclair lands?" His light tone was deceptive and dreadful.

No one answered, waiting to hear what Laird MacKay was contemplating. Malcolm turned his heavy gaze to the open door of his stronghold, the doorway opening to the east, as though he saw something in the distance. Perchance he could, at least in his mind's eye.

"Then, she should see *all* of the Sinclair lands. Duncan, Hager, join me, if ye will."

The two men jumped at his command while the rest of those gathered grumbled and retreated to their duties. The kitchen maids and ladies of the keep slipped beyond the interior passageways, back to their chambers. 'Twould do well for everyone to avoid the Laird's ire while he worked over a strategy in his head.

***

Rafe MacKay was one of those men who departed the hall, the tension of the Laird's reaction tightening in his neck and shoulders like a spear of apprehension twisting down his back. He tugged his plaid over his arms against the drizzling rain and made his way back to his lonely, narrow croft.

Border raids and reiving cattle, 'twas one thing. Mayhap 'twas common for one clan to take advantage of another, preoccupied clan who let their borders and overall strength waver. But to seek out a vendetta? Over what amounted to little more than a stunt? Rafe's face clouded with uneasiness as he sought refuge from the rain under his own thatched roof.

What manner of clan had his kinsmen become? Perched on the stool near the cold hearth, Rafe let the sins of his clan, of his own actions, clutter his mind, and he didn't care for what he saw. More often as of late, Rafe found himself standing to the side, distancing himself from the actions of his clan. When had his own clan become one of embarrassment? Of treachery? Of disdain?

Rafe thought better of himself. He had considered what manner of vengeance Laird MacKay would exact upon the Sinclairs, and Rafe knew one thing for certain – he didn't want to be a part of it. He was done with being part of a clan built on treachery and deceit. Who could say those same men, his very kin, would not turn on him one day if the opportunity presented itself?

His belongings were few – an extra plaid covering his shoulders, a fresh pair of leather boots on his feet, and several bannocks and dried fish thrown into his sporran were all he needed. Rafe stepped outside where the rain still drizzled, falling just as his respect for his own clan fell. Mud squished under his feet as he walked south, in much the same direction as the false English lass had supposedly ridden with John Sinclair.

Knowing his clan as he did, he guessed 'twould be more than a day 'afore anyone questioned his absence. He may be well on his way to the Great Glen if the rain held back its wrath. Or at least to Badanloch if it didn't.

He didn't have a plan, or even a final destination, unless King Robert the Bruce was willing to forgive the wayward nature of his clan and accept the pathetic sword of a lone MacKay.

Mayhap he wouldn't tell the Bruce that. Perchance 'twould be better if he forgot he was a MacKay completely.

Rafe ducked his head against the drizzle and soldiered on.

Chapter Sixteen: When We Reach Across the Divide

Days later, the rain clouds had finally parted, and the evening was mild as Aislynn nestled deeper into the crook of John's neck. A light film of their exertions covered them, cooling just as their ardor for each other cooled.

His breathing steadied, and Aislynn rose up on her elbow to study his face as he slept. His long, dark-maroon eyelashes rested on his cheeks above the light scruff of his beard. His hair, longer on the top and back, flowed over his bedding in a mottled river of red and brown, sparkling with burgundy, earth, and clarets in the moonlight. His nose, marred only by a slight bump courtesy of a break by Marcus when they were children, was strong, breathing easily. She marveled at his handsome strength, and the intensity that made her quiver whenever she gazed upon him.

"Are ye enjoying the view, lassie?" John asked, his eyes closed. Aislynn started with surprise.

"I thought you were asleep." Her cheeks flushed to match John's coloring.

"Almost. Ye wear a man out, my wife."

Her blush deepened, and again she was wonderstruck that she, a noble English lady with ties to the King of England, had her heart conquered by a rogue Scottish Highlander. Out of such darkness and travesty at the beginning of her life had come this remarkable chance for happiness.

"'Tis strange. I have not known you long, but I feel this pull to you. 'Tis as if I felt it almost the day we met. Is it the same for you? How's such a thing possible?" Her voice was barely a whisper in the night as her fingers traced the lines of his face.

John inhaled deeply, peeling open one eye to regard the luminous woman propped over his chest. Her hair hung over their faces, a chestnut curtain hiding them from the world. Her eyes were whiskey spilled over grass, the swirling hazel warming him and making his head spin, just like the drink itself.

"I think 'tis like a pull, as ye say. A calling. Ye ken when ye hear the wolves call across the moors?"

Her brow crinkled. Why was he talking about wolves? The memories of hearing those resonating cries when she lived at Dumfries sent an icy chill over her naked shoulders.

"Yes," she answered. "I've heard them."

"I think a lover's heart is like that wolf. Those wolves are lone wolves, roaming the empty moors, howling their solitary cries to the moon. Those howls echo across the moors for miles, calling to another lonely wolf, searching for companionship. Regardless of distance, they howl, hoping their voice is heard by their mate. Then they can find each other, and each will no longer be a lone wolf."

John lifted his hand to her back, holding her tightly while he spoke of this strange comparison, his lips close enough to brush hers.

"'Tis the same with us, my love. Our hearts called to each other, and regardless of distance, they called until we found each other." John pressed his forehead against hers. "My heart called for ye the first time I saw ye."

Aislynn traced his full lips with her fingertip, the power of his words making her heart flutter just like his body had done earlier.

"We are no longer lone wolves, my husband," she told him, her lips following the trail her fingertip left behind.

***

A busy day of tilling, weeding, and food preparation, one that included a small bit of laundry at the keep, caused a tight knot to form deep in Aislynn's belly. Though more than a month had passed since her unpleasant encounter with the Sinclairs the last time she assisted with laundering, the clan had not grown any warmer in their welcome.

Haleigh, of course, was as affectionate as Aislynn expected, as were Marcus, Oggie, and Etan. Mistress Eva Sinclair in the kitchens always had a bright smile and an open hand, and a series of chores, whenever Aislynn stepped into her domain. But for the rest of the clan – the elderly kinsmen, the jealous lassies who wanted a Sinclair brother for their own, those who harbored an unabiding hatred for all things English – their frosty reception continued.

Well, not all, she was forced to admit. Her maids, Mary and Esther, were giddy at their new, permanent positions in the keep. Part of their duties included assisting Aislynn as needed, a chore the young ladies truly seemed to enjoy. The wide smiles on their freckled faces didn't appear inauthentic.

And a few other maids in the kitchens welcomed Aislynn as well, happily showing her how to make every manner of Highland fare. But those outside the tower, well, they were a hardier bunch to break. And John told her that Highlanders had long memories – she feared they may never forget the atrocities committed against them or their hatred for the English, Aislynn included.

John more than made up for the misgivings of his clan. Aislynn smiled to herself every time she thought of him – his strangely long, vermilion hair cropped close to his ears, his wide and impossibly muscular chest, his formidable limbs that marveled her daily in how they could so violently swing a broadsword yet hold her so delicately. His dancing green eyes sent a shiver of excitement down her spine whenever she caught his gaze. And the sensations he gave her at night in their bed chamber. . .

She flushed at her own thoughts. Yes, she was willing to forgive the Sinclairs much for that.

Still, their days together were numbered, and when he returned to King Robert's campaign, she wouldn't have John's affections to offset the hard looks and grumbling of the clan. What would she do then?

She wanted to ask if she might accompany him when he departed for the King's army. Aislynn had seen enough wives and mothers join their men. And though her heart soared when she contemplated staying by his side, she knew down to her core that would *never* happen. The Scots King and Laird Sinclair sent her here for confinement and safekeeping, and John was his Laird's brother and the King's man. They would no sooner let her ride back to Dumfries than they would allow King Edward Longshanks to saunter into the Highlands.

She may be wed to the Laird's brother, but she was also aware that, as far as many Scots and the English King were concerned, she was still considered a captive in the Highlands, in hiding for her own protection.

At least she was a willing captive now, she joked to herself. In addition to the seductive beauty of the Highlands that yoked her soul to the land shortly after her arrival, John himself yoked her as a Highlander, heart and body, in full. Her mind flitted to John again, and another shiver of desire palpitated through her, recalling just how willing of a captive she'd been, with John's eager head between her legs in the most inappropriate way as he drove her to the brink of madness in divine ecstasy with his mouth.

Her smile widened. *Aye,* she thought in the Highland brogue, *willing.*

***

Yet, the novelty of the Highlands lost a bit of its luster as everyday life took over.

Baskets of bright fruit in hand, Aislynn walked past one of the open fires used for laundering – boiling thin woolens for draining the fruit and making cheese. The open yard was cluttered with women and children scuttling around in every manner of chore. Even animals joined in the chaos, adding to the general din of work. Aislynn had been tasked with bringing baskets of early fruits and berries to the kitchens, readying herself for a tiring day of making preserves. Bubbling compote would join more bubbling water and the entirety of Reay tower would be awash in hot, damp air and sweat.

The breezy air of early summer did little to cool their brows.

Small children, hurriedly filling the baskets, competed to see who might find the largest, most swollen berries, or as evidenced by their smeary purple faces, who could eat the most without getting caught.

Aislynn laughed at their antics. Their mams and elders may still be wary of Aislynn, but not the children. They ran around her legs, and one small girl, her full cheeks stained pink from exertion and berry juice, offered Aislynn a plump brambleberry in her impossibly tiny hand. Aislynn gave the little one a smile, plucked the berry from her up thrust palm, and popped it into her mouth. Sweetness exploded against her tongue, making her mouth water. The berries were perfect – no wonder the wee bairns were scrambling to eat more than they put in the baskets. The children's joy was infectious, and Aislynn spent more time watching the children than on her own work.

She sighed. Sloth was her sin of the day, 'twould seem.

Unfortunately, many of the children were also distracted – their attentions on their fun rather than the yard. Most of the older girls watched what they were doing, but the younger children raced around skirts, brushed past women carrying heavy baskets or pails, full of excitement in their task of collecting low hanging fruit. The women either ignored them or brushed them away, admonishing the wildlings to behave.

'Twas just Aislynn's luck she happened to be right next to the fire when the tiny girl who had offered her the brambleberry tripped over her own feet and struck her head against the rocks that ringed the fire. Blood exploded on her dainty face and the child screamed in pain and fear.

Without thinking, Aislynn dropped her basket, stepping on mushy berries as she reached for the girl and lifted her from the fire pit in a swift movement. One of the girl's braids had started to kindle, scorching her baby-blonde braid a stinky black, and Aislynn wrapped the bairn in her plaid to extinguish the small flame. The dense wool easily smothered the burning hair, and only the tip was tainted as a reminder of the fire.

Her poor forehead, conversely, did not fare as well. A knot the size of a duck's egg rose and strained against her thin skin, and the deep gash dripped blood into the sobbing child's eye. Aislynn wiped at the blood, trying to evaluate if the girl needed the wound sewn up, when a woman – from her coloring, Aislynn guessed her to be the girl's mother –

ran to them and fell on her knees, an aura of panic surrounding her in a wide cloak.

"Is she well?" the mother cried, reaching for her daughter whom Aislynn readily handed over. She couldn't begin to imagine what the mother was thinking, both for her daughter's safety or that Aislynn was the one who came to the girl's aid.

"Yes," Aislynn breathed in relief. The gash was wide, but once she wiped away the blood, she noted it wasn't as deep as it first appeared. "She has a gash that should be cleaned, and the lump may last a day, but she is awake, and the blood no longer flows freely."

The mother studied her daughter's face to confirm that, indeed, the blood had stopped and was forming into a bright scab right over the knot on the girl's fair head. Gathering the still weeping child in her arms, the mother rose and made to march off, ostensibly to care for her daughter, when she abruptly halted.

The woman swung around to regard Aislynn; her grateful eyes pinned on Aislynn's worried face.

"Thank ye," she said earnestly with a quick bow of her head. Then she spun around again and ran from the yard as quickly as her skirts permitted.

Only then did Aislynn rise and take a glimpse around the yard. Women of all ages, and some of the older clansmen helping with the harder labors, were watching her with shrewd interest. Feeling self-conscious at the stares, an unpleasant sensation swelled in her chest.

What did they think? That I would have hurt the lass more? Let her burn or bleed to death? What do they think of the English? Or of me?

Then her eyes caught Haleigh's strange gaze. Aislynn wasn't aware of it, but the Laird's handfast wife had stepped from the kitchens just as the child fell and watched the entire scene. She said nothing to Aislynn, but a tight smile spread across the strong features of her face. Giving Aislynn a nod, similar to the one the child's mother presented, Haleigh returned to the kitchens.

Most of the gathered on-lookers followed suit, returning to their own chores, and the yard resumed its drone of busy work.

The children, however, stopped running around as much and focused on their own tasks, the lesson of what can happen if one is distracted and misbehaves well-learned.

The Seduction of the Glen

***

For a change, the sun was blindingly bright when Aislynn woke, encouraging the Sinclairs as they bustled about their chores. Aislynn's arms still ached from the day before, dragging baskets and the boiling cauldrons in the yard to the tower. Today, she'd spent most of the morning in the kitchens, with much lighter work but hidden away from the splendor of the day. The first chance she had, Aislynn snuck out the rear door.

Breathing in the sweet air and letting the sunlight warm her face, she gathered up her skirts and took the short trail from the tower, letting the long grasses and heather tickle her ankles. She stopped before the land descended into the cove. From her vantage point, she smelled the salt on the water and took in the endless views of the distant sea. During the daytime, with the sunlight twinkling on the waves, it seemed as though she was looking at the edge of the world, where the water dropped off to the nothingness of the great beyond. Such grandeur was as awe-inspiring as 'twas invigorating.

And not for nothing, the breeze was lauded, appreciated, prickling her skin and wicking away a fair bit of the sweat that clung and clung. Aislynn pulled her kirtle away from her chest, trying to catch the cool breeze under her gown. She closed her eyes to enjoy this heavenly moment before she had to return to her work. Too soon she would be missed, and the last thing she desired was to appear to be a layabout.

"Mistress?"

A young voice called to her from her left, and Aislynn jumped, clutching her kirtle back to her breasts. Her cheeks flamed at being caught in such a compromising position just to cool her skin.

The young lad stood a few feet away, a mauve thistle clutched in his slender fingers. He appeared to be of an age shortly before a lad becomes a man – clean shaven and deep-set, wide amber eyes that bespoke innocence and naïveté.

"Mistress?" the lad asked again in his squeaky voice. "Mistress Sinclair?"

"Yes, young man?"

He extended the flower out to her, stretching as though he wanted to keep his distance. A *modest* young man.

"Your man, John, he asked if ye want to see more of the Sinclair lands this day?"

Her brow pinched at the question. Was this another surprise from John? It seemed that every day he did something, no matter how small, to surprise her and bring a smile to her lips. Lips that he then claimed with fervor. She recalled the last surprise trip John took her on, to the burn, and a grin pulled at her cheek.

"Well, my lad, if John wants to show me more of the Sinclair lands, I guess we shouldn't disappoint."

The youth spun on his heel and marched forward with determination, leading her west. He helped her across the shallow bog of the Sandside Burn, holding her elbow like a gentleman and ignoring her questions about their destination.

Once the ground grew firm under their feet again, she lifted her eyes to the horizon, watching as the infamous barn, the one she'd first viewed upon entering the Sinclair demesne a lifetime ago, rise into view. The Gateway to the Sinclairs.

"Is John in the old barn?" she probed, trying to get some answers from the reticent young man.

He was intent on his duty to escort her to the barn, and his behavior showed his intense focus. His dedication melted her heart. John was adored by his clan, without a doubt. And nearly as much as the charmer Marcus was.

They reached the edge of the barnyard. Aislynn searched the yard for a sign of her husband or his horse, but she found nothing of him. Perchance he wanted to surprise her in the barn? She recalled their long-ago conversation regarding the construction and etchings in the beams, and that memory confirmed her suspicions – he was hidden within, waiting for her.

The lad tugged on her arm again, to pull her toward the slightly ajar, rickety barn door, but she held up a hand to stop him.

"Give me a moment, young man," Aislynn commanded.

He pursed his lips, evidently irritated that he had to wait to complete his important task, then it was gone, and he dropped her arm.

Turning away from the lad, she used the damp hem of her kirtle to wipe at her face, hoping to wash away any lingering dust or grime from her morning endeavors. Aislynn pulled her kerchief from her hair and ran her fingers over the tresses in a pathetic attempt to tame the flyaway locks. While she didn't have Haleigh's deft fingers, she did her best to rework her braid.

The young man cleared his throat, his impatience showing, and she waved a hand at him to wait. She could at least *try* to look respectable before seeing her husband.

Her hair tight in her braid, she then flapped her kerchief to tie it around her wrist rather than hide her crowning glory from John.

Patting at her kirtle, and hoping she managed to make a silk purse from a sow's ear, Aislynn smiled at the young man.

"I'm ready, lad."

"'Tis about time," the young man said under his breath, and she chuckled.

As far as running errands for the Laird's brother, escorting his wife to a barn had to be one of the worst tasks. She pitied the poor boy and his lowly duty.

They reached the door, and the lad stepped back, letting her go in first.

"He's in there," he pointed past the door.

Aislynn gave the young man a bright smile. "Thank you, young man. You did your duty well."

He shrugged and turned away, walking southward. *Most likely taking the long way home*, she thought to herself as she pulled the decrepit door wide to enter the barn. She well understood the desire to avoid chores by taking one's time in returning to a task.

The door, it appeared, was ready to fall off the hinges as she swung it open. High pitched squeaking drilled painfully in her ears. What kind of romantic tryst was this?

The dilapidated exterior of the barn didn't do the inside justice. The ancient beams and slats held a particular beauty, holding what remained of the barn in place as dust motes danced in the pale light. A scuttling sound in the debris to her left drew her attention. Field mice or a small hedgehog? The interior of the barn was like a fairy land, untouched by man for ages.

"John?" she called into the depth of the barn. "John, where are you?"

She'd presumed he would be right by the door, waiting for her. Was he at the rear of the barn? Did he chance the broken ladders and climb into the lofts above? She lifted her eyes to those heights, noting the slanting sunlight that cut through the open spaces in the roof.

The second option didn't appear sound – much like the ladders and the door, the lofts were falling apart, missing floor slats, and the wood that remained was peppered with holes and splinters the size of her finger.

"John?"

Was he hiding? Was she supposed to hunt for her surprise? The grandeur of the barn was starting to wear off as she picked her way around the rubble and rubbish, searching for her husband. Why did he want her here?

He must be up in one of the lofts, Aislynn finally decided. She hiked up her skirts and tested the nearest ladder, tapping on the first board with her foot. Under moderate pressure it held, so she stepped up and did the same with the next rung. With slow precision and caution, she made her way to the top rung and heaved herself over the edge of the loft. Nothing but more ancient debris and animal droppings. She wrinkled her nose – 'twas difficult to ignore the unmistakable stench of the barn.

John was nowhere to be found. Bewildered, Aislynn scanned the other loft sections across the barn, one in each corner, but nothing. *Where was he?*

A sinking sensation churned in her bowels. Recalling the stories of spirits that John and Marcus had told her when she first came to Sinclair lands, she fretted that the ghosts had awoken. Or did something worse inhabit the barn?

She glanced down at her kirtle, now dirty and torn, a jagged rent near the hem. Her skin and hair probably resembled her soiled clothing, and as she sighed in frustration, her gnawing unease grew, and a warning voice whispered in her head. Why did the lad bring her here then, if not by John's command?

In a heartbeat, her unease exploded into potent fear. John wasn't here. Why was she?

The slamming of the barn door made her jump, and she lost her footing on the warped wood. She managed to catch herself before falling to her death over the edge and find her footing on the ladder.

"John, is that you?" she called as she made her cautious way down the ladder. "John?"

No answer, but the light on the main floor of the barn had dimmed considerably, the barn door now shut. Its mangled boards still let in rays of light, but why was it closed if not from John?

She thought she heard voices outside the barn.

"John, are you outside?"

She didn't bother to try to hide the fear in her wavering voice. She was afraid – more afraid than she'd ever been in her life.

And then she smelled smoke.

Chapter Seventeen: Fire

Marcus was flirting with a crofter's daughter, a comely lass with light, reddish blonde hair that danced in the bright sunlight. His task of hoeing dirt forgotten, his attention kept dipping to the neckline of the lass's kirtle, to the suggestion of cleavage that teased him without mercy. He pondered if the time was right to lean in and steal a kiss when he caught movement out of the corner of his eye. As much as he didn't want to tear his focus from the inviting lass before him, something of that movement struck him as wrong. Forcing himself to turn his head, he watched as a young lad spoke with Aislynn before they left together.

The boy didn't seem familiar, but Marcus had been gone from his lands for a while. Mayhap a young crofter's lad was starting to reach manhood. He stared after them for a moment too long, losing his chance with the lass who was called back to her mother.

Marcus quickly swung his head around and watched the lass return home. Disappointed, he resumed his task, assaulting the soil with his hoe, yet the image of Aislynn walking off with the lad didn't sit well. His thoughts about the comely lass were replaced by the mysterious air of Aislynn and the young man. John was toiling in the barn, tending the stalls before the cattle were herded back for the day. Where was she going? Who was that lad? And if the lad wasn't a Sinclair, was Aislynn trying to escape again?

Filled with doubt, Marcus threw down the hoe and marched briskly to the stables. John was filling the few stalls with hay, stalks of which caught in his hair as he worked.

"Brother!" Marcus called, and John stopped mid-pitch, shook his head at Marcus, and resumed his work.

"Why do ye bother me, ye layabout! Ye should be at your work. The plants won't tend themselves," he huffed as the hay pile in the stall grew.

"Nay, brother. I just wanted to ask ye what manner of husband are ye?"

John paused and rotated, holding the pitchfork in one hand. One dust-covered eyebrow rose high on his forehead.

"What question is that? Jealous, are ye? Not 'tis any of your business, but the lassie is quite satisfied with me."

"Are ye certain she does no' still feel a prisoner and want to escape?"

John stabbed the pitchfork into the mound of hay and reached Marcus in two long strides. His face came close enough to Marcus's that he felt the feverish heat of John's exertions and the underlying anger John struggled to control.

"She does no' want to *escape*." He sniffed a ragged breath through his nose. "Now, tell me why ye ask me such a thing?"

An anxious look crossed Marcus's features, and he was now glad he followed his instincts to find John. Something *was* amiss.

"I just saw the lassie leave with a young laddie, someone I dinna recognize. At first, I thought he was to bring her to ye, but they did no' come this way. They went west."

John's face went as hard as stone. "The MacKays?"

Marcus shook his head. "I dinna ken. Just something about it struck me as wrong."

John continued to breathe heavily; the subtle movement of his eyes imperceptible as he weighed the information Marcus shared. John knew Aislynn, knew her heart – or at least believed he did. After the tender moments and soft words they'd shared, she didn't want to leave, nay himself nor the Highlands. That he also knew. If she were being led toward the MacKays, 'twas under false pretenses. A shock of nervous fear shot up his back.

"Amiss?" John questioned. Marcus shrugged.

"Just a gut feeling."

John grabbed his upper arm and led Marcus to the horses hobbled outside.

"I trust your feelings. Get your horse, call for Etan and Oggie."

Marcus raced for his steed, hollering for all he was worth at Etan and Oggie to join him. They mounted and joined John, who rode west in a frenzy.

They had barely crested the hill past Reay Tower when they saw a distant line of gray smoke against the brilliant blue sky. An icy chill filled John's every pore. Even with the recent rain, the past few days had been dry and old wood burned with ease. The smoke appeared to be coming from the old Gateway barn.

John reigned his horse around in a panic. "Etan, ride back and gather as many as ye can! Bring every bucket ye can find! Hurry, lad!"

Etan was already wrestling his horse back to the yard, calling for buckets and men to fight the blaze.

John didn't know with any certainty that Aislynn was at the barn, that the smoke had anything to do with where Aislynn was. The coincidence of it, however, struck him as too convenient, and he wouldn't risk Aislynn's safety by assuming she wasn't there. Locking one's enemies in a barn or croft to burn to death was not uncommon in Scots history. Burning an English noble to death seemed a harsh way to strike at the Sinclairs, but John would not put it past the ignominious MacKay clan. And the unfamiliar lad that Marcus referenced, well, it raised every hair on John's body.

The gray smoke bloomed more fully the closer they rode to the old barn, and too soon they were upon the building, flames licking and consuming the old wood and daub like a starving man at a feast.

John leapt from the moving horse into a run, a fluid move that had him at the burning door before Marcus and Oggie were able to follow. The weak door, barred by an iron post, was rendered only weaker by the angry flames. Bracing himself against the scorching heat, he pulled the bar away and kicked with one powerful leg. The door splintered into a pile of ashen shards. Smoke and heat escaped the inside in a rush, and John coughed as he was overwhelmed, smoke burning his throat and eyes. Piercing fear struck deep in his chest. If Aislynn were in there, how could she survive that much smoke? That heat?

John took one step over the remnants of the barn door.

"Aislynn!" he called into the impenetrable interior.

***

At first she thought 'twas her imagination – fear and thinking of ghosts oft made anyone see or hear things that weren't present. The smell grew steadily denser, hardier, and she coughed. That was not her imagination. The barn had caught fire!

By the time she reached the bottom of the ladder, the mincing steps of the decrepit ladder slowing her progress, she saw how thick the smoke had become. What had been a gray haze when she was on the ladder had billowed into a thick fog filling the top of the barn. But coming down the ladder meant easier breathing, so she ducked, hoping the smoke would stay high off the ground.

Stumbling through the hay and debris that littered the floor, she tried to make her way to the barn door. Mayhap she could reach it afore the flames spread too far?

The heat grew as thick as the smoke – pressing against her in a way that made her want to run in the other direction. *Don't panic,* she commanded herself. *If you panic, you are surely dead.* She focused on keeping her wits about her, which was difficult as the flames increased. Sweat ran down her face and into her eyes, blurring her already smoke-pained sight. It seemed as if the heat and smoke singed her eyeballs, and she had to swallow a rise of bile in the back of her throat that tasted like fear.

The air by her feet swirled on her legs, cooler and clearer, so she crouched to the ground, crawling the rest of the way to the door. The heat against the wood was brutal, and when she tried to reach for the door to push it open, her hand blistered from the flames that licked the scalding wood.

She screamed and coughed and fell back into the dirt. Unwrapping her kerchief from her wrist, she wound it around her seared palm, hoping to calm the pain and shield it from further damage. With her hand protected from the flames, she had a flash of an idea. Pulling up her kirtle, and with a silent apology to Haleigh, Aislynn tore a handkerchief-sized swatch from the gown and wrapped it around her nose and mouth. If her kerchief protected her hand, perchance the swath of fabric could do the same for her choking breath.

Then, wrapping her hands in the hem of her poor, ragged gown, she attempted the door again, but to no avail. It was stuck. Or barred. Either way, she was trapped.

Crawling away from the door and the adjacent wall which was being licked away by dancing flames, Aislynn searched for an out – a broken set of boards, crumbling rocks in the foundation, somewhere she could find reprieve from the fiery death that would indeed consume her if she remained inside. The building was falling down around her, decrepit as it was – pieces of roofing and slats of wood; there must be a gap to the outside!

She wavered about, not moving too far from the door as she searched. If she ventured too far back into the barn, and there was no way out, she feared she would be stuck and overwhelmed with the slowly oppressing heat or the thickening haze. The door was a weak spot and an exit. Her conundrum froze her where she rested on all fours, indecision impeding her ability to choose the best option for escape.

A cracking sound at the barn door forced the decision for her. That rickety door would never hold against the fire, and her best, and probably only, chance to escape was through that exit. Abandoning any plans to move farther into the inferno, she kept her distance from the inflamed door, searching it for any sign of weakness.

Until the door exploded inward, throwing her backward onto the centuries-old hay and dirt.

***

"John! Dinna go in there!" Marcus screamed from atop his horse, riding at a heart-bursting pace to reach his brother before he entered the inferno and almost certain death. His voice was lost in the roaring of the fire as it consumed the ancient building.

The building itself was not completely engulfed in flames, though that inevitability was not far off. The crumbling thatch of the roof had not yet collapsed, fortunately for John, and possibly Aislynn. The few boards used as support still stood, but much of the daub and waddle was ablaze.

The stones at the foundation caught the falling debris and crumbled as it fell away.

What was worst, at least in Marcus's estimation, was the pungent odor of vitriol, sulfur, that hit like a hard punch to the nose. Marcus would rather have had to fend off an entire clan of sword-toting men than immerse himself deeper into that foul, hell-borne smell and its deadly heat.

Aislynn will no' survive this, he thought, hating himself even as the idea passed through his mind. *And neither will John if he stays inside that barn.* The lass didn't deserve such a fate, nor did his loyal brother who loved the English rose.

Snapping and popping made him jump, a horrifying sound that drowned out everything else in the glen. His horse reigned up, crazed eyes bulging and twisting in fear. Marcus slid off and slapped the horse away. Other riders appeared over the crest of the hill, buckets and blankets strapped to horses and gripped in panicked hands. An inlet from the sea trickled north of the barn, and before Marcus yelled a single command, the Sinclair men and several of the women scooped their buckets from the burn and came as near as the blazing fire allowed. Water splashed on the walls, foundation, and the surrounding grass to prevent its spread.

If there were any hope for Aislynn or John to escape the barn, 'twould be through the gaping maw of the door, fiery teeth dripping embers like drool from a rabid dog.

Marcus searched desperately for John inside that blazing opening. Surely, he didn't enter the barn to the rear? Risk his life? Was Aislynn clever enough to stay near the door?

Heat and water battled and rained down on him as he ventured farther, his eyes searing in the smoke that puffed from the interior not unlike warm breath on a frigid day. Buckets of water splashed against the flames, splattered, and dripped onto Marcus, but seemed to do little good. Ignoring the chaos of the fire and the yelling of clansmen, his attention focused on a dull shape that clung to the remains of the doorway. Wrapping his hand in his tunic, he shrunk back to prevent flames from singeing his arm hairs as he grasped the object.

The heat seared through the wool around his hand, but not enough to burn, and he plucked the item from the ashy remains. 'Twas an object that had no place on the ancient barn door, and he was baffled by what he held.

'Twas an iron bar, much like one used to fasten a cart to a horse's reins. *Why was it attached to the door?*

A sickening realization swarmed over Marcus, harder and more dizzying than the smoke that ached in his lungs. Someone barred the door.

The smell of oil of vitriol.

A fire after days of rain on damp, swollen wood.

'Twas no accident or work of nature that caused this fire.

This inferno was caused by human hands. And as his stinging eyes flicked inside the fiery mouth of the barn, hoping to see at least one dark figure approaching the door, he knew what did cause it.

Or rather, who.

Chapter Eighteen: Silver Linings Edge Dark Clouds

Flames licked against the skin of John's calves like a ravaging hell beast as he pushed past the door into the impenetrably dark barn. He opened his mouth to call out to Aislynn, but all he managed was a hacking cough as his lungs fought for clean air.

The smells and sounds of the scorching building were like nothing he'd experienced in his life. Even the battlefields alongside King Robert the Bruce, amid the screams of men and clanging of swords, were nothing compared to the aggression and raging of the fire in his ears and on his skin. He had to fight every instinct to race from the barn and seek fresh air.

If Aislynn were in here, 'twas an excellent chance she was unconscious, either from the pressure of the heat or the smothering smoke. He dropped into a crouch, sidling along the floor. A prayer consumed his mind in a steady mantra – *Please let her live. Please let her live. Please let her live.*

Sweeping his hands along the floor, he moved into the depths of the barn. His chest throbbed, and fear clutched him, plying him to escape and save his own skin.

If Aislynn dies, then what use is my skin? I should perish with her. The harrowing thought filled him with conviction and helped press his fear aside. Neither of them, he vowed, would perish this day.

He pushed a few feet farther inside, covering his face with his tunic against the noxious air, squinting to see something, anything of Aislynn. Hope was fleeting, escaping him just as the smoke escaped from the collapsed roof.

Then his hand struck an object that wasn't hay or old debris.

'Twas a leather-clad foot.

Hope surged in his chest, breathing new life into his lungs. He wrapped his hand around her ankle in his sturdy grip and pulled Aislynn against him. She was unconscious, and John couldn't tell if she were still breathing or not. He didn't bother to check – 'twas no time to waste.

Threading his arm around her chest, he stayed low, where the suffocating air was less stifling, and dragged her to the gaping, burning opening of the doorway.

Through the wavering heat and a blurry gaze, he saw Marcus standing by the door, holding a pole. John watched his mouth open, yelling, yet no sound came through. Only the continued roaring of the fire.

John fought to rise, clutching Aislynn as close to his body as possible, bracing them both to plunge across the threshold and out to safety. Flames whipped around the doorway, threatening to catch any rogue hair or clothing. John struggled against the oppressive heat that wanted to push them back into the now-fully consumed barn. 'Twas like fighting the Devil himself in the bowels of Hell.

Then a hand clutched his arm, a hand strong enough to pull both John and Aislynn across that threshold of death as John jumped, and they landed in a heavy heap just outside the doorway. John inhaled through his mouth, a powerful cleansing gasp as though he'd not breathed in months. The moments inside the barn had seemed just that. A lifetime in mere seconds.

Hands grabbed at the shoulders of his tunic, which ripped as he and Aislynn were dragged away from the burning ruins of the Gateway.

"His plaid!" someone yelled, and a splash of cold water shocked his senses.

Evidently flames licked a little too closely when he leapt across the fiery abyss with Aislynn. The icy blast extinguished the flames wicking across his plaid – a relief after so much heat. John coughed over and over, choking up smoke and carnage from his sore lungs.

Aislynn didn't cough. And as John regained his breathing, taking in clean air with grateful gasps, the panic that threatened to consume him inside the barn returned with a vengeance.

"Aislynn?" he croaked in a voice not his own. "Aislynn, lass?"

He pushed up on one arm to gaze upon her. She was singed, that much was clear. Swaths of fabric were marked with ash and burns – even her hair stank of fire. Her kerchief was wrapped around her hand, and John saw pulsing blisters on her palm. Ash covered her lifeless body from crown to foot. Someone had pulled the cloth from her face, hoping Aislynn, too, would take deep, gaping breaths of the life-giving Highland air.

A woman brought cloths soaked in water from the inlet to cover her, cool her skin and wipe away the lingering smoke from her in hopes that she might return to life.

Tears tracked through the soot on John's face, though he didn't realize he was crying. Marcus and several other men were speaking to him, but he heard nothing. The only thing he was aware of was Aislynn's seemingly lifeless body (he wouldn't say the words, he wouldn't give voice to the possibility that he didn't reach her in time) and the mantra in his head – the same mantra that echoed in him in the barn: *Please let her live. Please let her live. Please let her live.*

Aislynn's body jerked in a convulsion as she sputtered and gasped, ash and gray puffs escaping her mouth in wracking coughs.

The surrounding crowd breathed a sigh of thankful relief. John still didn't hear it – the only thing he heard over the roar of the fire was the blessed sound of Aislynn's breathing, gasping for the clean air to replace the poison in her lungs. John gathered her in his arms, holding her as hard as he dared while she continued to cough.

Other than her hacking, she was limp against him. His entire body ached, and he knew they would spend months recovering. John didn't care.

She lived. So did he. And that was all that mattered.

***

Oggie had parted from Marcus, grabbing buckets from the oncoming riders and taking them right to the marshy inlet. The smell of oil of vitriol permeated the air as he had ridden toward the smoky haze, a sharp tang that stung his nose and told him 'twould be useless to try and tame the beastly fire with water. Dry wood sucked up the water and extinguished the fire. Sulfur, however, did naught but cause the water to splatter, or even worse, splatter the flames and catch more of the glen ablaze.

"Nay the wood!" he yelled at his clansmen and women following him. "The roof! The stone! The grass! Stop the spread!"

His clan kenned at once what he meant – 'twas not their first time dealing with fire, let alone intentional fire encouraged by a coating of oil of vitriol.

Hastily hobbling his horse at the stones by the swampy inlet, he dunked his buckets and raced to the barn, pouring the water around the base of the foundation, as near as he dared to tread. As the Sinclair kin filtered in, they brought more buckets and formed scattered lines. Oggie, at the front of his line, raced around the old barn, saturating the surrounding grasses and ground, risking his own skin by getting as close to the barn as possible.

The rain from days before meant the ground was not as dry as they feared, but with the grasses and flora in the glen on a bright day, fire could spread fast, especially when urged on by sulfur that fed the fire like a mam feeds her babe.

Other Sinclair men did the same, working their way around the barn and the grass. Oggie's attention was on the Sinclair kinsmen and the barn, focused on stopping the blazing onslaught. When several of the women rushed to the open yard away from the barn, he diverted his gaze and watched as a smoking John and his British bride were dragged from the inferno.

He sighed in heavy relief. They hadn't been too late, and whoever sought to strike such a harsh blow against the Sinclairs was foiled. While he observed the tender scene of his clan trying to save the lass, the fire burned hotter, impossibly hotter. 'Twas as though it singed the hair on his legs.

Only when the woman extending a bucket to him screamed did he swivel around, noting that the heat of the fire didn't lessen, but instead worsened, scorching his backside.

What –?

The woman threw the bucket of water on him, but 'twas too late. The seeping, bubbling heat on his skin, caused by the flames that had caught on the edge of his tunic and the slippery vitriol, reached his hair and engulfed his head in a horrifying blaze.

Screaming, he ran the best he could manage toward the inlet, hoping to reach the water before the flames overwhelmed him. Cool waves of water splattered against him as those with buckets tossed the contents, desperate attempts to put out the flames that grew with every step Oggie took.

When he finally splashed into the mucky water at the edge of the inlet, his skin was blackened and suppurating. Oggie never rose again.

***

Aislynn was barely conscious when Marcus hefted her onto his horse, ready to ride like a madman to Reay Tower and Mistress Eva Sinclair's healing hands.

Etan led John to his own horse. He could finally look around the glen and see what had happened while he was occupied in the barn's crumbling inferno. What he did see left him in awe.

Only a blackened skeleton of the barn stood against the sun low in the sky, which was streaked with black and gray smoke. Few hardy wood posts stood up from the debris, testaments against the fire's havoc, their burnt ends charred and peaked. Little of the interior wooden structures remained, and most of the stone wall sections and foundation were seared, the only parts of the Gateway that weren't fully destroyed. An ancient marker, built by Northmen of old and an ancestor of the Sinclairs, gone in less than one afternoon. A harsh sadness accompanied those thoughts and that ruined vision.

Yet, the sight of the decimated barn was not what stunned him.

'Twas the sheer number of clansmen and women presently in the glen.

Most of the Sinclair men at Reay had ridden to the Gateway to give assistance, their own soot-covered bodies still hefting buckets of water on and around the carcass of the barn to prevent further spread of the fire.

What shocked him more was the collection of clanswomen who also helped, running buckets, giving water to working men, and even those who came to Aislynn's aid once John yanked her from the fire. These same people who didn't want to attend a festive wedding out of anger and vindictiveness arrived in droves to Aislynn's aid, putting their own lives at risk to help Aislynn and combat the fire.

Perchance, as 'twas with many dire events, a silver lining edged this black cloud of a day. Perchance the Sinclairs were able to put aside their hatred of the English when lives were at stake.

That thought helped clear his head and chest almost as much as the fresh Highland air. Etan gave the weary John a shove onto his horse, then mounted his own and escorted the Laird's brother home.

***

They arrived at Broch Reay to the open arms of Haleigh and Mistress Eva, with poor Mary and Esther wringing their hands right behind them. Haleigh had Marcus carry Aislynn to John's chambers, and Eva barked orders to Mary and Esther and the other maids in the kitchen. The household rallied to Aislynn's aid.

Marcus deposited Aislynn on the bed she shared with John, sending up his own silent prayer for her recovery. Then, leaving the lass in the capable hands of his good-sister, he made his way to the hall to await John's arrival.

The iron bar he had left in the care of Etan, with the dictate to bring it to Reay without delay. While he would eventually share his hunch with John and Haleigh so they could bring retribution against the MacKays, today was not that day. The Sinclairs had too much to recover from before that happened.

Marcus rested his lean, weary frame against the open door of the main hall, casting his gaze westward. The sky was a smear of sunset colors marred with gray plumes and streaks, and the smell of soot hung heavy in the air.

Aye, today was not that day, but vengeance would come, swiftly.

***

John spent the entire night and the next day by Aislynn's side. Her eyes remained closed, her face silent to the world. Yet she lived, her chest rising and falling in a steady cadence, and because of that, John kept his hope for her full recovery alive, too.

Aislynn's maids, Mary and Esther, also kept their hope for their mistress alive. The sisters had grown enamored with their British mistress, and to see her laid low was more than the sheltered lassies could bear. They waited on Aislynn, and on John as well, hand and foot. Mary and Esther brought food and water to John, emptied the chamber pot when he didn't want to leave the room, and brought fresh washing cloths in case John, who still bore marks of his passage through the fire, wanted to wash more than his face. And one of the girls remained with Aislynn at all times, as though they alone might bring Aislynn back.

More, 'twas to watch over her, to ensure nothing like this happened to their mistress again – guardian cherubs hiding in the shadows.

John didn't notice the girls or their efforts, his whole being focused on the woman prone in the bed. 'Twas as if he believed his own sheer force of will was enough to bring her back from wherever she was.

When they first got her into the bed, with Haleigh's tender hand taking the lead, the women had washed the soot and ash from her pale skin, treading with a light hand on the burned sections of her body, which were fortunately few. Her hand was the worst, peppered with a series of red, angry blisters.

Mistress Eva Sinclair prepared a honey and herbal salve to coat the blisters, then she re-wrapped Aislynn's hand in clean linens. The hand would scar, she knew that without a doubt. Mistress Eva Sinclair hope to save its usage, given Aislynn's talent with a sewing needle.

The tips of her earthen locks were singed in spots, fraying her soft waves. They had changed her gown, replacing the tatters with a fresh chemise, then brushed the grit and knots from her hair.

There she lay, the evidence of the nightmarish incident washed away. And still she didn't wake.

John watched over her throughout the night, her guardian angel as well. Marcus and Haleigh peered in, wanting to offer succor by way of kind words, yet held back by the sense of fixation John exuded. Mary woke in the middle of the night to check on her mistress, her burns, and her hand, and gave John a tender touch on the shoulder when she finished her tasks. He was still awake.

By morning, his eyes were ringed with purple fatigue. He'd begun talking to Aislynn, hoping she heard his desperate voice and wake.

He had worked his way into a spoken version of his prayer, saying it so often that he believed his ears to grow numb. Obviously, they must have, because he didn't believe it when she finally spoke.

"John?"

Please let her live. Please let her live.

"John?" she croaked a bit louder.

His exhausted head shot up, his sad eyes wide.

"Aislynn? Ye are awake?"

He choked with emotion, with gratefulness, with relief.

Chapter Nineteen: Slow Recovery

Aislynn opened her eyes, wondering if she'd arrived at the gates of Heaven. The dim lighting and the pain in her hand, however, made her question if she were actually in Purgatory. She wasn't in Hell, that she knew. She'd already overcame the test of Hell's flames. Whether she survived or not, though . . .

But when she turned her head, John was sitting next to her, and she lay on her bed, so she was tormented by confusion. Was John in Purgatory with her?

"John?" she croaked. "John?"

She wanted to ask where they were, if they had died together, but her dry voice didn't want to form any words. Even saying his name traumatized her throat, which throbbed as she spoke.

"Aislynn! Ye are awake?"

John stood above her and caressed her arms with the barest touch of his hands. His nearness overwhelmed her. *Why didn't he take me in his arms?*

She only nodded at his questions. Dropping to his knees, John pressed his face into her side and sobbed like a child. *What's wrong with me?* Terror filled her chest like lead, and her whole body ached.

Clearing her throat with an irritated grumble, she tried again. "What's wrong with me, John?"

It even hurt to move her lips.

John's head snapped up, and he surprised her by barking out a laugh. She flinched at his reaction and her mind floundered, more confused than ever. His worried, ruddy face smiled widely, joy reflecting in his normally formidable green eyes. She reached her hand out to run her fingers through his wild hair, only to see it wrapped in swaths of dusky linen. 'Twas the hand that ached the most.

"What happened, John?"

He couldn't control his joy. "Nothing! Everything! Oh, Aislynn, we so feared ye would nay wake!"

She cleared her throat again, and John jumped to his feet.

"Dinna speak. Let me get ye water."

Water. The mere word made her throat clench. She'd never felt so thirsty in all her life.

Esther had the cup ready, holding back even as her own joy made her want to rush forward and hug her frail mistress.

John brought the goblet to her lips. With the help of John's arm under her shoulders, Aislynn used her left arm to prop her head up enough to sip. Sucking at the cool liquid relieved her dry mouth and throat, holy water from God's own hand.

"What happened, John?" she asked again, laying her head back on the cushions. She squinted at him, trying to remember how she ended up in bed. "There was a fire. That I can recall. A bad fire at the old barn. I thought you were there. . ."

Her voice drifted off as she tried to piece the previous day together in her memory.

"I was there," John told her. "Marcus saw you leave with the MacKay lad."

Aislynn shook her head, a moue of pain flickering at the effort. "Nay, afore the fire. I thought you would be there."

John sat next to the bed, holding her injured hand as delicately as he would an injured bird.

"What do you mean, love? Why did you think that?"

"The boy, he made it seem like you were there. A surprise for me. To show off more of your land."

"Oh, Aislynn." John lifted her burned hand and kissed the top, avoiding the clusters of blisters that plagued her palm. Her words made him feel that he was somehow at fault. "Nay, 'twas a lie to get ye into the barn."

"You weren't there. I looked around the barn, and suddenly there was smoke, so much smoke, and then the door was on fire . . ." This time when her voice drifted off, it was accompanied with a shudder at the memory. She lifted her hand, peering at the bandage with weary eyes. "I tried the door with my hand. Is that how I burned it?"

John nodded. "Aye. When Marcus saw ye leave, he came and found me, as 'twas strange to him. He's always been astute when something raises the hackles on his neck. We saw the smoke in the distance then and assumed it had something to do with ye. Turns out 'twas a correct assumption."

Aislynn lay back on the bedding, trying to take in the news. Her brain was still in a fog.

"Why was there a fire? I dinna understand. Was there a lightning strike? I dinna recall any rain."

John's entire face clenched with a fury that frightened her.

"Nay. The MacKay lad, the lie to get ye to the barn, 'twas a ploy. I am nay certain, but we think the MacKays realized we had one over on them when ye dressed in your English finery to retrieve me. Haleigh and I believe 'twas a way to get retribution for our duplicity. 'Tis no other reason we can fathom for why they focused their actions on ye. 'Twould seem rather dire of them, and ye can be assured we will deal with their treachery swiftly."

"But they could have killed me, killed us --"

John's face tightened again. He looked almost haunted.

"Aye, and we will have redress. But ye, lass, I dinna want ye to overdo it. Ye've just awakened and ye dinna need to fret over such atrocities. Rest, regain your health. I shall be here for ye, as will poor Mary and Esther who've flitted about ye since we've returned."

Aislynn's face softened at the mention of the girls' names.

"Are they here? I would thank them for taking care of me."

"Most assuredly." John leaned back, searching the doorway. Esther stepped to the side of the bed, placing a tender hand on Aislynn's arm. Aislynn leaned into the girl's touch.

"I'm so verra pleased ye have wakened, mistress," Esther whispered, speaking aloud to Aislynn for the first time since she'd arrived at Reay. Though it pained her, Aislynn smiled at the girl.

"I'll find the other lassie for ye," John told her, rising. "Are ye hungry? Thirsty?"

"More water would be fine. And maybe something easy to eat? I don't have it in me for much else."

She closed her eyes, and John stepped to the door, calling softly for Mary. She appeared as if by magic from the depths of the hallway.

"Milady has awakened. She would like some more water and parritch and honey. Can ye see to that for her?"

Mary brightened at his words. She raced to the bed, placed a light kiss on Aislynn's forehead, then swirled around to the stairwell. "I will bring it right away!" she called with excitement.

When John returned to Aislynn's bedside, her eyes were closed. She had already fallen back asleep.

***

The next day, Aislynn felt well enough to sit up in bed and eat the parritch Mary brought to break her fast. Joy shone from the girl's cheeks, bright apples against her pale skin, rejoicing that her lady was recovering.

Haleigh made her appearance as well, an apologetic tone lacing every word. "I am so relieved that ye are faring well this day."

The Laird's wife sat on the edge of the bed, reaching across Aislynn for her uninjured hand, patting it in a motherly way.

"We were so afeared that we had lost ye."

John grumbled from the corner of the room, letting her know what he thought of that. Fleck stood near the door, giving Aislynn a light nod when she peered over at him.

"I am thankful we all made it back safely," Aislynn concurred.

An odd hush fell over the room. At first, Aislynn took this as a moment of grateful reflection on her survival. Then she noted that Haleigh,

John, and Fleck exchanged concerned glances, and perchance 'twas more that held their tongues.

She pushed her bowl of parritch to the side, her appetite gone.

"What is it? Is there something you aren't telling me?"

Haleigh patted her hand again, turning her face to John as she spoke.

"We have reason to believe the MacKay's are responsible for the fire. That 'twas retribution against ye for your ploy in retrieving John. 'Tis the only logical conclusion we can draw for why ye were led there."

Haleigh kept her gaze averted from Aislynn. Thus, Aislynn couldn't see her strange eye, and Haleigh's efforts to hide her gaze suggested 'twas more they weren't sharing.

"We will retaliate," John's gruff voice promised.

Of course, Aislynn knew the Sinclairs would not permit an insult to their clan go unanswered. But Haleigh's still averted her eyes.

"Is there more?" Confusion set into Aislynn's face, and she twisted toward John. *What were they not saying?* A piercing surge of apprehension rose in her throat. "Is it Marcus? Did he make it out unscathed?"

Fleck's voice resonated from the doorway. "Aye, Marcus did."

But someone else did not. 'Twas as though Aislynn could hear the unspoken statement aloud.

"Who?" Her voice was barely a whisper as she bit back her tears.

"Oggie," John answered, dropping his eyes.

Aislynn's hand flew to her mouth. *Oggie? The gentle man who was my guard as they traveled north? Who attended me and kept me company, who protected me?* This time the tears filled her eyes. Oggie was too good a man to find such an untimely death. Guilt filled her with leaden pain. Had she not gone to the Gateway barn, had she not followed the lad, Oggie would still be alive.

The ache of the guilty weight was too much to bear, and she wanted to beat her hands against her chest in lamenting disbelief.

"Oh, Haleigh, John, I am so very sorry." She couldn't think of what else to say.

Haleigh tugged on her hand, her voice hard. "Nay. Dinna apologize, for naught is your fault. 'Tis the machinations of the MacKays, and the MacKays only, who are responsible."

Aislynn wiped at her wet cheeks. Haleigh may have spoken the truth, but it didn't make Aislynn feel any less culpable. John joined her by her side, and she crumpled into him.

"We have much to hold the MacKays accountable for, my lassie. Dinna keep any fault for his death in your hands, for 'tis nay yours. We will bury our man, have our retribution, rebuild the Gateway, and ye and I, my wife, will build our lives here."

Until you must leave, she thought bitterly, then let the thought fly from her head. 'Twas not his fault that he must depart to the side of the Bruce soon, and 'twould not do to let those vain thoughts taint Oggie's memory or displace the importance of his burial.

"Now, lass," Haleigh's tone shifted, taking on that motherly quality again. "Dinna think on this now. Let Mary take your meal if ye are finished and try to rest. This news must have taken much out of ye."

Haleigh wasn't the only one who noticed how pale Aislynn had grown. Fleck escorted Haleigh from the chamber as Mary entered and retrieved the platter of food. John remained behind, still seated on the bed.

"Stay with me, John. I don't think that sleep will come easily, no matter what Haleigh advises."

John kissed Aislynn's forehead, sharing in her pain.

"Heed Haleigh's advice. 'Tis no' your fault, and we canna do anything now. Rest."

Aislynn took his hand in hers, searching for succor in the heat of his skin.

"It may not be my fault, but I still weep as though it were. And it shall be difficult for me to ever believe otherwise."

John had no words of solace to offer, only the steady firmness of his body as he stretched out next to her, holding her as she fitfully found her troubled slumber.

***

They buried Oggie on a gray day, wrapped in a shroud sewn by the women of his clan, and marked his final resting space with a heavy stone upon which his name had been carved. Aislynn wasn't able to attend, after being commanded to stay abed by Haleigh and Mistress Eva Sinclair.

John, his brother Marcus, and other Sinclair men drank in the hall afterward, sharing stories of their fallen kinsman, offering toasts to Oggie, and taking stock of their own lives.

Aislynn didn't anticipate seeing John that night, figuring he would wash his sorrows away with whiskey and shared memories. She remained in her chambers with Mary and Esther for company. Haleigh had popped in throughout the day, supposedly to socialize, but Aislynn knew 'twas to see how she fared. Though Haleigh and John both assured Aislynn she was not to blame for Oggie's death, his demise at the fire weighed on her shoulders. This day was the ultimate reminder of that.

Further, she feared how the Sinclairs viewed her now. Aislynn's presence had killed their man. Her standing with them had been precarious at best, and if anyone in the clan did hold her accountable, her acceptance would assuredly flounder.

Mary and Esther departed early in the evening, removing Aislynn's untouched evening meal with them. Mary "tsked" under her breath, fretting over Aislynn's health as she did so well, but said nothing more than "good eve" as she and Esther closed the door.

In the flickering candlelight, she took stock of her hand, and of her overall present state. Most importantly, her mind reeled back to the same recurring question: Was the love between her and John enough to overcome the obstacles in their path? Did John love her enough to accept all that came with their marriage? Not for the first time, Aislynn feared she made the wrong choice, condemning not just herself but John and his entire clan with her decision to wed.

Just as her personal laments reached their ultimate low, her chamber door banged open. John stood in the doorway, his hair dark in the shadows of the hall. He wore only his plaid swathed around his hips, with his bare chest and legs exposed to the world. His warrior stance, however, was a mask – he wobbled when he tried to step into the room.

"John!" Aislynn gasped, running to his side before he fell over. The sickly-sweet smell of drink emanated from every pore. "You're drunk?" she asked it as a question, but 'twas more of a statement. One with which John readily agreed.

"Aye," he said with a burp. He gave her a surprisingly boyish grin.

"Well, come then. Let's get you abed."

Aislynn wrapped her arms around him, trying to support his unstable gait, when he stopped her in the middle of the room.

"Oh, lassie," he breathed, threading his fingers through her hair and letting the tresses cascade over her shoulder. "Ye are so fine a lass. I dinna think I've seen a lass as lovely as ye." His words were a bit mumbled, drunk as he was, yet touched Aislynn's heart.

"Thank you, husband," she answered as she again urged him toward the bed.

"Do ye ken how much I love ye?"

She gazed into his drooping eyes. "You *are* drunk. Come to bed."

"Drunk or no. And ye should always trust the words of a drunk man. 'Tis the only time ye can be certain a man speaks the truth. Whiskey loosens the tongue. And my tongue wants to lick ye from your cheeks to your toes."

"John!" Aislynn threw up a hand at his bold words even as a smile tugged at her lips. He graced her with a sloppy kiss on said cheek and sagged against her.

"Well, if you are drunk enough to speak the truth, then tell me this. Do you truly not blame me for all that has happened these past days?"

His face screwed up at her question, and his voice was muffled as he talked into the curve of her neck. "Blame ye? Why would I blame ye for what the MacKays have done? I may be drunk, but ye are the one speaking nonsense, wife."

Whether she believed him more because he was drunk or because he had now told her several times she was not to blame, she accepted his words as truth. A glimmer of light shone on the heels of that thought – perchance the Sinclairs saw it the same. They already had grievances with the MacKays. Perchance these events helped focus that ire more directly.

"Then let's get your drunk self to bed."

Aislynn all but pushed him down onto the tartan coverlet, pulling at his stained leather boots.

"I love ye, lass," he said once more before he fell back on the bed, snoring.

She patted his steadily breathing chest.

"I love you, too, John."

Chapter Twenty: Acceptance

The inhabitants of Broch Reay awoke with the sun, as work in the gardens, fields, barn, and stables demanded attention. John managed to rise as well, shaking off any effects of his night of drinking, and kissed Aislynn's lips just as she stirred awake. Then he was gone, the needs of the day calling to him.

Aislynn pulled herself from the comfort of her bed, deciding that today she could resume her work. She poked at the burns, with new pink skin in its place. Mistress Eva Sinclair had removed the last of the bandages the day before, pressing on the skin and on Aislynn's fingers. She was testing the hand, Aislynn understood, trying to evaluate if the injury were more than skin deep. Aislynn's fingers moved well, flexing comfortably, and when Mistress Eva asked her to ply a needle, Aislynn held it in a nimble grasp. Mistress Eva declared her recovered.

No longer tender, her hand wouldn't impede her abilities any longer, not at sewing or elsewhere. At first, Aislynn thought to head to the kitchens. Then the basket of sewing caught her eye. *Might as well see what my hand can do,* she thought. Resigned to starting with her tapestry, she vowed to attend to the kitchens after she broke her fast.

Mary arrived shortly, knocking at the door before entering. Aislynn didn't raise her head from her tapestry as she bid the girl to enter, so Mary's words caught her unawares.

"Milady, ye have a guest," she announced in a low voice.

Aislynn's head snapped up from her needle to see a kerchiefed woman holding a small, blonde child. She placed the little girl on the floor, and the girl ran to Aislynn, her face clear and bright with joy.

"Oh, little one!" Aislynn cried in recognition. "Your head looks so much recovered!"

The girl hugged her skirts. "Aye! And it doesna hurt anymore." The girl pressed her head towards Aislynn to show her the mark was gone. Aislynn brushed her fingers over the girl's gossamer hair.

"That is good. I was worried about you."

The girl flicked her startlingly bright green eyes to her mother. "Mam said the same about ye, that ye had been injured, too. And that we should come to see ye. To say thank ye for helping me and give ye a gift to help ye feel better. Is your head injured, too?"

Her sudden question made Aislynn smile again. Ahh, the impetuous nature of children.

"No, sweetie. I hurt my hand, but 'twas near a fire, just like yours."

Aislynn held out her freshly pinked hand, and the little girl brushed against it with the tip of her nose, as though she were trying to investigate it with intense focus. Her mother stepped forward to pull the girl away from Aislynn's hand.

"We brought ye bannocks and compote," the mother said. "And Mera is correct, to thank ye. I did no' get the chance to thank ye properly. And when I heard ye were fairly injured, I was worrit for ye. We both were." The woman inclined her head at the girl, Mera.

Aislynn rose, taking the pouch the woman offered. She clasped the woman's hand in both of hers.

"Thank you for this. And for your kind words. You and Mera are welcome here anytime."

Mera lit up like the sunrise, excited at the opportunity to return to the impressive tower. Aislynn understood the child's delight. What young girl didn't love the prospect of being like a fairy princess in a tower. *It's not all it's reputed to be,* Aislynn acknowledged to herself as she beamed her own bright smile at Mera.

"My name is Leana Sinclair," the woman said.

"And I'm Aislynn. Aislynn Sinclair."

***

Leana and her dear daughter Mera left, their own day of work ahead of them, leaving Aislynn to herself. Mary had placed a small platter of cheese and dried fruit on the desk before she had slipped out of the chamber unnoticed. Aislynn added the pouch of bannocks and berry compote to the vittles and stared out the window at the bustling yard, deeply introspective.

While John loved her and wanted to assure her of her place in his clan, Leana's visit with wee Mera told her what she needed to know. John was right – his clan didn't hold her accountable. In fact, many were concerned for her welfare. And though she would eternally hold herself into account for Oggie's death, it relieved her to realize the clan, perchance, did not.

The humming in the yard soon became a crescendo, and Aislynn leaned from the window, trying to look around the side of the tower where the excitement appeared to be. John burst through the door again. *Did the man not know how to open a door?* Aislynn wondered.

John's face alighted with joy as he grabbed Aislynn's hand, dragging her from the room.

"Come, lassie! Asper has returned with a retinue of the King's! I would have him meet my wife!"

Aislynn couldn't help but laugh at John's infectious humor that painted him in childlike happiness. He almost passed for a lad.

"You just want him to know that you won the wager!" Aislynn joked as they ran from the tower into the yard. John gave her a sidelong look and winked at her. There was a shred of truth in her tease.

It seemed to Aislynn that everyone in the Sinclair lands gathered to celebrate the arrival of their Laird, with Haleigh at the front. After giving his handfast wife a suggestively appropriate greeting, amid the cheering and jeers of his clan, the burly man with the same wild, deep-russet hair as John and Marcus worked his way through the throng. John launched himself at his brother, enveloping the gigantic man in a bear-like hug.

"John, ye made it intact! And did ye deliver the asset as instructed?" His booming voice carried over their heads.

"Ooch, I did more than that. I followed the King's dictates to the letter. May I introduce my wife, the lovely Aislynn de Valence Sinclair?"

That same face that had frightened her months ago while she stood in the King's study now looked at her with an expression of pompous gaiety. Asper embraced her in his own powerful, suffocating embrace.

"Welcome, lass. I hope the Highlands have been kind to ye, and that ye have found all ye were looking for here."

Aislynn curtsied politely at the wild man, then resumed her position next to John.

"I think I chose wisely," she answered.

News of how the Sinclairs were to contend with the MacKays' egregious actions came to her from John after a late evening of conference and drink. Though he wasn't drunk this time, his words flowed as though he were.

"The King's retinue, under the command of Asper, and in the company of the Sinclairs, will ride to the MacKays," he explained. "As the King's men, they should welcome us. In reparation, the King is demanding that a significant number of the MacKays, including their Laird, must come south to Glasgow to serve the King's campaign. They must also return lands and cattle, and they must assist in rebuilding the Gateway."

John turned his gaze to the window, contemplative. His face pulled taut, showing his displeasure with the decision.

"Seems like an insignificant reparation for an attack on a man's wife and the loss of a kinsman. But the last thing the Highlands needs is more bloodshed. At least, 'twas the estimation of Asper and Haleigh."

Aislynn hugged John's hard body to hers. *The last thing, indeed.* An imperfect vengeance — yet was there such a thing as perfect vengeance? Aislynn didn't know.

Chapter Twenty-One: Finding Peace in the Choices We've Made

Preparations were underway for the celebration of Asper and Haleigh's wedding. A late summer wedding was full of colorful splendor, and as long as the rain held back, the day would be one fit for a queen. In all her finery, Haleigh would undoubtedly rival one, Aislynn was certain.

Aislynn stepped to the side of the cattle barn, where a bit of shade from several full rowan trees offered succor from the warmth of the day. If she looked to the right and squinted, she was able to make out the deep blue horizon of the North Sea. A full, flowering glen backed by high mountain peaks in the distance filled her view to the left, and a pair of horses approached her from the west.

One rider was much taller than the other. Both wore caps that blocked their faces from the sunlight that barely dappled through the clouds. Next to a rocky outcropping, they hobbled their horses, and the shorter rider slid off his horse.

Aislynn stiffened at their approach. She didn't recognize them as Sinclairs – not a red hair betwixt them – and a bubble of panic welled in her chest. *Were they MacKays?*

'Twas when the shorter rider started walking toward Aislynn that the panic dispersed and another, headier emotion consumed her. She recognized that walk. *No, it can't be. It's impossible!*

But was it impossible for her sister, disguised as a man, to have found her this far north?

Aislynn lifted her skirt and broke into a run, throwing herself at the lad – Agnes in man's garb.

"'Lynn! I almost didn't recognize you, dressed as one of these wild Highlanders!" Agnes's face was buried in Aislynn's hair as she spoke. Aislynn hugged her tighter.

"Oh, you are one to talk! Dressed as a man like you are! I had a moment of panic at the strange riders."

At this, Aislynn thrust her sister from her embrace. "Agnes! What are you doing here? You will surely be captured and gaoled if caught! Why risk such a venture?"

Confusion set into Agnes's brow. "Why? Aislynn, for you! We learned the usurper sent you north to survive in the wilds, and I couldn't get to you fast enough! I have Boldie here with me," Agnes flapped her hand at the rider behind her, "and you can ride with me. We will head south, first to our Uncle, then to England. You have suffered enough in this vile country."

Agnes tugged at Aislynn's arm, turning toward the horses. Aislynn stayed rooted in her spot. Agnes spun around and flicked her surprised face at Aislynn.

"What are you doing, 'Lynn? We must leave before someone sees us! We can escape if we leave now!"

Aislynn was unmoved.

Here it was, her chance to leave with her beloved sister, to go back home, resume her title as a noble, the niece of the King, and return to civilization.

But was it really home? Other than Agnes, she'd had no real home, only trunks of clothes thrown into the chambers of others. She barely recalled England proper. What was home?

A crossbill's call attracted her notice, and Aislynn closed her eyes, lifting her face to the sky. The high, sweet smell of heather and grass, the fresh salty air, the greens and blues and brown of the land and sky. And deep reds and greens, colors that well reminded her of John and sent an exuberant flutter up her spine whenever she thought of him. These people that, in spite of where she was raised, had started to accept her as one of their own, saved her life, gave her a place where she felt at peace. Where was home?

"Aislynn!"

She stepped away from her grabbing sister.

"Nay," Aislynn said defiantly, giving her own voice a Highland lilt.

"Nay? What--?"

"Much has changed since you left, Aggie. I am not the same person I was earlier this year. Nor would I want to be. I have found a place that gives me peace and serenity, and people who love me. I have a husband here –"

"A WHAT?" Agnes yelled in shock, her hazel green eyes wide saucers on her face.

A satisfied smile pulled at Aislynn's cheek. "Aye, a husband. I've been more at home here than anywhere else. I shall stay."

"WHAT?" Disbelief poured out of Agnes like a burst dam. Aislynn suppressed the desire to laugh at her sister's bafflement.

"I thank you for coming for me," Aislynn tried to soften the blow, "worrying for me. And you shall always be my dear sister. But I can't go with you."

In a quick move, Aislynn swept a shocked Agnes in a hard hug, then released her just as suddenly and stepped back toward the barn.

"Care for yourself, sister. Find your own home, a place where you feel you belong. I hope and pray to see you again."

Agnes stood with her mouth hanging open. This was not the way she'd expected her day to end. Instead of riding south with her sister, Agnes would leave the Highlands with only her English escort. It all seemed so *wrong*.

"Are you certain, Aislynn?" Agnes's voice was a breathless whisper, her eyes watery with unshed tears.

"Aye, my sister. I am certain. Go now. Find where you belong."

"But you belong with me," Agnes begged.

"Nay. I belong here." Aislynn took her sister's hand, trying to offer Agnes comfort. "You've spent the past months without me. And God willing, you will see me again."

Aislynn hugged her sister close once more, kissing her dirt-stained cheeks. "Now go. Hurry, before I cry!"

Agnes pursed her full lips, holding back her tears. She nodded once, held her hand over her heart, then spun and raced back to her horse. Aislynn watched her scramble into the saddle, lean over to speak with her escort, then the two rode off, heading back from whence they came.

"Are ye sure ye made the right choice?" John's voice asked from behind her.

Aislynn cut her eyes over her shoulder, then looked back at the silhouetted riders on the western horizon.

"How long were you there?" she asked.

John moved so he stood directly behind her, his steady chest pressing reassurance against her back, fitting so perfectly. He wrapped his arm across her chest, clinging to her with a sense of desperation. With their plaids flapping in the soft breeze, they appeared almost as one person standing against the elements.

"Long enough to hear ye say ye are where you belong." His voice was a brogue roll against her ear.

"Why didn't you come out? You could have taken her, another de Valence sister, as prisoner for the king. Why did you let her leave?"

"She was here for no other reason than to rescue her sister. I would have done the same for Asper or Marcus. How could I fault her for that? She was of no danger to us." He paused, inhaling before he spoke his next words. "The only danger I feared from her was that she would have convinced ye to leave."

Emotion choked his halting voice, and only then did Aislynn realize the dread John must have felt in seeing her with Agnes. She lifted her slender hand to rest on John's arm.

"Are ye sure you made the right choice?" he asked again, his voice raspy.

She twisted in his embrace, lifting her face to look into his stormy green eyes. She grasped his hand and placed it over her still-flat belly.

"Indeed, I did."

The End

An excerpt from the Celtic Highland Maidens series –

This new series will take us back in time, to a place where the Ancient Celts, the Caledonii tribe, fought for their land and their people against the Romans in 209 AD

The Maiden of the Storm

King Gartnaith Blogh himself who managed to run the Roman fools from the land, laughed with zeal as the Latin devils, in their flaying and rusted Roman armor, scrambled over the low stone wall. As though a minor *cnap-starra* would stop the mighty Caledonii warriors from striking fear into the heart of their Centauriae. Fools.

But when rumors blossomed of rogue Roman soldiers venturing far north of the wall, a foolish endeavor if Ru's daughter, Riana, ever heard one, warriors from her father's tribe and other nearby tribes traveled across the mountainous countryside, down through the wide glen to meet them.

Thus far, the soldiers had remained close to the wall, fearing to leave the false security it provided. Ru's warriors had struck down one or two that meandered away from that security, wounding them, perchance fatally, with a well-aimed throw of a spear. The diminutive Roman soldiers, clad in their hopeful leather and metal armor, were no match for the powerful throw of a Caledonii spear.

This most recent Roman soldier, however, appeared less resilient, less aggressive than his previous counterparts. Though clad in full Roman military garb, he wasn't paying attention to his surroundings — distracted as he was. The Centauriae had traversed the low mountains and lochs to their hidden land. And he was alone. Ru noted his lean-muscled build and made an abrupt decision.

"Dinna kill this lad," he whispered to Dunbraith, his military adviser and old friend. "We should keep him, enslave him. Melt his iron and armor into weapons. And use his knowledge against these pissants."

Dunbraith's face, blue woad paint lines mixed with blood red, was fearsome and thoughtful. "Severus is defeated," his growling voice responded. "The Roman lines are scattered. 'Tis a safe assumption they will not even try to retrieve the lad." A frightening smile crossed his face, one that Ru knew well. A cruel smile that didn't reach his eyes.

Ru nodded his agreement and waved his hand at his *Imannae*, a young, curly-haired Caledonii anxious to prove his worth. The young man positioned himself just beyond the leaves of the scrub bush in which he hid, narrowed his eyes at his prey, and launched a strong-armed throw of his sharpened spear.

The *Imannae's* throw was perfect, catching the young Roman's upper arm under his armor in a sharp retort. The lad cried out and dropped to his knees in pain and shock. Ru and his warriors moved in as silent as nightfall.

Coming Soon

A Note on History –

For this story, I took the character of the supposed niece of Aymer de Valence, the Earl whom the Bruce defeated at Loudoun Hill, and created a story for her. I love taking characters from history and writing them into my stories, inventing a narrative for them.

But it is invention. Here are some elements that are accurate: the construction of barns using Viking wedge technology, the capture and imprisonment of the Bruce's wife and daughter, and the issue of minor skirmishes, or even loyalties, between clans, and their relative geography.

Using those elements as my jumping off point, Aislynn and John are thrust together. And a wager between brothers is always fun.

Once again, I hope the history seems as real for you as it does for me. And if there are any mistakes in the history, those are completely mine – reconstructed for creative licensing, of course!

Book 6, tentatively titled *The Warrior of the Glen,* will release later this year!

A Thank You–

Thank you to the most amazing readers on the planet. That you keep coming back – that you want to read more, is what keeps me going. Thank you for your feedback, commentary, reviews, and cheers! This book is dedicated to all my readers: the ones I have now, and the ones I hope read in the future!

About the Author

Michelle Deerwester-Dalrymple is a professor of writing and an author. She started reading when she was 3 years old, writing when she was 4, and published her first poem at age 16. She has written articles and essays on a variety of topics, including several texts on writing for middle and high school students. She is also working on a novel inspired by actual events. She lives in California with her family of seven.

You can visit her blog page and sign up for her newsletter at:
https://michelledeerwesterdalrympleauthor.blogspot.com/
Amazon Author page: https://www.amazon.com/-/e/B07C784SJ6

Follow her on
Facebook: https://www.facebook.com/MDDauthor/
Instagram: https://www.instagram.com/michelledalrympleauthor/
Twitter: https://twitter.com/mddalrymple?lang=en
Goodreads:
https://www.goodreads.com/author/show/17969353.Michelle_Deer
wester_Dalrymple

Bookbub:

https://www.bookbub.com/profile/michelle-deerwester-dalrymple

Also by the Author:

Glen Highland Romance
To Dance in the Glen – Book 1
The Lady of the Glen – Book 2
The Exile of the Glen – Book 3
The Jewel of the Glen – Book 4
The Seduction of the Glen – Book 5

Celtic Highland Maidens:
The Maiden of the Storm – book 1, coming soon!

As M.D. Dalrymple
Men in Uniform
Night Shift – Book 1
Day Shift – Book 2
Overtime – Book 3
Holiday Pay – Book 4
School Resource Officer – Book 5, coming soon!

Printed in Great Britain
by Amazon

31315511R00118